# THE LAKE HOUSE

# JAMES
# PATTERSON

---

# THE LAKE
# HOUSE

BCA

This edition published 2003
by BCA
by arrangement with Headline Book Publishing
a division of Hodder Headline

CN 116256

Third reprint 2003

Typeset in Palatino Light by
Letterpart Limited, Reigate, Surrey

Printed and bound in Germany by
GGP Media, Pössneck

# THE LAKE HOUSE

This is for the *other* Max, Maxine Paetro, who has been involved with the bird-children from the beginning. She knows and loves them as I do. And they love her back!

## AUTHOR'S NOTE

It surprises some readers that *When the Wind Blows* (featuring Max and the gang) is my most successful novel around the world. Who knows why for sure, but I suspect it's because an awful lot of people, myself included, have a recurring fantasy in which they fly. They treasure it. On the other hand, there are plenty of folks who won't fantasize or play make-believe. They wouldn't have gotten to Never Never Land with Peter Pan. There is one other thing that might be interesting to those who read this book. When I researched it I interviewed dozens of scientists. All of them said that things *like* those that happen in *The Lake House* will happen *in our lifetimes*. In fact, a scientist in New England claims that he can put wings on humans right now. I'll bet he can.

So settle in, you believers, and even you Muggles.

Let yourself fly.

# PROLOGUE

---

# RESURRECTION

# The Hospital; somewhere in Maryland

A t around eleven in the evening, Dr Ethan Kane trudged down the gray-and-blue-painted corridor toward a private elevator. His mind was filled with images of death and suffering, but also progress, *great progress that would change the world.*

A young and quite homely scrub nurse rounded the corner of the passageway, and nodded her head deferentially as she approached him. She had a crush on Dr Kane, and she wasn't the only one.

'Doctor,' she said, 'you're still working.'

'Esther, *you* go home now. Please,' Ethan Kane said, pretending to be solicitous and caring, which couldn't be farther from the truth. He considered the nurse inferior in every way, including the fact that she was female.

He was also exhausted from a surgical marathon: five major operations in a day. The elevator car finally arrived, the doors slid open, and he stepped inside.

'Goodnight, Esther,' he said, and showed the nurse a lot of very white teeth, but no genuine warmth, because there was none to show.

He straightened his tall body and wearily passed his hand over his longish blond hair, cleaned his wire-rimmed glasses on the tail of his lab coat, then rubbed his eyes before putting his glasses back on as he descended to the sub-basement level.

*One more thing to check on . . . always one more thing for him to do.*

He walked a half-dozen quick steps to a thick steel door and pushed it open with the palm of his hand.

He entered the dark and chilly atmosphere of a basement storage room. A pungent odor struck him.

There, lying on a double row of gurneys, were six naked bodies. Four men, two women, all in their late teens or early twenties. Each was brain-dead, each as good as gone, but each had served a worthy purpose, a higher one. The plastic bracelets on their wrists said *DONOR*.

'You're making the world a better place,' Kane whispered as he passed the bodies. 'Take comfort in that.'

Dr Kane strode to the far end of the room and pushed open another steel door, an exact duplicate of the first. This time, rather than a chill blast, he was met by a searing wave of hot air, the deafening roar of fire, and the unmistakable smell of death.

All three of the incinerators were going tonight. Two of his night-time porters, their powerful working-man bodies glistening with grime and sweat, looked up as Dr Kane entered the cinderblock chamber. The men nodded respectfully, but their eyes showed fear.

'Let's pick up the pace, gentlemen. This is taking too long,' Kane called out. 'Let's go, let's go! You're being paid well for this scut-work. Too well.'

He glanced at a young woman's naked corpse laid out on the cement floor. She was white-blonde, pretty in a music-video sort of way. The porters had probably been diddling with her. That was why they were behind schedule, wasn't it?

Gurneys were shoved haphazardly into one corner, like discarded shopping carts in a supermarket parking lot. Quite a spectacle. *Hellish* to be sure.

As he watched, one of the sweat-glazed minions worked a wooden paddle under a young male's body while the other swung open the heavy glass door of an oven. Together they pushed, shoved, slid the body into the fire as if it were a pizza.

The flames dampened for a moment, then as the porters locked down the door, the inferno flared again. The cremation chamber was also called a 'retort'. Each retort burned at 3,600 degrees, and it took just over fifteen minutes to reduce a human body to nothing but ashes.

To Dr Ethan Kane that meant one thing: no evidence of what was happening at the Hospital. Absolutely no evidence of Resurrection.

'Pick up the pace!' he yelled again. 'Burn these bodies!'

*The donors.*

# PART ONE

## CHILD CUSTODY

# CHAPTER ONE

It was being called 'the mother of all custody trials', and that might explain why an extra fifty thousand people had poured into Denver on that warm day in early spring.

The case was also being billed as potentially more wrenching and explosive than Baby M, or Elian Gonzales, or O.J. Simpson's. I happened to think that this time *maybe* the media hype was fitting and appropriate, and even a tiny bit underplayed.

The fate of six extraordinary children was at stake.

Six children who had been created in a laboratory, and had made history, both scientific and philosophical.

Six adorable, good-hearted kids whom I loved as if they were my own.

Max, Matthew, Icarus, Ozymandias, Peter and Wendy.

The actual trial was scheduled to begin in an hour in the City and County building, a gleaming white neoclassical-looking courthouse. Designed to appear unmistakably judicial, it was crowned with a pointy pediment just like the one atop the US Supreme Court building. I could see it now.

Kit and I slumped down on the front seat of my dusty, trusty beat-up blue Suburban. It was parked down the block from the courthouse, where we could see and not be seen, at least so far.

I had chewed my nails down to the quick, and there was a pesky muscle twitching in Kit's cheek.

'I know, Frannie,' he'd said just a moment before. 'I'm twitching again.'

We were suing for custody of the children, and we knew that the full weight of the law was against us. We *weren't* married, *weren't* related to the kids, and their biological parents *were* basically good people. Not too terrific for us.

What we did have going for us was our unshakable love for these children, with whom we'd gone through several degrees of hell, and their love for us.

Now all we had to do was prove that living with us was in the best interests of the children, and that meant I was going to have to tell a story that sounded crazy, even to my closest friends, sometimes even to myself.

But every word was true, so help me God.

# CHAPTER TWO

The amazing story had actually started six months ago in the tiny burg of Bear Bluff, Colorado, which is fifty or so miles northwest of Boulder on the 'Peak-to-Peak' highway.

I was driving home late one night when I happened to see a streaking white flash – then realized it was a young girl running fast through the woods not too far from my home.

But that was just part of what I saw. I'm a veterinarian, 'Dr Frannie', and my brain didn't want to accept what my eyes told me, so I stopped my car and got out.

The strange girl looked to be eleven or twelve, with long blonde hair and a loose-fitting white smock that was stained with blood and ripped. I remember gasping for breath and literally steadying myself against a tree. I had the clear and distinct thought that I couldn't be seeing what I was seeing.

But my eyes didn't lie. Along with a pair of foreshortened arms, *the girl had wings!*

That's correct – wings! About a nine-foot span. Below the wings, and attached somehow, were her arms. She was *double-limbed*. And the fit of her wings was absolutely perfect. Extraordinary from a scientific and aesthetic point of view. A mind-altering dose of reality.

She had also been hurt, which was how I eventually came to capture her, in a 'mist net', and sedate her, with the help of an FBI agent named Thomas Brennan, whom I knew better as 'Kit'. We brought her to the animal hospital I operate, the Inn-Patient, where I examined her. I found very large pectoral muscles anchored to an oversized breastbone; anterior and posterior air sacs; a heart as large as a horse's.

She had been 'engineered' that way. A *perfect* design, actually. Totally brilliant.

But why? And by whom?

Her name was Max, short for Maximum, and it was incredibly hard to win her trust at first. But in her own good time she told me things that made me sick to my stomach, and also angrier than I'd ever been. She told me about a place called the School, where she'd been kept captive since the day she was born.

Everything you're about to hear is already *happening*, by the way. It's going on in outlaw labs across the United States and other countries as well. In our lifetimes! If it's hard to take, all I can say is, buckle up the seatbelts on your easy chairs. This is what happened to Max and a few others like her.

Biologists, trying to break the barrier on human longevity, had melded bird DNA with human zygotes. It *can* be done. They had created Max and several other children. A *flock*. Unfortunately, the scientists couldn't grow the babies in test tubes, so the genetically modified embryos had to be implanted in their mothers' wombs.

When the mothers were close to term, labor was induced. The poor mothers were then told that their premature children had died. The preemies were shipped to an underground lab called the School. The School was, by any definition, a maximum-security prison. The children were kept in cages and the rejects were 'put to sleep', a horrible euphemism for cold-blooded murder.

Like I said, *buckle up those seatbelts!*

Anyway, that was why Max had done what she'd been forbidden to do. She had escaped from the School.

Kit and I listened to what Max had to tell us, then we went with her to try and rescue the children still trapped at the lab called the School. Amazingly, we succeeded. We even got to live with the kids a few months at a magical place we all called the Lake House.

When the smoke cleared, *literally*, the six surviving children, including Max and her brother, were sent to live with their biological parents – people they'd never known a day in their lives.

That should have been fine, I guess, but this real-life fairy tale didn't have a happy ending.

The kids, who ranged from twelve years old down to about four, phoned Kit and me constantly every single day. They told us they were horribly depressed, bored, scared, miserable, suicidal, and I knew why. As a vet, I understood what no one else seemed to.

The children had done a bird thing: *they had imprinted on Kit and me.*

We were the only parents they knew and could love.

# CHAPTER THREE

Outside my battle-scarred Suburban, the crowd was flowing like lava down Bannock Street. I had read somewhere that Denver had the fittest population of any major city in America. I'd always loved it here – until now. I was about to force a joke when Kit said, 'Brace yourself, Frannie. The kids are here.'

He pointed to a black town car slowly parting the crowd and finally coming to a stop at a no-parking zone right outside the courthouse. The hairs on my neck stood even before the crowd started chanting her name. My heart was in my throat.

'Max! Max! Max! We want Max!' somebody screamed.

'The freak show has arrived!' yelled another voice.

Car doors flew open and somber-looking gray-suited bodyguards and lawyers scrambled out on to the sidewalk. Then a second car braked behind the first.

A bull-necked man in a tight-fitting black jacket opened the passenger-side door for a petite, blonde woman about my age. She opened the rear door of the sedan, then reached into the back seat.

Max emerged from the town car. There was a sudden hush over the crowd. Even I caught my breath. She was stunning in every way. An amazing girl with extraordinary intelligence and strength – and wings that spanned close to ten feet now. They were feathered in pure white, with glints of blue and silver shining through.

'God, she's beautiful,' I whispered. 'I miss her, Kit. I miss all of the babies. This just breaks my heart.'

I remembered how stunned I had been when I saw her for the first time, and the crowd was having the same reaction now.

'Max, Max, Max,' people started to chant.

Cameras flashed. 'Here, Max, look over here.' 'Max, here.' 'Max, smile!' 'Max, fly for us!'

Four people burst through the police line holding aloft a banner that read: *Only God can make a tree. That goes for children too.*

Other signs read: *Cell no! Say no to cloning!*

Another banner had birds stenciled on it and read: *Bake them in a pie.*

Then the news choppers came in, and it got really loud and unruly. Max swung her head around to take in the astonishing scene. My heart lurched.

We grabbed up our papers for court, and as Kit locked the car doors he said softly, 'She's looking for us, Frannie.'

'She's scared. I can see it in her eyes.'

Max has the ultra-keen senses of a raptor. She can hear a caterpillar wriggle from a hundred yards away. She can *see* the caterpillar from a half-mile overhead.

She called out now, her voice shrill with fear, 'Frannie. Kit. I *need* you. Ple-e-e-e-ase. Where are you guys?'

Her piercing cry was still hanging in the air as more cars pulled up to the courthouse.

Burly men with buzz cuts leaped out on to the street. Several cars began discharging the other kids. They were so hesitant, so young and vulnerable. They shied away from the cameras, hid their darling little faces.

'Spawn of the devil!' someone screeched. 'These children are demons!'

# CHAPTER FOUR

Courtroom No. 19 was on the sixth floor. It was the largest room in the complex by far, and would have to be to hold so many inquiring minds. As Kit and I approached with our attorney, we were besieged by a throng of reporters. 'Put your head down,' our lawyer advised, 'and just keep walking.'

'Agent Brennan, look over here. Dr O'Neill. Hey, Frannie! What makes you think you're a competent mother?' one of the press vultures shouted. 'What makes either of you think you can be good parents to these children?'

Kit finally looked up at the reporter. 'Because we love the little creeps,' he said, and winked. 'And because they love us. Life's simple like that.'

A couple of armed guards swung open the double set of doors to the courtroom and we disappeared inside. If the brouhaha on the street had sounded like a hurricane in motion, the one inside had the intensity of swarming bees.

The room was paneled in golden oak, and the gallery at the rear was furnished with matching benches that held over two hundred spectators. Every available space was filled with family members, scientists, and members of the press with real clout and, hopefully, better manners than those of the terrible horde outside.

Our lawyers and those representing the biological parents had gathered in small groups around the bar area. The lawyers' tables were situated in the middle of the room. Up front was the judge's seat, and it was vacant.

Our lawyer, Jeff Kussof, had told us that Colorado courts almost always rule in the 'best interests of the child'. I was holding on to that statement as tightly as I clasped Kit's hand when the door from the judge's chambers opened.

What I saw next kind of took my breath away. I suspect that it did the same thing to everybody else in Courtroom No. 19.

Eyes front, wings folded, the six children filed into the room, wearing their custom-tailored suits, and starched little smocks. They were eye-poppers, for sure. Dazzlers.

First came the four-year-old twins, Peter and Wendy. They were dark-haired, of Chinese descent, their snowy wing feathers glinting with dark blue lights.

Max's little brother, Matthew, an unruly towhead of nine, came next.

He was followed by the two handsome older boys, Icarus and Ozymandias.

And bringing up the rear was the lovely firstborn herself.

*Maximum.*

The crowd, as they say on the sporting pages, went wild.

# CHAPTER FIVE

A couple of paces behind the six children strode Judge James Randolph Dwyer, a large, fit man of seventy-three. He had a face like a crumpled paper bag, wispy white hair, and a no-nonsense set to his jaw.

There was a loud *whooshing* sound as everyone in the courtroom sat down.

While the bailiff called the court to order, and then read from the docket, I was keenly aware of the men and women across the aisle from us. They were the four sets of biological parents, and they had assembled a formidable legal team of attorneys, headed by Catherine Fitzgibbons, a former prosecutor known for her aggressive parry-and-thrust style and impressive winning record. I suppose it didn't hurt their case that she was married, and pregnant with her fourth child.

'Your Honor,' said Jeffrey Kussof, our lawyer, 'I am quite certain this case will stretch the heartstrings of all concerned. There are *no bad people* here.

'The real conflict is about what is in the best interests of the children. We will prove that their best interests clearly lie with Dr O'Neill and Mr Brennan.

'I'd like to quote Marianne O. Battani, Judge of Wayne County Circuit Court, Detroit. In 1986 she said of a test-tube-baby case, "We really have no definition of *mother* in our law books. Mother was believed to have been so basic that no definition was deemed necessary." Your Honor, all that has changed. Today, in our complex and sometimes confusing world, a child can have as many as three mothers. The one who conceived the child, the one who bore the child, and the one who raised it.

'Agent Brennan and Dr O'Neill have been surrogate parents under extreme fire. They actually put their lives on the line for these children. I'll repeat that – *they put their lives at risk.*

'They never thought of anything but the children's safety. Dr O'Neill lost her animal hospital and her home in the process. To take blows and bullets for others shows love as fierce as any natural maternity or paternity.

'That said, this case isn't about my clients or about the respondents. It's about the children and the Colorado law that mandates children be united with their family. There is a *new* kind of family here, a family that came together through terrible adversity. And this powerful, loving family, for the good of the children, must be kept together. To separate Kit, Frannie, Max, Ic, Oz, Matthew, Wendy and Peter would be an injustice to everyone involved. It would be exceedingly *cruel*.'

I wanted to hug Jeffrey Kussof, and he did look mildly pleased with himself as he sat down. 'It's a start,' he whispered.

But Catherine Fitzgibbons was already on her feet.

# CHAPTER SIX

'I'm here today to represent the rights of six American citizens, Max, Matthew, Oz, Icarus, Wendy and Peter,' said Attorney Fitzgibbons, 'as well as their *true* parents.'

'Why am I always the last one?' Little Peter suddenly spoke up from his seat in the second row. Everybody in the room laughed at the unexpected interruption from the small boy.

'No offense meant,' Catherine Fitzgibbons said, but she had turned the brightest red. Her face seemed to float like a balloon above the tailored navy-blue field of her maternity dress. 'Okay then – Peter, et al, I'm here to represent all of you,' she said, and smiled benevolently.

'I sincerely doubt it,' Icarus, who has been blind since birth, piped up next. 'You don't know us. As *blind* as I am, even I can see that.'

Once again, the room was moved to laughter and small talk, only quieting after Judge Dwyer's repeated gavel-banging and threats to clear the room. The kids finally settled down somewhat. They were all quick with a quip, though, probably because each of the six had a genius IQ. They tested off the charts – Stanford-Binet, WPPSI-R, WISC III, the Beery tests, Act III.

In her opening remarks, Fitzgibbons went on to laud Kit and me for what she called our 'heroic rescue' as a way of acknowledging our help in the past and putting it completely to rest. Then she began to make her critical points *against* us. Each was like a knife driven into my heart, and Kit's, and, I was quite certain, the children's.

'Your Honor, Dr O'Neill and Mr Brennan, for all their altruism on the part of these children, have *no legitimate claim* in this courtroom,' she pronounced. 'None.

'They are unmarried. They've only known each other and the children for a matter of months. Furthermore, and this hardly can be said strongly enough, the children's parents have done nothing whatsoever to forfeit their parental rights. To the contrary, we will show cause to irrevocably declare them the *lawful, legitimate,* and *exclusive* parents of their children once and for all.'

When Fitzgibbons had finished her opening remarks, Jeffrey Kussof stood up immediately and called Kit. I watched with pride, and love, as he took the stand.

Jeffrey cited Kit's law degree from NYU and his twelve years as an FBI agent. And he gently elicited the personal tragedy that was like a dark hole at the center of Kit's life. Four years ago, while he was working on a case, his wife and two small boys had left for a Nantucket vacation without Kit. Their small airplane went down and there were no survivors.

Kit testified calmly, yet passionately, and with a spark of humor and wit that defines his personality. I thought anyone seeing him for the first time would be entirely convinced not just that he was a brave man, but that he had been, and would be again, an unimpeachably good father.

Then, for two unrelenting hours, Catherine Fitzgibbons expertly filleted Kit's career – and just about every moment of his private life.

# CHAPTER SEVEN

'**K** it isn't your given name, is it?' she asked.
'No, actually it's Thomas. Thomas Brennan. Kit is a nickname. Frannie and the kids call me Kit. It's a long story.'

'Mr Brennan, you've been with the FBI for twelve years?'

'That's right.'

'Have you ever heard of Fox Mulder?'

Kit snorted and shook his head. He knew where this was going already. 'That's very cute.'

'Please instruct the witness to answer, Your Honor,' said Fitzgibbons.

'Mr Brennan, please respond to the question.'

'Fox Mulder is a fictitious character on a television series,' said Kit.

'Do you have an opinion of this fictitious character?'

'Yeah. He's a frickin' nutjob.'

The spectators laughed. So did I. And the children twittered with delight. They *adored* Kit.

'Have you any idea, Mr Brennan, why your colleagues at the FBI call you "Mulder"?' asked Fitzgibbons.

'Objection, Your Honor! Argumentative. Move to strike,' shouted Jeffrey Kussof.

Fitzgibbons bowed her head as if to show she was contrite. She wasn't, of course.

'I retract the question. Mr Brennan, do you consider yourself a workaholic?'

'Maybe. At times. I'm definitely committed to my work. I even like it sometimes.'

'And would you describe yourself as a stable person?'

'Yes, I certainly would.'

'But you've been medicated for depression.'

Fitzgibbons turned her back on Kit when she said this. It was good to see that even she could feel some shame.

'Yes. I was depressed, damned depressed when I lost my entire family,' Kit said, his voice rising sharply.

Catherine Fitzgibbons turned round to face him. She held her stomach in profile to Judge Dwyer.

'I see. So you *understand*, then, how the respondents must feel about losing *their* children?'

Kit didn't speak. Across from me, the twins sent up frightened, high-pitched screeches in protest at this attack on Kit.

'Agent Brennan, shall I repeat the question?'

'You heartless—' he said in a whisper.

'Permission to treat the witness as hostile, Your Honor,' said Fitzgibbons.

'Mr Brennan, please answer the question,' said the judge.

'Yes. Yes, I understand how it feels to lose a child,' Kit finally answered.

'And still you persist in this action? You say that *I'm* heartless? That will be all, Agent Brennan.'

# CHAPTER EIGHT

I was feeling sick in the pit of my stomach when Jeffrey Kussof rose and spoke in a clear, confident voice.

'I call Dr Frances O'Neill.'

I immediately wondered *why* Jeffrey seemed so confident. Did he know something that I didn't? Why did he have more confidence in me than I had in myself?

As I stepped up to the witness seat, I think I had some idea of how it felt to be a four-hundred-pound lady in a wading pool. I looked out at the gallery and the gallery looked back at me. A little more than two hundred people staring right at me, waiting for me to convince them that I would be a great, no, a *flawless* mother for six unusual and very special children.

Well, that was what I planned to do.

Because I knew in my heart that I would be. Wasn't that worth something?

Jeffrey gave me a reassuring smile, then, under his direction, I cited my academic and professional credentials: the Westinghouse Science scholarship, my DVM from the Colorado State Teaching Hospital at Fort Collins, and all the rest of my laurels.

This prompted a little cheer and a round of whistles from the six kids, right under the noses of their seething parents. Even the twins were laughing. I chanced a quick look over at Kit, and he gave me a wink and one of his famous crooked smiles.

As the interview went on, for well over an hour, I began to feel a little more confident. I *knew* I would be a great mom; I *loved* these kids more than anyone else could. Because I was a veterinarian *and* a human being, I understood how complex they were. Jeffrey asked me to speak about my own recent tragedy – my husband had been murdered in a holdup two years before. And I talked about my successful one-woman animal practice on a squiggle of dirt road in Bear Bluff, a one-traffic-light town about fifty miles northwest of Boulder.

Jeffrey then went on to depict me as a woman with a heart as big as the Rockies, with an open door to every chipmunk and mule deer and pound puppy in Colorado. Okay, so I started to blush.

But most importantly, he told about my having operated on Max when she was near death. How I had saved her life when no one else could. That was a fact that no one could dispute, not even Ms Fitzgibbons.

Or so I hoped.

So I prayed.

A few moments later, Catherine Fitzgibbons came over to the stand and smiled as sweetly as if she were my own dear sister, Carole Anne. But she didn't waste much more of the court's time on niceties.

'Dr O'Neill, what is your annual salary?' she asked in her trademark huffy tone.

'I can't really say. It differs from year to year. Depends on whether I'm working on more chipmunks or horses in that particular year?'

'On average, more or less than thirty-five thousand a year.'

'Less,' I said, more emphatically than I'd meant to.

'And you expect to support six children—'

'I wouldn't do it alone! These kids need love more than money. They're depressed now.'

Catherine Fitzgibbons' eyebrows arched. 'You say the children are depressed. How do you know that? You aren't a psychologist, are you?'

'No, but—'

Fitzgibbons cut me off. 'You aren't any kind of a *people* doctor, are you, Dr O'Neill?'

'No. But these children are—' I started to say, but she rudely cut me off again. I was tempted to speak right over her next question, but I stopped myself. My mistake.

'You've never been a mother, have you, Dr O'Neill? Please answer yes or no.'

'No, but— No.'

*I wanted to punch Fitzgibbons, I really did. She deserved it, too.*

'You've been cohabiting with a man who is not your husband, is that correct?'

'I wouldn't say we're cohabiting.'

*I definitely wanted to strangle her to death, then punch her lights out for good measure.*

'Correction. Okay. Have it your way, then. You're having sex with a man not your husband?'

Jeffrey Kussof objected to the question, and he was sustained.

'Is this your idea of how to be a role model to underage children?' Fitzgibbons stayed on the attack.

Jeffrey was up in a flash. 'Objection, Your Honor. Calls for a conclusion on the part of the witness.'

'Sustained.'

'Dr O'Neill, if you were to have custody of the six young children, how would you manage to both work and care for them? Have you thought about that? Would you drive them to their various schools? Or would you just open the door and let them fly?'

'OBJECTION, Your Honor! Counsel is badgering the witness,' said my lawyer.

But Catherine Fitzgibbons gave him a curt, snide wave of dismissal. 'I have no further questions for this witness.'

She proudly waddled back to her seat.

# CHAPTER NINE

Judge Dwyer gave us the most special gift that night, and I hoped it didn't come out of some combination of pity and guilt. He made a decision that the kids could spend part of the night with Kit and me. He kind of threw us a bone.

What a treat! Unforgettable.

The kids were brought to our hotel, the venerable old Brown Palace, by a phalanx of US Marshals. The first order of business was deciding on a place for dinner. Everyone was superstarved. The choices were room service, the Ship Tavern right there in the hotel, or the Little Italy in the Sixteenth Street Mall. Little Italy won in a landslide, six to two. Supposedly, they had great veggie pizza, the kids' all-time favorite food on the planet. Say no more.

We arrived at the Italian restaurant around eight thirty and the usual rules were in effect: no staring contests with other people; no food fights, especially under the circumstances; absolutely no flying inside Little Italy; no snide jokes about 'Uncle Frank' or 'little Joey', who were pictured all over the walls.

The kids were a dream to be with that night. Part of it was because they were on their best behavior, but part was because they were so smart, and they were growing up so fast. Max was twelve, but in human years she was probably twice that. She was even starting to look like a young woman in her midteens. And then there was Ozymandias, who was more handsome than Prince Harry on a good hair day.

This was the first time they had all been together to talk and 'vent' about their new parents.

Ozymandias started off by saying that his mom was a 'really good, really sweet person', but that she just didn't get the bird part of him, and kept suggesting that he would 'grow out of it'. He also revealed to us that his mother had engaged an agent and an entertainment lawyer because 'we don't want to be taken advantage of by Hollywood types, do we?'.

'I like her, you know,' he said, 'but she really isn't equipped to handle me. The press are always sniffing around the house, and she thinks it's okay. She likes the attention, I think. Not in a mean way. She's just human.'

All of the kids had horror stories about the press constantly being at their houses, at school, just about anywhere they went. The Chens had sold interviews with Peter and Wendy; the Marshalls would have, except that Max *forbade* it. She had also smashed up a camera during a particularly obnoxious interview.

'If goddamn ET shows up here tonight,' she warned, 'I'm going to take away their cameras, and film *them*.'

While we were waiting for various desserts to be served – gelato, sorbetto, chocolate zuccotto cake – Max took the floor. God, she was magnificent: looks, bearing, everything about her said *Hero. Follow me. I am the special one you've been waiting for*.

Imagine heightened mother-of-pearl and you would come pretty close to getting the color of her wings right. They had an iridescent sheen, flushed pink where the shafts emerged from her nearly translucent skin. They reminded me of the wings of ospreys or swans, but, of course, spanning ten feet, were much larger. The wings grew from behind her shoulders, but Max's arms seemed elegant and natural. Clearly, she represented the best of both species.

'Unaccustomed as I am to public speaking,' she said, and we all laughed. Actually, Max had been on just about every TV news and talk show going over the past few months. And of course, she was very good.

'Win, lose, or draw,' she continued, 'I just want Frannie and Kit to know how much we appreciate everything they've done for us, and I mean everything, from saving our pitiful butts, to getting shot at, and having Frances's wonderful house burned to the ground, and then coming here and offering to take all of us into their new home. My God, they're even willing to take in Icarus!'

'Sure, pick on the blind kid,' yelled Ic as he laughed hysterically. He actually loved it that Max always took special care to include him.

'Frannie said in court today that we belong together, that we should never be separated, and I swear, that's the way it will be. It's the right thing to do, the only thing. Anyone with even half a brain has to see that. So we may be in trouble,' she said and winked, 'because our fate is now in the hands of this country's justice system.'

Then Max came around the table and gave Kit and me the biggest, warmest hug and kisses.

'We love you both,' she said. 'Mom and Dad.'

# CHAPTER TEN

That night, a man who looked very much like Dr Ethan Kane walked through thick woods toward Frannie O'Neill's cabin in Bear Bluff. He'd flown into Denver that morning and actually watched a part of the trial. Dr Kane was extraordinarily interested in the bird-children, especially Maximum, who not only represented a forward step in evolution, but who might also know things *she shouldn't*.

Amazing to Dr Kane, the vet had left the door to her animal hospital unlocked. There was a note taped to it: handwritten instructions to someone named Jessie.

Ethan Kane proceeded inside the small house, preferring to use a flashlight rather than turning on the lamp in the foyer.

He found his way through a small office, then into some kind of operating suite, which seemed to double as a pharmacy.

The animals at the clinic already knew he was there. Dogs, cats, and Lord-knew-what-else began to bark, howl, hiss and chirp from the room in the back.

'*Shut up*, you *imbeciles*,' Kane said through gritted teeth. He hated pets, and even more, those who kept them. Did no one understand natural selection nowadays?

He made his way back to the office and started a search for Dr O'Neill's notes on Max. They had to be somewhere in the files – and they were. He located two manila folders thick with scribbly handwriting. *No computer nonsense for our Dr O'Neill, no sirreee!*

Dr Kane began to make mental notes from the examination findings . . .

*Max is a human who has been 'improved' by genetic engineering,* Dr O'Neill had written.

*Injected with avian DNA as an embryo . . .*

*Examination specs:*

*Massive chest, fully three times deeper than that of a human . . . needs the extra musculature to support her wings.*

*Overlapping ribs and a protruding breastbone or 'keel' that runs the length of her ribcage.*

*No breasts or nipples . . . Max will not deliver live young.*

*Exceptionally long trachea or windpipe . . . thirty inches . . . folded accordion-style . . . fills with air during long flights.*

*Bones are hollow to keep her body light for flight.*

Then Dr Kane heard a faint noise on the front porch. He too had exceptional hearing. Plus, he was paranoid.

*Now who?* he wondered.

'Frannie? . . . Are you in there, sweetie? . . . Fran? It's Jessie . . . I thought you—'

A very large woman was at the door that led into the office – Jessie from the note on the door. She must have weighed two hundred fifty, and not even soaking wet.

She saw him.

'Hello, Jessie,' he said. 'I suppose there's no harm in telling you that I'm rifling through Dr O'Neill's notes on Max. And that it's vitally important for mankind. I'm sure you won't tell.'

Kane then pulled a handgun from his jacket pocket and shot the large woman twice. That was nothing. Not a problem. Getting rid of Jessie's body, making it disappear, now that took some real thought and effort.

But in the end – Jessie disappeared *as if she had never been.*

That was the genius of Dr Ethan Kane.

# CHAPTER ELEVEN

The custody hearing began again at nine sharp the next morning. This was the big day, had to be. Catherine Fitzgibbons shot to her feet and called Oz's mother to the stand first thing. I thought I knew why, and it troubled me. The story that Anthea Taranto would tell now was sad and affecting. *It might even win the case for their side.*

Anthea was a pretty, graying woman of forty-nine. She wore a lavender silk skirt, white blouse, and a navy-blue blazer. She was recently widowed, her husband, Mike, having died of cancer the previous year. Ozymandias was her only child, and her only living relative.

Mrs Taranto spoke haltingly, but she told her story with heart-wrenching simplicity and tact. She and Mike had tried for years to have children. They had gone to a well-known, highly regarded *in vitro* fertilization clinic in Boulder. There had been false starts, but, finally, Anthea Taranto had conceived.

'I went in for a routine checkup at eight months,' she told the hushed room. 'I remember how happy Mike and I were that day. Dr Brownhill told us that it was all routine, then as he examined me, he became concerned. He told me that the fetus was in trouble and would have to be delivered right away. I had an emergency C-section on the spot. *I was told that my baby had died*. Can you imagine how I felt that day?'

Mrs Taranto touched her stomach unconsciously, and seemed to drift out of the courtroom and into her memory before she resumed her tragic and affecting story.

'When I found out my son was *alive*, not dead, it changed everything for me. Oz is the most important person in my life. He is my reason for living. I would do anything for him. Just give me a chance, Oz. Please let me be your mother, my angel.'

Then Anthea Taranto looked directly at Kit and me. She fired the next few breathtaking words at us.

'It doesn't matter that these children are different or that it is a challenge to parent them,' said Mrs Taranto. 'They are our children. No one should be allowed to take them from us again. Please don't take my baby away! I am Oz's mother. That has to mean something, even in this brave new world we're living in.'

There was a long pause. All eyes were on Anthea. Finally, Catherine Fitzgibbons said, 'I have nothing else for Mrs Taranto. Thank you so much.'

'I have no questions, Your Honor,' said our attorney.

In fact, Jeffrey had few questions for any of the biological parents who took the stand that morning. They were from different backgrounds, different socioeconomic groups, but all seemed like nice people. The issue was, *could these seven people raise such special children, and also keep them safe?*

I honestly didn't think so. Especially the *safe* part.

Jeffrey gently suggested to Max's father that he might be overly enjoying his fifteen minutes of fame. He got the Chens to admit that major advertisers were negotiating for Peter and Wendy to do product endorsements. He brought out that Oz had an agent in Hollywood. But even the lightest jabs made me squirm with embarrassment. Attacking the parents could only backfire. And it just wasn't fair.

But one thing about the parents did bother me. It bothered me a lot. None of them said, 'I want to do whatever is best for my child.' And none of them acknowledged the safety issue either.

The court recessed for lunch, which Kit and I both skipped. We went up on the roof and held hands and were unusually quiet for us.

We also prayed for the kids, and for their parents. When the trial resumed, it was with a thunderbolt.

Jeffrey Kussof stood and turned toward the children. 'I call Max Marshall to the stand.'

# CHAPTER TWELVE

When Max heard her name called, her heart started to pound *at flight rate*, close to one hundred and twenty beats a minute.

It was her turn on the spit. She'd seen what the lawyers could do to witnesses, and now she would be grilled. Almost every minute of her life had been classified as Top Secret. And she had been warned very explicitly:

*You talk, you die.*

It was that simple, that crystal clear.

She was supposed to tell the truth, the whole truth and nothing but the truth in this courtroom, right? But what if she did?

It would make everything worse than any of them could imagine. Max knew things that no little girl should be burdened with. And she knew the secrets had to remain that way.

*You talk, you die.*

The courtroom had gotten very quiet, and Max realized that every single person was gawking at her. She was in the dreaded spotlight, and she hated being there. Her *freak-meter* was sounding loud and clear.

'Max, *go*,' said her biological father, Art, who was a nice enough guy, though bossy sometimes. 'Go on now. You can do this, honey.'

'You'll be fine,' said her mother, Terry. 'Go ahead, Max. You're safe here. Just tell the truth.'

*Yeah, right*, Max couldn't help thinking. *Tell the truth, and die a horrible death.*

Such was her fear that when Max finally stood, she beat her wings and hovered a few inches off the ground.

The crowd whispered, '*Ohhhhhhhhhh.*'

Max grimaced and forced her wings to her sides. Then she made herself walk the twenty-five feet or so to the witness stand. *Just walk, Max. Be a normal twelve-year-old.*

She looked up and saw the two flags behind the bench: the American stars and stripes; and the Colorado state flag with its alternating blue and white stripes and the big red letter C with a yellow circle inside. Behind the judge was an inscription on the wall: 'In God We Trust'.

*What did that mean right now? Could she really trust in God? Had God made her – or was it man?*

A clerk offered Max the Bible and she placed a hand on it and swore to tell the truth. Her body was still shaking a little. This was so bad, almost unbearable.

*You talk, you die. And so do the other five kids. And maybe Kit and Frannie, too.*

'Don't be afraid,' said Judge Dwyer, as if he knew what she was thinking. 'We're all friends here.'

'Yes, that's right,' said Jeffrey Kussof. 'Just tell your story, Max. We want to hear it. Everyone does.'

Max nodded okay, though this wasn't okay at all. She flipped her long blonde hair back over her shoulders. She cleared her throat, then leaned in close to the microphone in front of her.

*Damn, she didn't want to do this. What she wanted to do – was to fly away.*

But instead, Max did the unspeakable.

She spoke.

# CHAPTER THIRTEEN

'**I** know I'm just a young girl,' Max began in a whispery voice. 'I don't know a whole lot of things, because I haven't seen too much yet. But let me tell you some things I do know. All of this is the truth, so help me. I was there, you weren't.'

Max could see Kit and Frannie watching her from their seats up front. Frannie winked at her, and she could almost hear her say, '*Go, girl,*' which Frannie said all the time. It was their mantra, one of the countless small, silly things that connected them, and always would.

'People did obscene, really horrific things where we used to live – at the lab called the School,' Max finally said, her voice like aspen leaves quaking in the breeze. Just thinking about the School made her incredibly angry.

'Little babies were put to sleep there, which means they were *murdered*. I saw it happen. I saw dead bodies of kids just like me. *Look at me, please*. Look at Matthew, Ic, Oz, Peter and Wendy. Aren't we cute? Well, we were treated like lab rats. Usually, a lot worse than rats. There are *laws* to protect lab rats.'

Max twisted in her seat to Judge Dwyer. Maybe he could help her. She desperately wanted to fly out of here. Her wings rustled. It was the only sound that could be heard in the courtroom.

'We were put up for sale. People *still* want to buy us! To experiment on us horribly. To see how we work,' Max said. 'Visitors came to the School to check us out, to test us. We were just property to them. Their *creations*, right? We were going to be used in further experiments. That's why my brother Matthew and I escaped. Then we were hunted. I was *shot* down out of the sky by the same people who said that they loved me. If Frannie and Kit hadn't helped us, we'd all be dead now. I'm not exaggerating, am I, Frannie?'

'No, you're not, sweetie.' I spoke from my seat. 'You're just telling the truth.'

Matthew jumped up from his seat. He whooped, 'We made it, though, Max. We escaped. The bad guys were burned to crispy critters! So don't mess with us! Ever!'

It took several minutes for the crowd to quiet after that. When it did, Max said, 'Try to understand. We can't have rules like other kids. We can't be told what to eat for breakfast or how to say our prayers. We have to fly when we want to, especially at night. As you can see for yourselves, we're not exactly like the rest of you.'

The judge was listening to her. He was really listening, and he wasn't threatening or scaring her in any way. Max took solace in that. For the first time, she allowed herself to hope that people could do the right thing. It was a real long shot. But *maybe* it could happen.

'We look like little kids,' Max continued. 'But we've seen a lot of suffering and death.'

Her throat caught, then, and she had to stop. She willed herself not to cry, which was what she ached to do. 'We really, really love Kit and Frannie. I know they aren't our biological parents, but they are the best for us. We found that out when we all lived together at the Lake House. We lived there for a glorious four months. It was heaven. The Lake House is the only place where we've ever felt safe in our lives. The only place! We only feel safe when we're all together as a family. *We must be kept safe!* Please believe me, it's dangerous for us out in the world. It's so dangerous. You can't *believe* how dangerous. We have enemies out there! People want to use us, abuse us. Take us apart and put us back together again!'

When she looked around, Max saw that little Peter and Wendy were shivering, holding on to each other. Kit and Frannie had tears in their eyes. So did a lot of the spectators seated around the courtroom. Even the Marshalls. For a moment, anyway, they all believed her. They got it. Finally.

Slowly, spontaneously and one by one, the rows of spectators rose. They began to applaud Max. They called out her name, and then the names of the other kids.

'Thank you, Max,' said Judge Dwyer, as the courtroom quieted. 'Thank you for telling the truth, painful as it is. You may step down.'

Max got up and moved away from the witness chair. She had told a lot of the truth. But she hadn't told it all. She hadn't told *why* it was so dangerous for the six of them, and how she knew.

The judge was speaking again.

'The court is in recess. I want to see the parents, and Mr Brennan and Dr O'Neill and their attorney, and the children's advocate, Mrs Fitzgibbons. In my chambers. Now.'

# CHAPTER FOURTEEN

M ax's mother came rushing over to her. 'Max, you must stay right
here in the courtroom, okay? I mean it, young lady. It's the
safest place for you and the other kids. I *do* understand safety. Your
father and I have to go in with the judge. I think he's made his
decision.'

Max felt a surge of resentment. She liked Terry Marshall well
enough, but her biological mother didn't understand a fricking-
fracking thing about her, or her safety, or the other kids. The other
parents were nervously trying to quiet their children, too. She could
hear the twins screeching, 'Leave us alone, please leave us alone . . .
*Back off!*'

Max felt tension and fear mounting throughout her body and her
head was throbbing. *You talk, you die.* She had to get away from all
this, at least for a couple of minutes. She had to get out of this
claustrophobic room. All the noise, the rude and pushy people. And
worst of all, the press. Tamping their sneaky IFB earpieces in place.
Twisting their network-logo-flagged microphones. Never taking their
nasty, beady eyes off her.

She needed space.

Even if it might be dangerous.

As soon as the Marshalls disappeared into the judge's chambers,
Max practically flew through the open doors and veered sharply into a
double-width hallway.

There was an elevator bank up ahead, shiny metal doors. Max looked back and saw Frannie and Kit holding back the crowd as best they could. She could hear Frannie saying, 'The kids just need to talk. They'll be fine. They're frightened and upset right now. Trust their instincts.' Then she heard the other kids coming, a rush of wings.

'Wait, Max! Wait up, for cripes' sakes,' yelled Oz. 'Max, let's stay together.'

Max listened to the grinding sound of an elevator as it climbed to the sixth floor. The elevator arrived, and the kids piled in.

*Yes, trust our instincts.*

'It's going up,' said Oz.

'Excellent,' Max said. 'I like *up* very, very much.'

The six of them whooped! They all liked *up*.

# CHAPTER FIFTEEN

U*p! Up! Up!*
  The elevator doors opened again and the kids filed out into a wide, empty space. Max saw a metal door with bright red letters: *ROOF*. She used both hands and pried it open.

'Roof! Roof! Roof!' the other kids chanted. 'The roof is the place to be!'

'Let's just vamanos!' shouted Icarus. 'I'm talking *escape*. Let's go to the Lake House. *Please*, can we?'

'The Lake House! Go to the Lake House!' the kids chanted.

The afternoon sun beat down on the roof of the courthouse, but the breeze riffling Max's feathers offset the heat. The wind was coming from directly behind them. It was blowing from the north and that was perfect.

Just right.

For flight!

'Let's do it,' said Ozymandias, who stood poised on the roof like a handsome young prince. 'You know we should, don't you? They're going to screw us over. There's no such thing as justice in America. It's all a fairy tale.'

'C'mon, let's go,' said blind Ic. 'If I don't have you guys around, I can't fly at all.'

'Can we, please, Max, can we, please?' Wendy begged. 'We can, can't we?'

'*Fly, fly, fly,*' came the chant from the street below.

'We should fly the hell away from here and from all of them down there,' Oz said darkly. He was the eldest next to Max, the strongest, the alpha male. 'We should fly away and never come back. I mean it, Max. That's what my instincts tell me. You know I'm right about this. We won't survive in these separate little families.'

Max sighed and shook her head. 'I like the woods too, but I hate to tell you, Ozymandias, winter is coming.'

Matthew said, 'So, we'll steal blankets. We'll sock away SpaghettiOs and big red fart-your-brains-out beans.'

Max laughed at the image from her precocious younger brother. 'Sure, but you know, we also like *pillows* and *Timeports* and *vegetarian pizza* and the latest *videos*.'

Matthew looked crestfallen. She thought that he might actually start to cry.

'Hey, don't be sad,' said Max. 'Buck up, buckaroo. At least you'll be with me.'

'We're just *things* to them. Like toys from FAO Schwarz,' said Oz. 'They want to tell us what to do. They're total control freaks. They think they're superior to nature, to animals, plants, and birds.'

'Maybe,' Max said, 'but we wanted to live in the world with other people. You know, we begged for it. We almost died for it. So maybe, just maybe, we should do what they say we should do. For a while anyway.'

'Well, guess what they say we should do,' said Oz. '*Listen* to the people, Max. What do you hear?'

The never-ending chant floated up to them from the street, where crowds were watching. 'Fly, fly, fly.'

Max cupped her hands in front of her mouth. 'Okay! Sure! Fine!' she shouted down from the eight-story-high rooftop. 'Okay!' she called out to the mass of people flooding the park, eddying around cars on the street below. 'But we're doing this because we *want to*. We're doing this *for us*. And we're not going to fly very far.'

Glee lit the children's faces, and they knew just what to do. They positioned themselves at ten-foot intervals around the curve of the roof. Hundreds of camera lenses were pointed upward. This was *the* picture the media had been waiting for.

And it only got better.

With a sudden flourish, the kids spread twelve magnificent wings and *thrssssssshhh!* their wingtips sailed up above their heads almost of their own accord. Sunlight glinted and sparks flickered off bright white-feathered wings.

At Max and Oz's signals, they bent their knees, pushed off hard, and launched themselves into the air. The people below sucked in their breath.

There was no hesitation. The kids flapped their powerful wings effortlessly in the heated air. They soared above the state capitol building, its golden dome glinting in the sunlight. Higher and higher, the six of them flew. *The flock.*

Max could see several of Denver's landmarks spread across the landscape: the public library, the art museum, the Pepsi Center, Six Flags Elitch Gardens amusement park. And, of course, the majestic front range of the Rocky Mountains off in the distance. The city, the entire state, was so gorgeous, and it had the most perfect skies anywhere.

They *chittered* as they flew so that blind Ic would know where they were. '*Cheee-rup. Chee-rup,*' Matthew screeched at the top of his voice. 'Let's go to the Lake House now! Let's go, let's go!'

Max reached forward with the tips of her fingers, then deflected the air with her wings. It was almost like rowing! She did it again and again. Found her rhythm. Nice.

Her magnificent body rose higher into the warm current. She felt her headache fall away. Suddenly, she was in another, better world.

'Stay with me, now,' she called to the others. 'Keep up. You too, Ic.'

'Don't pick on the blind kid,' he yelled back, his favorite joke, *their* favorite joke.

Max tipped her right wing and banked gracefully to the right. The others followed her lead. She tipped her left wing and banked left. This was effortless pleasure.

She kept her left shoulder down and completed a wide and generous loop around the imposing, gray-granite capitol building with its golden dome. The kids were flying wing to wing at her sides.

She had to smile as she looked down. She even allowed herself to feel a little hopeful. The people on the streets were cheering and waving, motioning them to fly faster and higher.

Max knew what every one of them was thinking: *We want to fly. Oh God, we wish we could fly like you.*

# CHAPTER SIXTEEN

B ut not everyone in the huge crowd wanted to fly like the six biological wonders.

Not everyone wanted the children to fly at all.

A gunman named Marco Vincenti was crouching beside piles of lumber on an unfinished floor of a building under construction not far from the City and County building in Denver. He didn't feel one way or the other about the flying kids, except for the fact that they were definitely little freakazoids. They were good-looking and all, even beautiful, but it just wasn't right, what they were, *whatever* the hell they were. Goddamn freaks of nature.

Still, they were fun to watch – until he got his orders to shoot them down.

Actually, he had no idea what the hell would happen next. Whatever it was, he was ready. If he had to take one of them out, it wouldn't be a problem.

He even figured he could take all six down if that was the job requirement. That wouldn't be a problem either. All hell would break loose after the murders, but he didn't give a crap about that. He had his back covered.

Slowly and smoothly he moved the sight of his rifle over the faces of the six of them. The Japanese-made sight was amazing, and he could see tiny imperfections – like a pimple or an ingrown hair – on the kids' individual faces.

He kept bringing the rifle sight back to the blonde female. She was the most impressive, the natural leader. Either she was, or the handsome boy they called Ozymandias. He was sleek and slender, but already had muscles like a laborer.

The rifleman wore a set of earphones, and he patiently waited for his orders to come. For all he knew, there were other snipers out there – *maybe one for each kid.*

Then he heard his name in the earphones. 'Marco, you there? Marco?'

'I'm here,' he said into the mike perched below his lip. *Where the hell else would I be?*

'Can you take out one of them now?'

'It's not a problem. Any of them. Which one do I hit? Your choice.'

'How about all of them?' the voice asked.

'Not a problem either. Just tell me when. *Now* would be a good time. Now is perfect. Not too much wind.'

There was silence for several seconds. Marco Vincenti's finger pressed lightly on the trigger. He was *so* ready.

'Put down the rifle,' said the voice. 'That's all we need for now. This was just a practice run. These children are incredibly valuable to science, and we hope there's another way to solve our problem. Please leave Denver as soon as possible. You're to go by car. You'll be paid for your time. As always, Marco, it's a pleasure to work with a professional. We'll be talking with you again.'

'I look forward to it,' said the contract killer.

And then his earphones went dead.

He held his sight on Max's left eye, then on her right one, and finally on a spot between the two about the size of a dime.

'Catch you next time, kid,' he whispered.

# CHAPTER SEVENTEEN

I felt as if the whole world were about to end. *This was it, wasn't it?* My head was spinning, and it also hurt like hell. I couldn't even think about the *possibility* of losing the kids.

I took a seat in a brown leather wing chair in Judge Dwyer's spacious chambers. The wood paneling in the office was supposed to give off warmth and a feeling of security, but I didn't feel in the least bit secure, and the air-conditioning had made the room freezing cold.

Kit entered the crowded room, searched me out, and came over and took my hand. Finally Judge Dwyer arrived, followed by the court stenographer. The doors were shut with a bang.

'I've called you together,' Judge Dwyer immediately began, 'because I want to let you know my decision in advance. That way, you can tell the children privately.'

I almost couldn't breathe. I squeezed Kit's hand harder as I looked up at him, and he kissed my hair. I couldn't help thinking about what an absolutely terrific guy he was. I brought my attention back to the judge. He was talking about the experimental laboratory that the kids called the School.

'I read the reports on what happened at the School, that horrifying lab that defies description, and my mind nearly rejects the words . . . Had experiments been conducted on rabbits or chimpanzees, I could cite chapter and section finding criminality in the heinous way the victims were treated. But the crimes that have been committed against these children bear no resemblance to science and medicine as it has ever been practiced, even in the darkest ages of human understanding.'

There was a sob from across the room. It came from Anthea Taranto. She looked like she couldn't take any more. Others in the room burst into tears.

Judge Dwyer continued. 'I understand that the people who committed these acts are gone, jailed or dead. Over the past three days I have seen the tragic results of their unspeakable crimes. There are innocents involved. And I don't mean just the children. As Mr Kussof said in his opening statement, there are no bad people here. But my job is to concern myself with the children, and what is best for them.'

The judge took off his reading glasses and placed them on his desk. He gazed around his chambers.

'Here is my decision . . . The petitioners, Dr O'Neill and Mr Brennan, have taken on the task of demonstrating that the custody of these minors by their parents would be detrimental to their well-being. They state that the children will not be happy, or *safe*, with their biological parents. The children seem to believe this as well. That's important to this court. It carries weight with me. But Dr O'Neill and Mr Brennan have not sufficiently proved their case. Not today anyway. Accordingly, I must rule that the children stay with their parents.'

Suddenly, I felt incredibly empty and hollowed out, as if I had lost my own children. Hot tears were streaming down my cheeks. I held in a scream of despair.

'However,' Judge Dwyer continued, 'this is a temporary order. There is a contingency mandated by law that I hold another hearing at a later date. If, as Dr O'Neill posits, this "flock" fails to thrive, I will reverse this ruling. Dr O'Neill, Mr Brennan, please accept my regrets. I'm sorry. I know you love these children like your own.'

A clerk slipped quietly into the room and handed the judge a note. He put on his glasses, read the note, and then he did something unexpected – he smiled.

'Mr and Mrs Stern, Ms Taranto, Mr and Mrs Chen, Mr and Mrs Marshall, the children have returned from a spin around the Capitol building and are waiting for you in Courtroom Seven. You may take them home.'

# PART TWO

---

# FLYING LESSONS

# CHAPTER EIGHTEEN

## The Hospital; Fantasy Room B

Charlotte Donahue's ample body tensed as the stainless-steel earphones were tightly secured on her head. She felt as if she were in a spaceship. *This was getting weird already.*

The sounds of the busy operating room disappeared once the earphones were secure. Then Charlotte heard a voice *inside* her head!

'This is Dr Ethan Kane. Please don't fight the anesthesia, Charlotte. Are you comfortable? Anything you need? It's important that everything is perfect for you.'

Charlotte was feeling stranger and stranger by the second – but *good* strange. Her body was floating; her mind was still sharp. 'I think so. I think I like it.'

'Can you feel this?' the doctor asked as he inserted a long hypodermic needle into the twenty-three-year-old Cincinnati native's acne-scarred lower back.

'Nope. I don't feel anything,' Charlotte said.

Oh God, she wanted to laugh, though. Her longstanding fear of hospitals had evaporated completely, and her excitement was bubbling over. Something incredible was happening to her, something good, something exceptional.

Suddenly, Charlotte smelled a salty sea breeze. Was that possible?

Where had it come from? *Isn't this the weirdest experience ever!* It certainly was.

Then she heard seagulls calling. Seagulls – she was sure of it.

And then she could *see* the SS *Nautica* looming above her, nine stories of pristine, shining white luxury. She looked down at herself in total amazement and befuddlement. Everything about her had changed. *When had this incredible makeover happened?* She was wearing a dress of thin red silk, and red slingbacks dusted with sparkling rhinestones. Her heels clacked pleasantly as she walked up the gangway toward the main deck of the *Nautica*. The decking was teakwood, and teak deckchairs were everywhere.

At the top of the gangway stood a blond-haired steward wearing a smart blue sailor's hat and crisply pressed blue uniform. He handed Charlotte a drink in a crystal glass and welcomed her aboard. 'Miss Donahue,' he said. 'A pleasure.' He even knew her name.

He winked at her, but Charlotte's thoughts were elsewhere. *The captain,* dressed all in white, peered down at her from the bridge. No doubt about it – he was actually watching her. Charlotte brazenly turned her face up to him, looked directly into his silver-blue eyes.

Ridiculous or not, she felt a wave of desire. Her skin was pleasantly warm – then Dr Kane spoke again.

*Spoilsport!*

'Can you still hear me, Charlotte?'

Somewhere on the deck a steel band had started to play a song she recognized as 'Mockingbird'. The band was halfway decent, too. Bob Marley-ish. Maybe a hint of Jimmy Cliff.

'Ms Donahue?'

'Go away, Dr Kane,' she said, and drank deeply from her champagne cocktail glass. 'I'm fine. I'm okay. This *is* perfect. Now let me have my fun in the sun.'

'What are you drinking?'

'It's pink,' she said. 'I think it's passion-fruit champagne. Delicious.'

The drink was sweet and pungent and made her feel a touch giddy. She didn't know where to look next, or what to do first. The bouncy rhythm of the steel drums called to her. The band had already found a nice groove. Oh yes, she wanted to dance! *With the captain!*

'Charlotte, go over to the railing and look down. You'll see me in the crowd. Wave to me, please,' said Dr Kane.

She wasn't sure why, but Charlotte did what she was told. She made her way to the railing and looked down at the cheering mob of well-wishers gathered on the pier. As she leaned against the rail, she could see lifeboats jutting out slightly from one of the decks below.

*There he was!* The very handsome, if somewhat cool and restrained, Dr Kane. He was looking up at her.

'Goodbye,' she called out to her doctor. She lifted her hand and waved and started to laugh. She couldn't stop laughing. Streams of pink and baby-blue confetti streaked the air. Ropes fell heavily against the hull. The ship's bullhorn blew three deeply satisfying blasts.

'Bye-bye,' she called gaily.

The doctor spoke once more. 'Bon voyage, Charlotte. I'm sorry you have to die now. But you're helping someone . . . who is so much more important than yourself.'

# CHAPTER NINETEEN

E than Kane stopped talking to silly ass Charlotte and went back to work on her.

The surgeon had nerves of steel, and hands that were even steadier. His instrument was a bovee, a scalpel that used heat rather than a blade. It burned blue at the tip and emanated a whispery sound as he made the first incision three millimeters deep, running laterally from one of Charlotte Donahue's shoulders all the way to the other.

The red bloodline turned black almost instantly and left a ghostly trail of smoke. The air filled with the unmistakable odor of burning flesh.

His next incision formed a T with the first, starting at the throat and ending at the pubic bone, a line so crisply defined it might have been drawn on the girl's milky skin with a fine-tip marking pen.

His third cut went deep into the subcutaneous layer, the thick yellow fat that rounded out Charlotte's voluptuous shape as a woman.

He then slid his hands inside her. Arteries were held with a guillotine clamp designed to press on one side, cut on the other. Dr Kane worked carefully to sever connective tissues and any adhesive attachments.

Within eighteen minutes, the woman's most precious organs floated freely inside the open cavity of her body. Bypass machines kept them shining and pink. Her heart still beat a strong sixty beats a minute.

Suddenly, there came an otherworldly hum from overhead. A stainless-steel mechanical device, looking like the jaws of an earth-moving apparatus, traveled over a metal track. A medical tech lowered 'the Scoop' by hand, then positioned it over the woman's body.

A slight, tinny, musical sound could be heard coming from Charlotte's earphones, an Island tune. *'Hot tea, rice, salt fish is nice and the rum is fine any time of year,'* Dr Kane sang along. He was being ironic.

'Okay, then,' he said, as he surveyed the work. 'I'm through in here. *C'est fini.'*

The anesthesiologist glanced at a monitor above Charlotte's head. Pictures aboard the SS *Nautica* flickered on the screen. 'Want to give the young lady a few more minutes to get laid? One last fling?'

'You're so sentimental,' Kane said, and frowned. 'No. My time is much more valuable than hers. Cut her off.'

The anesthesiologist shrugged, then ripped the cord from Charlotte's earphones and the music stopped.

'Thank you,' said Kane. 'I hate that reggae shit anyway.'

He flipped a switch, and the guillotine clamps made their cuts. Blood immediately drained through large plastic tubes out of the body and into a huge stainless-steel canister. Charlotte Donahue's organs began to turn gray. The neon-colored tracers on the monitors went crazy.

Then they flat-lined, with the resultant high-pitched *bleeeeeee-eeeeeeeep.*

'Okay, everyone,' Dr Kane said to the room at large. 'Let's shuck her.'

The open jaws of the Scoop closed. With a whine and a hum, the Scoop lifted the woman's internal system out of her body in one piece.

Charlotte Donahue had been shucked as clean as an oyster at DC Coast in nearby Washington, one of Dr Kane's favorite places to eat and drink. He might even grab the wife and go there tonight.

# CHAPTER TWENTY

C olorado.
    *Another day, another school,* thought Max to herself. *But hopefully, this will be a good school. No, a great school! And a great beginning.*

The jarring ring of the bell marked the end of third period. She'd been listening to a talk on the diminishing populations of endangered species in Colorado: the black-tailed prairie dog, Hops Blue butterfly, peregrine falcon, osprey. It was her eleventh day of classes, and she was trying hard to do everything *imperfectly.* Smart, but not too smart; funny, but not too funny; humble, but not a smarmy kiss-ass.

She grabbed her very cool bicycle messenger bag from under her desk, stuffed her textbooks inside, and rose to join the bubbly throng flooding out of the classroom. The crowd included a dog. Her teacher, as usual, had brought his brown Labrador retriever to class. Kind of goofy, but kind of cool too.

Max never actually reached the doorway.

A scream coming from somewhere outside the building stopped her cold. She spun around. *Matthew! He was in trouble!* Max was sure it was her brother; his voice was impressed on her brain, hardwired into her nervous system.

None of the other kids heard it – but her sensitive hearing picked it right up. *Matthew!*

Max dropped her book bag, ran to the window, and looked two stories down into the dusty plain of the schoolyard. There he was! A pack of boys was chasing Matthew, a couple of them waving hockey sticks. And cans of something. *What the hell were they doing?*

She saw a flash of metal and a yellow mist fill the air. Then she got it. They were trying to paint Matthew's wings. It was the third time since they'd been at the school that a gang had gone after him.

'Hey,' she yelled. 'Hey, stop that! STOP IT NOW!'

She beat on the windowpane with her fists, but no one looked up. Of course not. *Their hearing sucked!* Max ran from the classroom, charged down the crowded flight of concrete fire stairs, and barreled out into the playground. She was careful not to fly at school. Not even now.

She could see the bully-boys at the far end of the playground. Oh so cool in their Aeropostale, American Eagle, and Abercrombie garb. Five boys, ninth-graders, had formed a semicircle near the chain-link fence. Nine-year-old Matthew was trapped in the middle of them. Their faces were twisted with hate and anger as they taunted him. Thank God the press wasn't around today or she and Matthew would be *Live at 5* again.

She could hear everything they said, but certain words stabbed into her heart. 'Freak show.' 'Carnival boy.' 'Maggot carrier.'

The biggest kid, a stocky, pear-shaped bully wearing baggy gangsta pants and an Avalanche sweatshirt, grabbed Matthew by the arms as another kid held up a can of spray paint. Red!

Max heard the harsh rattling of the metal ball inside the can, then the fizz of airborne Rustoleum.

*'Stop that right now, you little brats!'* she screamed.

The boys were momentarily startled and broke apart from their huddle. Matthew wrenched free from the biggest kid's grasp and immediately fell to the ground. His wing feathers and clothes were soaked with paint. He was forcing himself not to cry. Brave Matthew! What a damn good kid he was.

'Matty, I'm here,' Max said, gathering her brother to her, kissing the top of his head. That was all it took to break the bullies' ceasefire. Spray cans fizzed again.

'Who are you calling a brat, you freak bitch?' yelled the leader of the pack.

'Oh, I'm sorry, I was talking to *you*.' Max spat out venom. 'You're the one I want a piece of.'

The boy was probably fifteen and already weighed at least one-seventy. She knew him by reputation. His father had played pro football for the Denver Broncos, or something terribly impressive like that. He laughed at Max. 'Bring it on. Let's tussle.'

Max had promised the Marshalls never to hurt a kid at school. So had Matthew. She wanted to take this creepy punk apart, but she held back, which was really hard. Almost impossible.

Then she saw the bright red paint smeared on poor Matthew. It got her furious all over again. *Bring it on? This obnoxious jerk had no idea what he was asking for.*

'What's your name, punk?' she asked.

'You don't know who I am? Shit, girl, I'm Bryce Doulin. Everybody knows me.'

'*You* don't know who you're messing around with, bitch,' Max growled. 'You and your friends don't get it. But maybe you will in a minute.'

Doulin was a little fat, but muscular. He came at her, but Max grabbed him in a tight headlock. He pulled at her arm with both of his hands. 'Hey! Leggo!' he yelped.

Max's fingers were like steel pincers. They didn't budge. Doulin was gagging. His piggy eyes were bulging. She yanked the spray can out of his hand. Easily.

What they'd done to Matthew was a desecration. It was a hate crime. She knew that much. Now what should she do? Maybe paint Bryce Doulin from head to toe. Or mark him with the words *MAX'S BITCH*. And then what? She'd be the bully, wouldn't she?

She finally loosened her hold on Doulin's neck and shoved him away from her. He stumbled and fell over backwards on the lawn. The rest of the gang was looking on in disbelief. Bryce Doulin was on his ass, and a girl had done it.

Max crushed the spray can until it crumpled and *popped*. It was easy. She took her time and stared right into the eyes of every kid in the circle, but especially Doulin's.

'Matthew could have hurt you, too. He's almost as strong as I am,' she said. 'He chose not to because he's such a goddamn good kid. Don't ever mess with him again. *Ever.* Until the day you die and maggots eat your worthless guts.'

She helped Matthew to his feet and together they watched as the pack of older boys backed away, grumbling and cursing, but mostly scared out of their gourds. Max would remember the faces. She would remember every one of them for as long as she lived.

*Why do they hate like that? Where does it come from?* She was afraid she would never really understand humans.

But maybe that was a good thing.

# CHAPTER TWENTY-ONE

On a Saturday morning about a week later, Max heard shouts, then a loud scream come from upstairs in the Marshall house. She turned to her brother, but he was lost in a game of *Grand Theft Auto* on his PlayStation II.

'We better go see,' Max finally said. 'C'mon, Matty. Put down the game. *Matthew*, now!'

'All right. I heard you the first time.'

Although they were forbidden to fly inside the house, they flew up to the second floor and then down the hall to the master bedroom.

They found Terry Marshall at the door to the room. She had on her cleaning outfit: a plaid kerchief, cut-off jeans, a T-shirt that had *Einstein Brothers Bagels* printed on it.

'It got in when I was airing out our bedroom,' she said. 'It will break everything I love in there. Can you help me, Max? I don't want to hurt it.'

Max took a peek inside the bedroom. 'It' was a female mourning dove that apparently had flown in through an open window and was trapped.

A couple of the poor girl's feathers were stuck on the closed picture window that looked out on to a small pond. There was a smear of blood on the dove's beak.

'Poor baby, easy, baby,' Max whispered to the dove. 'It's okay, sweetie.'

'What can we do? Can't you talk to it?' Terry Marshall asked in a shaky voice. 'Get it out of here! Please.'

'*It's* petrified,' Max scolded, but then she went on; 'We'll take care of it, Moms.' Moms was what she usually called Terry, mostly out of respect, but sometimes just because it was the practical thing to do.

'We know how to do this. We'll talk to the dove,' Max said, then gently nudged Moms out of the room. 'Leave it to us,' she said. Then she closed the door.

Matthew immediately rolled his eyes at his big, usually smart sister. 'We'll talk to the dove? What are we gonna say to it? *Get a grip, dumb bird?*'

'I don't know, Matt. Something will come to me.'

'Should we rush it? I can be kinda gentle.'

'I don't think so, Matty. She'll freak. She's petrified to be in here.'

Max went and opened the French doors that led from the bedroom on to a small terrace.

The dove continued to fly against the picture window – the one way it *couldn't* get out of the room. It was so beautiful, warm brown in color, with pink feet and a pinkish cast to its breast feathers.

'Sit down with me, Matt,' said Max. 'Sit by the open door. Just *sit*, Matthew.'

Matt rolled his eyes again – his absolute favorite communication that meant something seemed particularly crazy to him – but he sat down. 'And now, we – what?' he asked.

'We talk to it,' said Max. 'It's called a mourning dove because of its call – *oooh-a-oo-whoo*.'

'Oooh-a-oo-whoo?' Matthew said, then snorted out a laugh.

'That's it, Matty. You've got it,' encouraged Max.

'Oooh-a-oo-whoo.'

'Oooh-a-oo-whoo.'

It took a couple of minutes, but the dove finally noticed the two of them. She didn't want them to know, but the female was checking them out. Also, she wasn't smacking herself against the picture window any more. Fluttering wildly, yes; but no more smacking her brains out against the glass.

'Oooh-a-oo-whoo,' Max and Matthew continued to whisper.

'Oooh-a-oo-whoo.'

'C'mon, sweetheart. You can do it,' Max coaxed.

'Oooh-a-oo-whoo.'

'This door is the way out. Come right through here.'

'Oooh-a-oo-whoo.'

'Oooh-a-oo-whoo.'

'It's so easy, dummy!' exclaimed a frustrated Matthew. 'Go. Out. The. Door.'

'Coo, Matty. She's a mother. She's worried about her young ones. Just be patient with her.'

'Oooh-a-oo-whoo.'

'Oooh-a-oo-whoo.'

'Oooh-a-oo-whoo.'

'Oooh-a-oo-whoo.'

Then very suddenly, and without so much as a thank you, the mourning dove darted out the terrace door to freedom. It flew at its absolute top speed across the mill pond, and disappeared into the thick grove of pines beyond.

When Terry Marshall finally came back to check, Max and Matthew were sitting on the bedroom floor, whispering 'oooh-a-oo-whoo' over and over.

'How strange,' their biological mother said. 'You two are really weird, you know that?'

*Frannie told you*, Max thought to herself.

# CHAPTER TWENTY-TWO

After the custody trial had ended, I went home to jump-start my life again in the beautiful Colorado boonies.

Kit went back to Washington, DC.

I'm not sure that either of us knew why we were separating, but I think it had something to do with losing the kids, and needing to grieve. Kit said that his job was in Washington, at least for the time being, but he would be out to see me a lot, as often as he possibly could.

We phoned each other in the beginning, and sent e-mails, but there was not a single visit from him. I honestly believe we had sunk into depression. It wasn't admirable, but I suppose it was understandable, and human, but mostly cowardly and dumb on both our parts – if I may speak for Kit as well as for myself.

Life went on in Colorado, though there was one strange and very sad event – a good friend of mine simply disappeared. Jessie Horvath was there one day, and then she was gone. All traces of her, all two hundred and fifty pounds. Just gone.

It was about four on a Sunday afternoon and I was up to my wrists in blood and guts. My usual gig at the veterinary hospital.

I was in the room that doubled, tripled, actually, as the surgery suite, examining room, and pharmacy area. All around me were supplies ranging from cotton balls and tongue depressors to hundreds of plastic bottles filled with pills, all of them white. A single picture hung on the wall, a news photo of me at the head of the 'Cause for Paws' benefit hike in Boulder.

A tuna-fish sandwich lay half eaten on the sink ledge where I'd left it at noon when a cat-rescue lady brought in a carload of feral cats to be altered.

Thankfully, the end was in sight.

I was closing up my ninth and last patient, a big homeless tabby named Sophie, when I heard an ungodly racket out front.

It was an extremely loud police siren – *and the car was right outside my door.*

I hoped somebody in a 4x4 hadn't hit a deer or a horse. Clearly, it was some kind of emergency, though.

*Damn.* I didn't need this at all.

I knotted the last stitch in Sophie's incision, put her into a cage with a fluffy pink blanket, then hurried outside to greet whatever trouble the cops were bringing me.

'I'm coming,' I called ahead. 'I'm coming! Hold your water! Turn off that damn siren!'

# CHAPTER TWENTY-THREE

The Inn-Patient, my small animal hospital, is a 2,000-square-foot glass-and-timber box that sits twenty feet off the highway near the intersection in Bear Bluff, a precious town, but one so tiny you could pass through it a couple of times without even noticing. The state troopers' barracks is only two miles up the road, and I've gotten to know most of the 'staties' from the hard-luck strays and hit-and-runs they've brought me over the years.

The cruiser's rotating beacon was still on when I stepped out into the parking area outside my front door. Suddenly I hoped this wasn't about my friend Jessie.

I saw Trooper James H. Blake get out of his car. A former fullback at Colorado State, he's a massive six-three with huge arms and torso. His strong arms carried a dun-colored sleeping bag, and it was soaked with blood.

*Oh c'mon, James H,* I said to myself.

I took another look at the cruiser, and saw a couple of plaid-shirted teenage boys in the back seat. A blond and a redhead; long shaggy hair; angry, pouty faces.

My sinking heart told me that whatever was in the sleeping bag had been hurt by these two boys. I've heard all the rationale, so don't bother to argue with me. *I hate hunting, and I always will.*

James Blake was obviously upset too. I could tell he was trying hard not to lose it. He's tried to date me a couple of times, and though I've declined, I do believe he's a nice, decent, stand-up guy. So why don't I date him? Because I'm a dumb bunny. Also, I'm holding out for Kit.

'Frannie, I hope you can do something,' James Blake said as he approached. Blood from the bundle in his arms was dripping on to the gravel underfoot.

I pushed open the glass doors for James, led him through reception, then past hospital Wards 1 and 2.

'Nothing on Jessie, I assume,' I said.

'Nothing,' answered James.

As we passed number 2, a looney-tunes black Lab who'd been dropped off to have his choppers cleaned started howling. That set off the basset hound with gastric torsion, and the stray shepherd-cross.

Also Pip, my own Jack Russell terrier who hangs out with the boarding dogs and can't say no to a good barkathon.

The clamor disturbed the animal in the sleeping bag, and it started a panicky stir.

'*Shut-UP, you guys!*' I hollered at the dogs.

I showed James into an exam room and shut the door behind us. A stray dog was napping on a window seat, snug in a pile of pillows. I started to unwrap the folds of polyester-filled bag.

Dog, cat, raccoon, or whatever, this was going to be an awful mess. That much I knew already.

But I was totally unprepared to be staring into the glazed-over eyeballs of a *Gymnogyps Californianus* – a bird that, to my knowledge, hadn't been seen in Colorado in two hundred years.

'What the hell is it, Frannie?' he asked.

'It's a California condor,' I told him. 'I've never seen one in the flesh. That's because their flesh isn't supposed to be around here.'

And it was weird-looking flesh at that. My newest patient had a bald head about the size of a large mango, with a longish hooked beak partially cloaked in pink wattles. There was a patch of stiff black feathers on its forehead, and where its neck met its shoulders was a wild ruff of thin black feathers that continued down the whole of its body, making this poor creature look like a weary old man wearing half of a gorilla suit.

'He sure is pretty,' said Blake.

I laughed. 'Pretty rare anyway. There are only about a hundred and sixty of these left in the world, and of those, sixty are wild and the rest are in captive breeding facilities. Or so they say.'

It was the sad truth. Once ranging freely, by '87 all but a dozen of these birds had been poached, poisoned, and shot nearly out of existence. With dedication and hard work, they'd been brought back to their current number in captivity.

I could tell from the orange tag on its good wing that this bird was from the Vermilion Cliffs colony in northern Arizona, some three hundred miles away. That's actually a short hop for a condor. They can coast for hours without once batting their wings and can make speeds of fifty-five miles per hour.

Of course, this particular marvel might never fly again. The hunter's bullet had shattered its wing, maybe beyond repair.

As if it understood, the condor cracked its beak and *hissed* at me. 'Okay, buddy,' I crooned to the bird. 'Let's cross our fingers, James,' I told the trooper. 'It's lost a lot of blood. All I can do is my best. Might not be good enough.'

James H. Blake sighed. 'I'm going to take those two bad boys down to the barracks,' he said, 'and see what I can slap them with.'

'Go for it. I'm hoping fifteen to life.'

He smiled. 'You're such a softie. I'll check back with you, Frannie.'

'I *am* a softie,' I said. 'I'll be here.' But I'd already almost forgotten Trooper Blake.

I scrubbed my hands with antiseptic and went to work. Work was the only thing that had been saving me lately. It sure as heck beat rational thought.

# CHAPTER TWENTY-FOUR

My fatigue had been replaced by an edgy kind of energy. And dread.

Operating on this rare bird was an awful responsibility, and I was going to have to do it unassisted. The dogs in Ward 2 were still in full throat, so I flipped on the radio and found a good music station. Good for my nerves, and good for the bird's nerves too. I recognized a cut from the latest Moby album. Good deal – I liked his stuff a lot.

I shone a light into the condor's eyes and hoped for a reflex. There was none. His condition was deteriorating by the minute.

'Come on, big boy. Don't give up on me. You've got a real big heart. Let's show it.'

I strapped a gas mask over the condor's beak, then cranked up the isofluorine mixture to five to knock him down fast.

The gas hissed through the tube. Only after the bird was out cold did I dare to entirely open the wraps and lay him out fully on the examination table.

I gently extended the shattered wing and, as I thought it would, it flapped open at a hideous and unnatural angle. I pushed the feathers away from the injured site and saw that the fractured bone had broken through the delicate, almost transparent skin. Worse, the wound was starting to turn green.

This big boy was a mess, all right.

I hoped I could keep him alive. But I also worried that if he lived, but couldn't fly, he'd be doomed to life in a cage.

Macy Gray was singing as I rummaged around in the cabinet over the sink for materials I would need. I liked Macy a lot too. The problem with pinning broken bird bones is that they're hollow and metal pins can't hold them together. I'd done a lot of work on hurt birds and had come up with my own MASH-unit-type surgical procedure, and frankly, it worked beautifully most of the time.

I stretched out the wing bones, then began to tease a small number 5 endo-tracheal tube into the break. It takes laserlike focus and a steady hand to do this just right. I held my breath and carefully threaded the tube through the broken bone, then back up to the proximal point of the fracture, where it held securely, and I could breathe again.

There's not much soft tissue in a bird's wing, but I cut away the damaged flesh, flushed out the wound with antiseptic solution, then closed the skin with a simple interrupted pattern of stitches.

I was satisfied. The surgery was pretty clean.

*Bravo, dottore!*

I folded the condor's wing and stabilized the fracture by securing the wing up against its body with a figure-eight, splintlike wrapping that works like a Chinese finger trap. If the bird tried to flap its wing, the bandage would only tighten more firmly.

Then I carried the thirty-pound condor into the storage room that my part-time assistant, Janna, and I use for medical supplies. There was no bow-wow chorus back here, but there *was* a large cage in the corner – a perfect Motel 8 for this fellow, who had certainly been hatched and raised in captivity.

I put the condor gently inside, covered the cage with a blanket, and turned off the light.

'Goodnight, big guy. Sleep well, you prince of Colorado.'

Finally, I went back into the operating room to clean up.

For the two hours that I'd been working on the condor, I'd been fighting off a feeling that I couldn't identify. Now that the surgery was done, I was overtaken by exhaustion, and also sadness. It was the kids.

Working on the condor had reminded me how much I missed each and every one of them.

I pictured their faces.

Counted their fingers and toes.

I threw the dead tuna-on-eight-grain into the trash, and stuffed the bloodied sleeping bag in after it. I swabbed down the stainless-steel table, washed out the sink, and went to bed.

# CHAPTER TWENTY-FIVE

'Frannie, if you're there, *pick up*,' said a whispery voice. 'C'mon, c'mon.'

I had been falling asleep, but suddenly I was awake. I reached out – and for at least the fourth time that month knocked over an ashtray from the original Hotel Boulderado, circa 1909. *Somebody was trying to tell me to stop smoking.*

*Max?* I thought to myself.

'Max, oh Max,' I said, grabbing up the phone. It was her voice on the answering machine. 'I was just thinking about you. Must be telepathy, kiddo. This is great. How *are* you?'

'Okay, I guess,' she said, but that *I guess* pierced my heart.

'What's wrong, sweetheart? Talk to me. I don't care if it's late. What's going on?'

'Oh, nothing,' she said in a false tone. Max can be such a twelve-year-old sometimes.

'Well, I guess you're not going to talk about yourself tonight, huh? How's Matthew?'

'Aw, Frannie,' Max said. 'It's real hard for him being so different than other kids.'

'Tell me all about it,' I said.

I managed to get my old flannel robe on without disconnecting the phone as Max told me about crimes of hate in Pine Bush, Colorado. Every day at school there was at least one incident of serious taunting, or much worse.

I struggled to find the right words to tell Max, even as the accusatory voice of Catherine Fitzgibbons echoed in my mind: *'You've never been a mother, have you, Dr O'Neill?'*

'Kids can be kind of mean sometimes, Max,' I told her. 'I really think you handled everything right. You know human kids aren't the only ones who try to hurt each other. Sometimes, in a nest of birds, the oldest chicks try to push the newly hatched ones out so that they can have more food. It happens.'

'Yeah, I suppose,' Max said, but sounded unconvinced. It was hard to forget she has an IQ in the 180s. Plus a photographic mind.

'So, anyway. Moving on to cheerier things,' Max started to say, then changed the subject, maybe a little too quickly. She told me about a cute, 'sensitive' boy named Mickey whom she liked at school, 'and he seems to like me, wings and all,' she added. Then she asked about the goings-on at the new and improved Inn-Patient. I told her all about the condor I'd just operated on.

'Wow, I'd love to see that patched-up bird,' she said. Some of her old spark was coming back. 'I miss you, Frannie. All of us do. Matthew sends major hugs and kisses. So does Ozymandias. And Ic.'

'I miss all of you too, honey,' I said gently.

I was careful not to make things harder for her by adding my own strong longing to hers. I expected her to sigh and agree as she always does, but I heard something different. Max's voice suddenly choked up. 'I gotta go.'

'Max, what is it? What's going on? There's something else, isn't there?'

'I can't talk about it. *Can't,*' she said. 'But it hurts so much to keep it a secret. It's bad, Frannie. Sorry, sorry, I've gotta go.'

'What are you talking about, Max? You're rambling. Slow down, honey.'

There was dead silence on her end of the line. So I asked again. I begged her, cajoled, reassured her. 'C'mon, Max. You're scared. I can hear it in your voice.'

'I *can't* tell you,' she said. 'It's dangerous, and hopeless. Frannie, it's worse than the School. The people there are worse, what they do is worse. Seriously. I even think somebody's watching Matthew and me. I know they are. I saw them twice. Gotta go! Gotta! I love you.'

Then Max hung up on me.

# CHAPTER TWENTY-SIX

Max tried real hard not to think about the troubles ahead; about whoever was spying on her and Matthew. Even though she'd seen them again – *three* times now. She put her mind elsewhere – into small-town life.

As clever and smart as she was about some things, Max found herself in a tricky situation a few days later. She was kind of on a date, and it was with one of the real 'cuties' in her school – a tall, blond, athletic hunk named Mickey Bosco. She'd basically been anti-hunk – until Mickey asked her out.

She and the hunk didn't talk much as they climbed the steep, rocky hill that rose along the west side of Schoolhouse Road. As she pushed her way through the overgrown scrub brush, though, she suspected this might be a bad idea.

She was going to show Mickey what it was like to fly. She'd promised him.

'We need to climb that rocky outcropping over there.' She sounded confident, but there was this Darth Vader warning voice in her head that wouldn't shut up. The voice said: *This is really stupid, Max. Smartest girl in the classroom; dumbest girl out on the street.*

'You're kind of quiet, Max,' Mickey said as he rock-climbed. 'You usually like this?'

'I'm just trying not to lose my balance. You might try the same.'

'Oh sure,' said Mickey. 'It's no problem. I was just checking on you. Making sure you're okay.'

'I'm fine. I am. Thanks for asking.'

Max's Reeboks grabbed on to the grain of the next rock. Mickey was right behind her. *So close.* Far below them was a noisy, fast-flowing highway. And across the highway, a vast stretch of open pastureland that looked promising. And much safer.

Finally, they were at the top. 'Ready?' Max asked. 'We don't have to do this if you don't want.'

'Are you kidding? I'm totally psyched. This is gonna be the best adventure ever! Talk about *extreme sports.*'

Max groaned as she bent at the waist, placing both hands on her knees. 'Climb on. Don't worry, I'm strong.'

Mickey Bosco climbed on to her back, hooking his legs around her waist. He wrapped his arms around her chest, under her wings. And he *was* kind of heavy.

'This isn't so bad,' he said, 'for me. You sure you're okay?'

'A one, and a two, and a three,' Max counted off. 'I'm just *ducky.*'

Then she pushed off the rock and they were airborne.

'Holy shiiiittt!' Mickey yelled. 'Awesome! Do the Dew! This is out-rageous! We're flying! I'm really flying.'

Max didn't think the adventure was quite so terrific. Actually, it went kind of wrong from the first second. Instead of gaining altitude, she dropped several feet toward the crowded lanes of speeding traffic. Mickey was a lot of extra weight to carry – even for her.

So Max beat her wings frantically. And suddenly she was scared! She'd only been aloft for a short time, and her lungs ached some. Her wing muscles burned like an engine about to catch on fire. *Not good.*

From the sound of Mickey's insane chortling, Max could tell that he had no clue how bad it actually was, and how scared he ought to be right now. She reached forward into the heavy air and pulled at it with her powerful wings. She finally caught a mild updraft and her body lifted.

'Having fun?' she managed to say a couple of seconds later.

'This is the bomb!' Mickey shouted into her ear. '*You* are the bomb, baby. The best ever!'

Max guessed that was a good thing, and she finally smiled. Maybe this could work out after all. She beat her wings again. She wouldn't feel totally safe until they had crossed the highway and were cruising over the pastureland.

Then she felt something shocking and totally unexpected. Mickey Bosco was moving his hands over her chest, exploring.

He was feeling her up!

# CHAPTER TWENTY-SEVEN

'**S** top it!' Max yelled. 'Right now! Take your hands off me!' She twisted her neck to look into the blond boy's eyes. He kept right on rubbing her chest.

'*You don't have boobs.*' He shrieked with laughter. 'You're flat.'

Max felt her emotions collide. A while ago she'd kind of liked Mickey Bosco. Now she was sick with shame, and more embarrassed than she'd ever been in her life. She hated him for being so crude and rude and totally thoughtless.

'I don't need breasts,' she tried to explain.

'Well I do,' Mickey Bosco said, and laughed again. He sounded as if he were playing machoman in a locker room filled with his pals, and Max knew that this story would wind up there.

Her eyes had started to tear up and she couldn't see real well. Her heart felt incredibly heavy. She saw that there was a farm pond looming ahead. Canadian geese flew up from the water's edge in a honking flurry.

'I asked you to stop,' she pleaded. 'Please?'

'What am I hurting?' the boy said, roaring with laughter. 'Nothing to hurt, right?'

'Just somebody's feelings,' she muttered. '*Oh, screw you!*'

Then Max swooped down toward the acre or so of muddy water. When she was just about at the center of the pond, she closed her wings and made a tight, spiraling *dive.*

'I call this little stunt "the bullet",' she turned and said to Mickey Bosco. 'Isn't it *the bomb*? Do the Dew, right!'

She felt his grasp loosen, his hands and legs slide down her back. '*He-e-e-e-e-y-y-y-y*,' he shouted. 'Cut it out. Jesus Christ, Max. Slow down! I'm gonna fall.'

Max didn't answer. 'I call *this* "the roller coaster"!' she yelled again. 'Talk about extreme. Bon voyage, tricky Mickey!' She executed a sharp nose-*down*, then nose-*up* maneuver.

Mickey Bosco screeched as he lost his grip and began to slide off her body. Then he plunged at least fifty feet into the murky brown water. He made a satisfying splash, like the one she'd seen a couple of nights before in the movie *Shallow Hal* with one of her all-time favorites, Gwyneth Paltrow.

Max watched Bosco sink, then resurface with a sputter. She flew an unhurried circle to make sure that the stupid boy didn't drown. When he finally paddled his way to shore through pond scum and stink-weeds, he gave her the finger. Max blew him a kiss.

'To first love,' she called.

Her emotions were jangled, though, and she needed to figure out some things. To the north of the pond was a thicket of evergreens. She picked out the tallest lodgepole pine, dropped into the crown, and straddled a solid-looking branch.

She leaned her head against the rough bark of the tree. There were tears in her eyes and she hated that. She hated to be weak. How could she have let somebody like Mickey Bosco hurt her? Never again, she vowed. Not in this lifetime anyway.

Then she stopped and listened to the sounds around her: the constant *creak* of branches, the *rustle* of leaves, insects rubbing their wings. Her heartbeat began to slow to its resting rate: sixty beats a minute. Her breathing finally normalized.

Soon, the relevant issues became very clear in her mind.

She wanted to be accepted here in Pine Bush, Colorado, but she wasn't going to be.

She wanted to be able to trust people, but she couldn't. *No! Not even close!* She needed to accept that, to live with it.

The only ones she could count on were the bird-kids from the original School. And Frannie and Kit. Seven people in the whole world, and she couldn't even tell *them* the secret thing that scared her most. She had been warned not to.

*You talk, you die.*

No, she couldn't tell anyone about the horrible things that were happening at a place called the Hospital.

She would never, ever tell.

Not a word.

Besides, who would believe her?

# CHAPTER TWENTY-EIGHT

It was getting dark and really nasty-looking to the west and south. Black rain clouds were gathering as Max finally flew back to the Marshalls' ranch house on Ames Road in Pine Bush. She was only a block away when she saw an old black Honda in the driveway and a tall, thin woman talking to her mother.

*What was this all about?*

She didn't recognize the visitor at first.

Then it clicked.

Denver!

Max recalled the visitor's face, even remembered the name of the woman who'd been at the custody trial. Linda Schein. A reporter with the *Denver Post*.

*Why has she come here? What does she want in Pine Bush? Oh God, why can't they just leave us alone!*

*I won't do any more freak-show stories. I just won't! Forget about it!*

Max pushed back on the air, effectively putting on the brakes. She dropped down to the front lawn, and saw the reporter's eyes go wide. She was probably pissed she hadn't brought along a cameraman.

Then Linda Schein smiled as she did when talking into a TV camera. 'Hi, Max. Nice of you to drop in,' she quipped.

'I live here,' Max said dryly. 'What do you want?'

Terry Marshall stood in the doorway under the light. 'Max, this is an important reporter from Denver. She drove all the way out here to see you.'

'Linda Schein,' the woman said, holding out her hand. She was around Frannie's age, sort of attractive, but too made-up for Max's taste. Max tried not to judge her because of her lipstick and mascara, though.

'I remember you, Ms Schein. I *think* you're the forty-seventh reporter to come to the house. Something like that. *Rocky Mountain News*? No, you're with the *Denver Post*, right?'

'Not now. I'm writing a book. I know I should have called first, but I just took a chance that you'd have a few moments to talk. I'm really sorry, Maximum. Your mother said it would be okay. If you agreed.'

*My mother said?* Max shook her head, but then she surrendered. 'C'mon inside, Ms Schein. Or would you rather we do the interview in a tree? Somebody asked me to do that once. Really creative, huh? But the best was the TV personality who wanted to jump out of a plane and interview me in the air. I said *OK* – if he didn't wear a parachute.'

Max walked inside the house and let the writer follow if she wanted to. Her bedroom was painted a creamy white with a floral border under the moldings. She had a tangerine-colored iMac desktop computer with a flying goose screensaver, a canopied bed, several shelves holding books and fossilized rocks and other found treasures. The Marshalls had tried to make it nice here for her. Score one for Moms and Pops.

Max sat on the edge of her bed and watched as the woman writer perused the wall hangings. She commented politely on Max's funky star map of Hollywood and her *40 Days and 40 Nights* movie poster, but it didn't take long for her to get to the real point of her visit. Which was—

'I'm interested in child abuse. I was abused,' Linda Schein said as she settled into the chair beside the desk. Max wasn't sure whether to believe her. She already knew that some reporters would lie about anything, even in their news stories. 'After I listened to you and the other children at the custody trial, I got interested in institutional abuse. I especially wanted to know more about the School. Please tell me what happened there, Max. It's important – for both of us. I think you know it is.'

'That's in the past,' Max answered softly. 'The School is gone. The people who worked there are dead or in jail.'

The writer's eyes narrowed, focused. Max could tell she was a smart one. Wily. 'I don't think so,' said Linda Schein. 'And I don't think you do either. They're not *all* in jail. I'm not wrong, am I?'

'What do you mean?' Max asked. She couldn't keep an edge of concern out of her voice. She stared hard at the writer, the intruder.

'I *know* things, Max. I do. I have a contact in Washington with access to sealed government documents. I did some digging myself and found a memo from a Dr Brownhill mixed in with a sealed Grand Jury indictment. It was pretty terrifying. It detailed an ongoing project, an offshoot of the School. I know it exists. I know about something called the Resurrection Project. What is Resurrection, Max? Is there a place they call "the Hospital"? There is, isn't there? You have to tell me.'

'You really have to go,' Max said abruptly. 'You're way off base. This is too crazy. Why can't you reporters just leave us alone?'

She stood quickly and flung open the bedroom door for the reporter. Then she had an attack of conscience. She felt compelled to add something. 'Don't dig into this subject, Ms Schein. Please believe me. If you talk about it, you could die. I'm not exaggerating. *You talk, you die.* You're way off base, but you could get hurt anyway.'

The reporter found herself being led out into the hallway. But she wouldn't go away. Not that easily. 'Max, you can't leave it like this. I can see you're frightened. I guess I understand that. Give me a few more minutes. Talk to me, please. What is the Resurrection Project? Where is it?'

Max shook her head. 'I don't have anything to tell you. You're looking in the wrong places.' But then she had to add again, 'If you talk, you could die. Please remember those words, Ms Schein. Now go back to Denver. Drive safely.'

Panting with fear and close to tears, Max shut her door and leaned up hard against it. When she heard the writer's car finally drive away, she collapsed on to her bed, fully dressed. Wired, and coming apart, all at the same time.

She'd done it now – talked to a writer. An investigative journalist.

She would be found out. Then all the children would be in terrible danger.

*You talk, you die.*

*Especially if you talk about Resurrection.*

# CHAPTER TWENTY-NINE

*Y*ou *talk, you die, you talk, you die, talk, die, talk, die.*

It was two in the fricking-fracking morning and Max had been twisting and thrashing in bed for hours. Her head ached from the pressure of too many thoughts, and she couldn't stand it any more.

She made a call with her cell phone.

Her best friend in the world answered, and they talked for less than a minute. Just in case somebody might be listening.

Then Max threw off her blankets and dressed for a cold night flight. She had to meet her friend. *Right now.*

It didn't matter that night flights were against the rules set down by Terry and Art Marshall. Their absurd, tight-assed rules didn't matter to her. Not any more. Not ever, really. Most parents made up rules to keep *themselves* comfortable, right?

She had to see Ozymandias. Somebody knew about *Resurrection*. A reporter knew, and they weren't exactly known for keeping their big fat mouths shut.

Max crept down the back stairs and through the silent house. She went straight to the mudroom.

There, she took her silver vest down from a hook. Zipped it over her shirt and jeans.

She knotted the laces of her sneakers together and slung them around her neck. She tucked her CD player into one pocket, cell phone in another.

Then she left the Marshall house quietly, carefully, through the back door.

It was two twenty in the morning.

Time to rock and roll.

*You talk, you die.*

# CHAPTER THIRTY

The moon was hidden behind thick clouds as Max ran barefoot down the entire length of the backyard. *Dewy, dewy, cold, cold.*

Max thought: I wish we were all back at the Lake House. I wish it was the way it used to be. Veggie pizzas and cookouts, long, long talks with Kit and Frannie, overnight hikes and fly-aways. But then Max stopped herself. The Lake House was in the past; ancient history; it was over. This was now. *You talk, you die.*

She pointed her arms forward and stretched out her beautiful wings. As the wings swung out, the joints opened automatically, and her flight feathers spread. *Bernoulli's principle in action, Jackson.*

As air flowed across the tops of her wings, Max rose as if she were being sucked right into the sky. Once aloft, she beat her wings until she was high above the treetops – and then she soared!

*God, I love to fly. I was born for this*, she thought.

*Who wouldn't love a night flight?*

*Maybe George W. Bush? Nah, he'd like it a lot!*

Max headed southeast over Pine Bush, rising like a jet through the moisture-laden clouds that dispersed as she cleared the town. The clouds didn't feel like much of anything as she passed through them – froth from the top of a latte? Spider webs? – but they were mysterious, ethereal, and she felt her face bead with water drops. The moon was so bright, and the stars were sharp white holes punched out of the fabric of a deep black sky.

And it was so *quiet* up here – so unearthly quiet and peaceful. If she wasn't so nervous and worried, and *scared half to death*, this would be perfect.

Max found the North Star by following the line connecting the two pointers in the Big Dipper. Then she adjusted her flight path so that she would travel along the eastern edge of the Roosevelt National Forest – toward the town of Fort Collins, about thirty miles away.

Oz lived near Fort Collins, and he actually liked the city a lot. God, she couldn't wait to see him. To talk to Ozymandias. To lean on his shoulder.

*You talk, you die.*

Max had her wings fully extended, catching the updrafts off the ridges, and glided for as long as ten minutes without beating her wings a single time. Fantastic! She knew bone deep that this miracle of flight was worth all she'd suffered for it.

She tried to put aside any fears and worries and surrendered herself to the pleasure of flying. Below her were thousands of acres of rolling hills against an awesome backdrop of snowy mountain peaks that rose up and pierced the clouds. Moonlight made the tiers of spruce and pine trees below her look like fantastical castles with silver spires. Oh hell, the poetry in her head didn't do it justice, not even close.

Max had been flying for about an hour when she picked out the metallic sheen of the Cache la Poudre River seven thousand feet below.

She flicked on her CD player and sang along with Nelly Furtado as she followed the river's course.

The cool night air buffeted her body all the way down to her tippy-toes. She could fly just fine with shoes, but bare feet gave her more rudder control. Felt better on the tootsies, too.

The Cache la Poudre ran parallel to a big four-laner, Route 287. Max followed the twisting ribbon of highway and flew above the subdued lights of Fort Collins, and from there about five miles east to her destination, the tiny town of Warren, Colorado.

*Ozymandias was down there. The strongest of the six children, maybe even the future leader. Absolutely her best buddy in the world. Her secret hero.*

She closed her wings a few degrees and descended to about a hundred feet. Then she skimmed the tree line until she could plainly see the Warren Raptor Center.

'Permission to land,' she whispered to nobody. Then, 'Permission granted.'

Max's night vision was superb, the moonlight as bright to her as klieg lights would be to an ordinary person. The wildlife refuge was made up of a timbered administrative building with a little lawn in front and dirt paths leading from it.

At the edge of the sanctuary was a cluster of small screened-and-slatted pole barns that housed the raptors, the birds of prey.

Max dropped and braked on the cool, wet ground.

'Oz,' she called. 'Oz, you here? Of course you are. But where? Come out, come out wherever you are. C'mon, Oz. Oz?'

A barn owl called, *can-you-cook-for-meeee*. Max called back, 'I can cook for you.'

Then there was silence again.

'Oz? Don't play mind games with me. Not tonight. I'm scared. I'm really, really scared, Ozymandias. I *need* you, good buddy.'

'Max, I'm in the hawk house. Come on up here, you silly goose.'

# CHAPTER THIRTY-ONE

I t was cozy and warm and, most important, safe in the low rafters of the hawk house.

Moonlight the color of butter slipped through the slatted roof, striping the faces of Max and Oz, who dangled their legs over the crossbeam and talked from their hearts.

'It's really good to see you,' Max whispered, and felt a lump in her throat.

'Good to be seen. But three in the morning? What's the matter? This better be good. And I'm sure it is, knowing you, Max.'

'We'll get to that. Maybe. I see that your friends are up late too. The hawks.'

The two red-tailed hawks that lived in the barn were perched nearby. The male, who was nearly blind, ruffled his feathers; and his mate, who had only one wing, moved closer to him. The hawks didn't mind their presence and Max found their sounds and smells comforting.

'*Cheeeeee*,' Oz called.

'*Cheeeeee*,' the male responded.

Max found herself smiling. Oz could be so gentle and sweet sometimes. Most of the time, actually.

She thought he had really changed since she had seen him last. He was small when they'd lived at the School. Now, although he was younger by a few months than Max, he was so much bigger. And stronger. The boyish twinkle was gone, the softness of his cheeks and jaw too. Jeez, Oz had grown into a real hunk. And she knew all about hunks, didn't she?

'Can I see your tattoo?' she asked.

'Yes. But then you have to tell me what scared you back at Bush League. You don't scare, Max.'

'Yeah, I do,' she said. 'So let me see your tat.'

Oz pulled up his black sweatshirt so that she could see the brown-and-red-and-yellow image of an American bald eagle depicted in full flight across his chest. The eagle held a shield in one talon and lightning bolts in the other. The motto, *Live Free or Die*, was etched underneath. It was magnificent.

'That is so damn cool,' said Max. 'Must've hurt like a bastard.'

Oz shrugged and said, '*This* one hurt.' He opened his palm and showed Max another tat. This one was an amateur job, clearly inked by Oz himself.

Max bent her head and read aloud: '*Ozymandias, King of Kings.* A little full of thyself, sire?' she asked.

'I mean it the way that poet Shelley meant it,' Oz said. 'Vanity means nothing, right. Even mighty Ozymandias, Rameses II of Ancient Egypt, died and turned to dust. You ever wonder why I was given that name?'

'How can we understand anything they did at the fricking School?' Max said. 'Those nutjobs.'

'I still hate them so much. Can't stop hating,' Oz snapped. 'I wonder all the time what our lives would have been like if they hadn't messed with us. Sometimes I think we have more in common with these hawks than we have with people.'

'You're reading my mind,' Max said. 'Now *that's* scary. Brrrrr.'

'So what happened in lovely Bush League, I mean Pine Bush? Why did you want to see me?'

Max picked through a myriad of troubling thoughts before answering. This was going to be a *lit*-tle tricky. 'I took a boy on a flight,' she said. 'I know, *dumb*. The bastard felt me up. He really hurt my feelings, Oz. He rubbed up against me, and then he told me I was flat-chested.

Like I didn't know already. Like I should care. Like I give two and a half shits. Which, obviously, I do.'

Oz shook his head and thought a few seconds before speaking. Very grown-up of him. 'I'm sorry that it happened, Max. But, honestly, I've been expecting something like this.'

Max couldn't believe what she'd heard. She searched Oz's face for an explanation. 'What are you talking about? *Honestly*, you've been *expecting* this?'

'That's what I said. Have you looked at yourself lately? You have any mirrors in that house?'

Max blinked her eyes rapidly. 'Sure,' she said. 'All the time. *And?*'

'You're beautiful, Max. You're gorgeous. You make Lara Croft *and* Angelina Jolie look like shit!'

Max felt a flush across her breastbone. The warm feeling shot through her veins and her stomach felt hollow, exactly the way it did when she did a barrel roll in the sky. Something a little weird was going on here. She wasn't ready for it. 'You need an eye exam, buddy.'

'One of us does,' said Oz. 'So what's really bothering you? Tell me true, Max.'

'You know already. Nothing. Everything. The kids at school can be unbelievably nasty, snide, cruel. You already know that. The press are even worse. They're clueless and they're everywhere we go. You know that, too.'

Oz grinned. 'Fox is filming us right now, Max. Sorry, I sold us out. I *needed* the cash. "Who Wants To Marry A Beautiful Girl With Wings?" '

Max stopped talking, and she looked around.

'Now *that* hurts my feelings. You thought, just for a nanosecond, that I might invite the sleazy press here.'

Max kissed Oz on the cheek. 'No, I didn't really. But yes, I am paranoid. I am very, very paranoid, Oz.'

*You have no idea.*

They sat there in the hawk house, neither of them saying a word for a moment or two. Usually that was okay, but right now it felt uncomfortable. She wanted to talk about Resurrection, the danger, but suddenly she couldn't get the words out. Maybe because she didn't want to drag Ozymandias into this mess.

'I have to go hunt,' Oz said finally. 'It's my nature.' He grinned.

'Now? I need to talk some more.'

'You can come with me. I'd like the company. But I *need* to hunt.'

Max had never hunted, and she didn't think she could. 'No, I'd better get going,' she said. 'It's almost morning.'

'Well, okay. I guess so. I wish you could stay. Safe home,' Oz said. 'I'm glad you came. I missed you.'

'Me too,' said Max.

'You're drop-dead gorgeous, Max. Live with it!'

'I'm a freak.'

'Gorgeous. You're a gorgeous freak. A beautiful creature.'

They hugged awkwardly. Then they hugged a second time, and Oz lightly kissed Max's cheek. Then they went their separate ways.

Max deeply regretted she hadn't talked about what was really bothering her, but she couldn't tell Oz about Resurrection yet. Why was that? Because she didn't want to put him in danger? Or was it that she didn't totally trust Oz in that area? He might get reckless. Try to be a hero. That was his nature, wasn't it? Oz *was* heroic, and heroes could get you hurt, or dead.

She flew home through a transcendent pink-and-baby-blue sunrise, but Max didn't much notice the sights.

*Somebody knew about Resurrection. Somebody who really shouldn't. A snoopy reporter. A writer.*

*The horror-and-creep show was starting to warm up again, wasn't it?*

Then Max felt the need to put her mind somewhere else, somewhere nice.

'*Oz thinks I'm beautiful,*' she whispered to the stars.

# PART THREE

---

# HOUSE CALLS

# CHAPTER THIRTY-TWO

## The Hospital

The place was jumping tonight. Doctors, nurses, dozens of gurneys on the move.

Seventeen-year-old James Lee nervously counted the passing fluorescent lighting panels in the dropped ceiling as the serious-faced, blue-gowned medical attendants rushed his gurney along the corridors of the Hospital. He was scared stiff, but also excited.

Dr Kane had already told him that he'd been selected to be a 'finalist'. 'Mr Lee, Mr Lee,' he'd said. 'You're a special young man. That's why we chose you. You have all the right stuff.'

'Do you have the tape I recorded?' Lee had asked. 'I need my tape for this.'

'We have it,' Dr Kane assured him. 'It's waiting for you in the OR. We wouldn't forget something like your tape. We're very buttoned-up here.'

'I've noticed that.'

James Lee clasped his fingers tightly together under the sheet so that his hands wouldn't shake. He licked his dry lips. He swayed against the sides of the gurney as it rounded a corner. Finally, the attendants arrived at the stainless-steel doors to the operating room. They opened with a loud *whoosh*. The gurney was wheeled forward, then parked parallel to an operating table.

'What, exactly, am I being operated on for?' James Lee asked.

'It's just a little exploratory operation, James. We're looking – *inside* you. Believe me, you won't feel a thing.'

The antiseptic smell was really strong in the operating theater, and the constant *pinging* sounds of medical equipment made everything a little too real. For a moment, James Lee's fear almost got the best of him. He had an impulse to say, 'Forget it. I've changed my mind.'

Then a deep voice directly above him said, 'On my count.'

He felt hands under him, two sets of strong male hands.

'One, two, three. Upsy-daisy, James.'

He was lifted easily on to the table and immediately covered with thin flannel sheets.

A nurse then swabbed the vein inside his left elbow with alcohol and pierced the skin with a needle. The IV drip began.

'You feeling okay, Mr Lee?'

It was Dr Kane, who always inspired supreme confidence in James. The doctor had a compact, muscular physique – even his hand felt hard and unyielding where he placed it on the young man's shoulder. The face looming above him was square and tanned beneath a blond brush cut. Intelligence radiated from the clear silver-blue eyes. Dr Kane was a real winner.

'I'm fine,' said James Lee as a nurse fitted a metal helmet over his shaved head. 'This really isn't going to hurt?'

'Not at all. Your tape is sensational, by the way. The best we've seen yet.'

# CHAPTER THIRTY-THREE

J ames Lee couldn't believe what was happening inside his head. *Wow!* This was close to perfect. Just what he had imagined. Maybe even better! He clenched and unclenched his fists and prepared himself for his debut. This was the best!

He was on the stage of the world-famous Stardust Lounge in Las Vegas. In his mind anyway. But it felt as if he were really there.

And he was ready. Oh man, was he ready.

This was his tape! He'd been fantasizing about this exact scene for years! God, this was *exactly* what he'd had in mind.

Lee ran his small hands down the fitted bodice of his strapless white cocktail dress, and flounced the layered organza skirt. He pressed his freshly lipsticked lips together and touched his lacquered bouffant hairstyle. Everything was so right. So real.

Suddenly, a pin light in the ceiling came on and illuminated him with a small blue light. There was the rustling sound of people shifting in their seats and *ohs* of surprise coming from the audience. Hundreds of pairs of eyes were trained on him.

The opening notes from the orchestra rose from the pit and spilled on to the stage – followed by a dominant seventh chord that served as the transition from the intro to the main melody.

His tape was even better than he'd imagined. Fuller and richer.

James Lee heard the gasps and the moans of the audience as the stage lights blazed. Through the smoky haze, he could see friends and family who'd come to watch him perform. There was his mother smiling up at him from the front row. She'd always had faith in him. Man, he was about to prove himself to the one person who really loved him.

Lee slowly raised the mike to his mouth. Then, in a breathy Astrud Gilberto voice, he began a song made famous by the incomparable Brenda Lee.

'*I'm sorry. So sorry . . . for treating you the way I did.*'

Jesus, he sounded great too. The audience in the Stardust Lounge were eating him up. How could they not?

'*Mr Lee? Jimmy?*'

Someone was interrupting his performance. James Lee's head snapped around. It was a friendly, authoritative voice that seemed to speak *inside* his head!

'*Ground control to James. Mr Lee, Mr Lee. Oh Mr Lee?*'

*Now* he remembered. This was a medical procedure. The stage show was all in his mind – just a distraction, but *what* a distraction. In some forgotten place, his naked body was lying on an operating table at the Hospital in Maryland.

'Yes,' James said. 'I hear you, Dr Kane. Now, *please* go away. You're ruining my performance.'

'Are you comfortable?'

'Yes, thank you. I'm in heaven,' he sighed.

'Not yet, but soon,' said Dr Ethan Kane. Then he whispered, 'Okay, shuck him.'

# CHAPTER THIRTY-FOUR

D r Ethan Kane got to leave the Hospital early that night; at least it was early for him. He decided to go to his second home, which was out in the rolling, wooded hills of Maryland, where he could have a little privacy.

Forty minutes later, as he climbed from his Mercedes at the house, he heard the dogs start to bark and it brought a rare and mischievous smile to his lips. 'Jesus, they're well-trained animals. Keep out the riff-raff.'

He unlocked the front door of the large fieldstone house and went inside. The dogs continued to bark.

A tall brunette woman wearing an apron over a flowery blue dress emerged from the kitchen. She was stunningly beautiful, and had the warmest, most open smile this side of Ohio. 'Oh, you're home, Ethan. I'm so happy. Your dinner will be ready at eight thirty. The *Washington Post* and the *Wall Street Journal* are laid out in the study, as is a Johnnie Black rocks. Go relax. You've earned it.'

Ethan Kane never said a word to his wife, Juliette. He didn't move to hug or kiss her. Instead, he pulled a compact black case from his pocket. It was similar to the locking device he used with the Mercedes, though considerably more complex.

Dr Kane pressed his forefinger to one of several buttons, and Juliette stopped talking immediately, stopped moving, shut down altogether. She just stood there frozen like a department store mannequin, in the center of the foyer.

'You're perfect, darling,' he muttered. 'The completely *evolved* woman. What would I do without you?'

Kane then pushed another button that turned off the barking of the dogs.

He walked to the study, where he read his favorite newspapers while he sipped his Scotch. Just past eight thirty he went into the kitchen and ate dinner: chicken marsala, fresh asparagus and broccoli rabe, risotto with morels, a sliver of apple crisp and cheddar cheese. All expertly prepared by Juliette.

Before he went upstairs, Dr Kane returned to the foyer and switched on the security alarms. He then turned Juliette back on.

'Hello, sweetheart,' she said and smiled demurely.

'Let's go up to bed, darling,' he whispered against her ear as she lightly stroked the front of his trousers. He put one hand on a pert, nicely rounded breast, the other between her legs. What waited there for him was the perfect *fit*. Kane knew that for certain. He'd measured.

'I need you, Ethan,' said Juliette – and there was that dazzling smile of hers again. 'You're such a wonderful lover.'

'*Carry* me up to bed, darling,' he whispered.

# CHAPTER THIRTY-FIVE

L inda Schein's work desk faced a blank white wall without a single adornment. On purpose.

Her picture window afforded a stunning mountain view from her condo on Fourteenth Street near Market in Denver, but Linda couldn't handle the distraction when she was writing. And at the moment, she was drafting the story that would both make her career and make her rich.

As she typed on her laptop, Linda heard a creaky whine somewhere in the apartment. She ignored the sound.

She was in *the zone*, that rare and special creative state where time has no meaning and every word falls into place poetically and logically. The Resurrection Project story had incredible scope, scientific and ethical and religious implications. Potentially, it was more explosive than the original exposé of the School, and even the revelation of the bird-children themselves.

And it was *her* story.

No one else was even close to this. At least she hoped and prayed no one was. It was so ground-shaking she didn't mind having lied to Max about being abused as a child. Actually, her childhood in Ridgewood, New Jersey, had been splendid.

Linda imagined her story running serially in a major newspaper, ten or twelve installments of three thousand words or so spaced over a two-week period. She would pitch it to the *Washington Post*, the *New*

*York Times, The Times* in London. Maybe *Time* and *Newsweek,* and *People.* Let them fight over her. Let them pay the big bucks. And then – *the Book.*

Linda drained her morning's fourth cup of coffee and blew a few pesky bangs off her forehead. She was polishing her lead, bracketing the letters TK where facts were still to come, and punching up the kicker.

She heard a squeak on the parquet floor in the foyer.

'Mrs Martinez?' She called out her housekeeper's name. 'Is that you? Hello there?'

Linda Schein felt a movement of air a fraction of a second before she felt something cold and hard at her temple. She took in a sharp breath.

Then she peeked, and almost wished she hadn't.

*Gun.*

'Be quiet, Linda. Do exactly as I say,' said a man's voice. Linda Schein soundlessly expelled the breath she'd inhaled a moment before. Her back muscles went slack.

She squelched the compulsion to cry out, or to struggle. She didn't turn her head any more than she had to see the *gun.* She hoped to God the intruder was wearing a mask because she didn't want to see his face. She suspected that her life depended on it.

'The only money here is in my purse,' she said. 'I'm not going to cause any trouble. I get the picture.'

'Well that's very good to hear. But I honestly don't know if I can believe you. My name is Dr Ethan Kane. You're writing a story about my life's work, so I thought we should talk. Hmmm? Shall we?'

Linda Schein felt total fear shoot through her body. He had *identified* himself. Oh God! Oh no!

*Dr Ethan Kane.*

*The Resurrection Project.*

'Am I supposed to know you?' she asked, pretending ignorance, trying to sidetrack him if she could.

'No, Linda. You're *not.* But you do. Now, let's talk.' He pressed the gun barrel harder against her temple. 'I want to hear everything.'

Linda Schein talked and talked until she realized she was repeating herself. 'That's fine,' Dr Kane finally said. 'I *believe* you, Linda. You *do* get the picture.'

There was a muffled explosion, then an intensely bright flash behind her eyes, and everything – her thoughts, her fantasies about fame, her fears of bodily violence – came to an end. The writer never knew that a nine-millimeter bullet had blown through her brain at about two thousand miles per hour.

'That didn't hurt, did it?' asked Dr Kane. 'Any more questions about my life's work? No? Well then, I guess we're through here. Excellent interview, Linda. Brief and right to the point. So rare with journalists today.'

# CHAPTER THIRTY-SIX

**M**ax was up very late that night, getting absolutely nothing accomplished, futzing around in her room.

Anxious.

Uncomfortable.

Angry without reason.

Couldn't sit still.

*Could not.*

*Sit.*

*Still.*

She played her electric guitar, and she was getting pretty good. 'Watch out Sheryl Crow, Eric Clapton, B.B. King.'

Then she was 'down with' a Tony Hawk video game – skateboarding at its best.

Max went online, played a game of cribbage with a girl from San Diego. Her screen name was UPDRAFTGURL38.

She won at cribbage.

Of course.

She wrote in her journal, her *third* journal since she'd been at the Marshall house.

|  *Current Likes*  |  *And Dislikes*  |
| --- | --- |
| Leather pants (all colors) | N'Sync |
| Buffy | *Chicken Soup for the Teenage Soul* |

| *Current Likes* | *And Dislikes* |
|---|---|
| Mary Karr | *Bag of Bones* |
| 'Firestarter' | Reality TV |
| 'Under Rug Swept' | Sunday nights on CBS |
| Shania, Fiona, Sheryl | Reporters who lie their asses off |
| 'The pellet with the poison's in the vessel with the pestle' | Righteous reporters who think they tell the truth, but lie |
| Watermelon lip gloss | The 'Mummy' movies |
| Josiah Bartlet | The way 'Moms' try too hard |
| The Flock | Bush League, Colorado |
| Especially Ozymandias! | Men's professional sports |
| Frannie and Kit! | The kids at school (most of them) |

Max stopped writing her crazy, dumb, self-involved gibberish and cocked her head slightly. She heard a noise outside. Something just slightly out of sync with the other sounds of the night.

The wind?

Someone calling her name? Oz?

*Come fly with me, Max.*

Maybe it was time for another strictly forbidden night flight.

She picked up her cell phone, then put it down again.

She heard another noise outside.

Definitely not the wind. Something that really sucked.

*Hunters!*

# CHAPTER THIRTY-SEVEN

Ethan Kane personally led the small team of three down the leaf-strewn slope of brambles and underbrush behind the house on Ames Road where the Marshalls lived. They all wore seamless black clothes and black ball caps; greasepaint smeared their faces. Even in moonlight, they seemed more like shadows than real men.

They had come for the two children, but the others in the house would probably have to die. They shouldn't take chances on detection. Not with Resurrection so close.

Ethan Kane held up his hand, a signal to the others to stop. 'Max and Matthew are very fast. They're also strong, and clever. Please don't underestimate them. In fact, don't think of them as children,' he said in an undertone.

Kane turned and studied the Marshall house. An unimpressive, slightly depressing ranch house. Dark at midnight. Not even a television glow at a single window.

This *might* be easier than he'd expected. They had no logical reason to have their guard up. Kane hadn't bothered to bring in professionals like Marco Vincenti. He felt he could trust his team tonight; he wasn't so sure about Mr Vincenti. He wanted the kids alive – for a while anyway.

He had his reasons. Extraordinarily good reasons that only he understood.

He signaled again, and the others fanned out around a jungle gym, then the brick patio and fireplace in the backyard. 'Just watch the house. I'll do the work inside,' he whispered.

Dr Ethan Kane walked directly to the mudroom door. He opened the lock with a twist and turn of a thin L-shaped pick.

Then he made his way silently through the mudroom to the kitchen, and to the stairs that led to the bedrooms.

He reached into a pocket in his jacket and took out a black case that held several syringes.

Silently, he climbed the stairs. The girl's room was on the right, the boy's on the left. Matthew and Max. The biological parents were in the master bedroom at the end of the hall. Terry and Art.

*You talk*, he said to himself, *you die. Or at least you get sold to the Chinese.*

Whatever the cost in human lives – Resurrection was worth it. And so were these amazing, amazing children – who could fly like eagles.

He gently pushed open the door to the girl's room. This was it. The moment of truth. As he entered the room a flashlight beam *blinded him!*

'What the hell?' he muttered.

'You got that right, pal.'

Almost simultaneously, someone crashed into him, took the wind right out of Dr Kane's sails, nearly dislocated his shoulder.

*My God, it was the girl! It was Maximum herself! Strong as a horse!*

'Run, Matthew, run!' Max called out. 'They've come for us. I knew they would.'

But the two of them didn't run.

They flew!

Straight down the upstairs hallway and out an open window, like a pair of guided missiles.

'Don't shoot the little bastards.' Kane issued a fierce command. 'Catch them! Don't let them get away! Bring them back to me. Alive!'

# CHAPTER THIRTY-EIGHT

'I'm really, *freezing* cold,' Matthew whispered to Max a few moments later. 'I'm fricking shivering. I'm mad as hell too. What was that about? Who were they? Who *are* they? What's happening to us, Max? Do I want to hear the answer to these questions?'

He and his sister were in their flannel PJs, huddled together in the top of a wobbly fir tree. They were maybe two hundred yards away from the Marshall house, fifty feet off the ground. Max figured they were pretty much invisible from the searching eyes below.

'Shhhh, Matty!' She was still panting from fear, still pretty much in shock herself.

The men were inside the house. The hunters. Were the Marshalls safe from them?

*Or had they been put to sleep? Please, God, don't let that have happened. Please protect Art and Terry*, Max prayed. *Please, oh please. I do love them.*

As she watched, a plain black panel van pulled up to the house. Her eyes followed the four men who crept from the shadows around the house. The tallest was holding his arm against his body and limping. *Good, she'd hurt his sorry ass. Good, good, good. Shame he could still walk.*

The men got into the vehicle, and it raced away. They were retreating.

'They were trying to kill us, weren't they, Max? To put us to sleep? Those worthless bastards. Those lousy, crummy shitheads.'

'I think so, Matty. I guess they were. OK, yeah, they were trying to kill us.'

She hugged Matthew so hard that he protested. 'Hey! That hurts. Jeez, Max. You know how strong you are. First you save me from the baddies. Then you almost kill me yourself.'

'Very funny. Glad you haven't lost your very strange sense of humor.'

Max gave him a big kiss and released her grip. Then she turned on her handheld and clicked to an Internet application. Oz was online.

Max sent him an instant message, one she hoped couldn't be captured or traced.

'SOS,' Max typed. 'Leave home NOW. Get Ic, NOW. As in NOW.'

'Meet at the Mine?' Ozymandias came right back to her.

'K,' Max affirmed. 'CU soon.'

Max and Matthew zipped back to the Marshall house to get their gear and check to see that everybody was all right. Amazingly, Art and Terry had slept through it all.

Then they did what Max had known they were going to do sooner or later – *they flew the coop*.

# CHAPTER THIRTY-NINE

The old rutted roads that once led to the Mine near Prairie Divide had been totally consumed by the encroaching forest. Now it was only accessible from the air.

That worked.

Oz and Icarus ran out of the Mine entrance as Max and Matthew dropped out of the dark night sky. There was a flurry of excited but nervous greetings.

'I'm free, I'm free!' Icarus kept saying over and over. 'And a blind man shall lead them! I *am* that blind man!'

Max noticed that Ic had grown since she had last seen him. His white-blond hair was shoulder-length and he was almost as tall as she was. His sightless blue-gray eyes seemed to actually focus as he picked Matthew up and held him.

'Put me down, Icky!' her brother yelped. 'I'm not a fricking baby any more. I'm grown up!'

Breathlessly, Max told Oz and Ic about the men who'd broken into the Marshall house with murder or mayhem on their minds.

'I think one or more of them were doctors. It's a feeling I had,' said Max.

'It's starting all over again,' said Ic. 'We should go get the twins. The little ones aren't safe either. Damn, we should go get them now, this instant.'

'They're doing *cereal* commercials,' Matthew said. 'They're probably safe.'

Max raised her voice. 'They're *not* safe.'

There was no further dissent, so, with some agitated warbles and whistles, they took off one at a time, falling into formation at two hundred feet. They headed southeast toward the town of Fort Lupton, where Peter and Wendy lived with their biological parents, and were supposedly *safe*.

# CHAPTER FORTY

The flight was so much different from the one Max had taken just two nights before. Everything had changed. She took no pleasure in the moonlight or the play of light and shadow on the forest below. As the eldest by a couple of months, she was the leader of the flock, and the others looked to her and to Oz for guidance. Max had already figured it might be hard to take the twins from their home. They were still babies really, hard to predict, hard to control.

But it had to be. There was no alternative.

*Someone was coming for them.*

They passed over the little town of Fort Lupton and soon neared the Chen farmhouse. It sat on a knoll a quarter of a mile up a driveway, at the end of a narrow dirt road. Their closest neighbor was more than half a mile away.

*A perfect place for murder*, Max thought. *Or capture. Or whatever the creeps in black are up to.*

She and the boys landed in a clump of pines that gave them a clear view of the farmhouse.

A flagstone path, which bisected the front lawn, led up to a wraparound porch that was full of wicker furniture and shaped three sides of the house.

Oz pointed to the Garfield the Cat doll stuck to one of the upstairs windows. 'Wendy loves that dumb cat.'

'Okay,' said Max, nodding. 'That's their room. I'll go up. I don't want them to be frightened yet.'

Max flew to the porch roof, landing softly. Then she crept over to the twins' bedroom window.

It was unlocked. *Uh-oh*. She opened the casement window and began to climb inside.

*Please don't let me be too late.*

'Boo! Hey, Max,' said Peter. 'We saw you coming a mile away.'

'Heard ya too,' chorused Wendy.

If Max had worried that she would have to convince Peter and Wendy to join them, she was wrong. The four-year-olds grabbed her, hugged and kissed her, and trembled with happiness. There was a blowup of one of their cereal ads spanning the twin beds. *Disgusting,* Max thought. *Makes me want to start a war with Battle Creek.*

'Oh, wow, a night flight,' said Peter. 'Let's skedaddle.'

'A *flock* flight, we're going on a flock flight!' Wendy whooped.

There was a pounding on the wall. Then the muffled voice of Warren Chen. 'Knock it off, Peter and Wendy. You kids go to sleep right now! You know you have an important film shoot in the morning.'

'We're stars,' Peter whispered, and winked.

Max froze. She listened to her heart pounding. She waited until she was sure no footsteps could be heard outside the room. Then she helped Peter and Wendy dress and pack. Carefully, quietly, quickly.

Moments later, they were crouched on the porch roof. Shades of *Peter Pan*. Kind of cool, kind of crazy, kind of nuts.

Wendy whispered, 'Where are we going?'

'It's a secret,' Max whispered back.

They pushed off into the clear black night and followed Max's lead.

'*It's a secret!*' shouted little Peter and Wendy. '*It's a big secret.*'

# CHAPTER FORTY-ONE

They were elated to be together again – the flock!

The tribe!

The family!

Just like it had been for a few precious months at the Lake House.

They did fancy aerobatics high above the snow-dusted woodland. Their innocent laughter floated clear and wide for miles and miles around. They were a miracle to watch. Better than any show the US Air Force had ever dreamed up, or ever would.

Matthew, at the advanced age of nine, led the 'junior squadron' in dive bombs and incredible triple-barrel rolls. He took the twins on a chase over and around a distressed pair of horned owls who were hunting. Oz and Ic were also having the time of their lives. Because he was blind, Ic needed Oz to help him 'see'. The kids had developed a verbal code or flight language to guide Icarus.

*Chee-rup* meant fly straight; *caw* was turn left; *cree* was the signal to turn right. A *talondrop* was a free-fall, feet first, and nothing in 'bird talk' satisfactorily replaced the fantastic power of the words 'climb' and 'dive'.

The kids combined some of the words together. *Caw-roll* meant roll to the left and *Chee-rup-te-rup-te-rup* meant to fly up and down like a roller coaster. When they were relaxed and gliding, Oz and Ic exchanged short whistles and tongue clacks and hoots, or sometimes they sang the lyrics to 'Bad to the Bone' and 'My Sharona'.

Max was filled with pride. They had survived the sick hellhole of the School, where they were forced to work in the labs, kept in cages, and lived under the constant fear of being put to sleep. Until last year, they had never ridden in a car or gone to a movie or a city, and they had never, never done what they were made to do.

*They had never spread their wings to fly!*

As she was having the brief happy thought, mischievous Matthew's enthusiasm overflowed. 'Snacks for the road,' he called out in a squeaky-high voice. 'Who's hungry as hound dogs?'

Matthew had spotted a 7-11 convenience store on the highway that ran through the town of Lyons. Blinding neon green and orange glowed up at them. He whistled to the twins, and they shot toward the inviting open doors like arrows toward a bull's eye.

All Max could do was yell, 'No! Guys! *No way!* Please, stop! Don't do this!'

She might just as well have saved her breath.

She watched helplessly as the kids buzzed the store shelves, spilling and knocking over jars and cans in their wake.

'Ring Dings!' Wendy shouted, grabbing a couple of packets of the chocolate cakes from the rack.

Peter hovered in front of the salty snack section before selecting a giant-sized package of Cheez Doodles corn puffs.

Matthew ripped off a box of Cracker Jack candied popcorn and some Tostitos tortilla chips. Finally they flew shrieking joyously out of the store, leaving the wide-eyed, grunged-out teenaged boy at the cash register bedazzled, and befuddled.

'Never again,' Max scolded when they'd gotten back into flight formation. 'What you did is stealing and that's wrong, wrong, wrong. That poor boy is going to have to clean up your mess.'

'We'll be good, Max,' Peter said, licking orange crumbs from his lips. 'Pinky swear. We'll be good *from now on.*'

Max wanted to smile, but she couldn't. She wasn't worried about the petty theft so much as she was about the fact that they'd been seen.

Now there was a witness only twenty or so miles from Bear Bluff. And Frannie's house.

# CHAPTER FORTY-TWO

I was having a pity party on the back porch of my place, with a nicely chilled bottle of Turning Leaf Chardonnay at my elbow, when I heard the phone ring. *Screw it.* I didn't pick up.

My medical emergency calls were being shunted over to my relief, Dr Monghil, in Clayton, the next town west. Right now I felt too low to inflict my blues on some innocent caller, whoever it might be.

I sat just soaking up the atmosphere: the crickets, the blinking stars and the all-you-can-drink vino, when the phone rang again, and now it really tweaked me.

*World.*

*Leave me the hell alone.*

Then I heard a police siren in the distance.

*Now what?*

I left my wine on the porch and went inside. I'd just about rewound the answering machine when I heard the infernal siren come to a stop. *This bud was for me.* I ran outside.

I saw a bright torchlight come shining through the woods. It was Trooper Brian McKenna. I called out, 'Hey, Mac.'

'Hey, Frannie. I *thought* you were here. Why didn't you answer your phone? You had me worried.'

'I punched out for the night,' I said. 'What's up?'

'The kids are missing,' said Mac, putting one heavily shod foot on the porch step and his meaty hand on the railing. Big Mac had tried to date me, too, and he was *married*. 'You know anything about that? I hope that you don't, Frannie.'

A shudder passed through me. '*Missing?* What do you mean? Who's missing?'

'All of them, Frannie. They're all gone, the six of them just vanished. Do you have them here, or have any knowledge of where they are? If you do, tell me, and that'll pretty much put an end to any kind of trouble for you.'

'I don't have them here, Mac,' I said. 'And I haven't heard a word from any of them.'

'Mind if I take a look inside?' the trooper asked.

'That hurts my feelings. But knock yourself out,' I said. 'Jeez, Mac.'

He gave me a sidelong glance that told me he disapproved of my attitude, or maybe I was slurring my words, I wasn't sure which. I definitely wasn't drunk, but I had made some progress in pain management. Still, I was stunned by the news! I talked to the kids a couple of times every week. Although I missed them terribly, I had lulled myself into thinking that they were safe, if not happy. That dull comfort had just evaporated.

I followed the serious young statie into my house and watched him poke around. When he was satisfied that I didn't have six young children under the bed or in the washer-dryer, he apologized for any rudeness and asked me to please stay in touch.

'If you hear from or see those kids, call me, Frannie. Beep me or you can talk to anyone at the barracks, okay? The parents are frantic.'

'I understand.' I actually did. I felt frantic myself.

The trooper touched the brim of his hat and went back down the wooded path toward the road.

The little buzz I'd been cultivating was completely gone. I had been lonely and self-pitying a few minutes ago. Now I was sick to my stomach and too scared for words.

There was only one person I could truly depend on for advice and solace right now.

And that would be Kit.

# CHAPTER FORTY-THREE

I threw on every light in the kitchen, and I had no real idea why I did it. *Because I was scared?*

The tap was dripping, so I wrenched the knob to stop the relentless *pinging* in the stainless-steel sink. I slammed a couple of cabinet doors shut, then I perched on the edge of a stool.

I took a few deep breaths, then finally pressed buttons on the cordless phone.

I listened to the ringing sound in my ear.

It was half past midnight, so I wasn't surprised that I caught Kit at home sleeping. Happily for me, he recognized my voice and didn't hang up. I said as much.

'Why would I hang up on you, Frannie?'

Well, the last time I'd actually *seen* Kit had been after the custody trial in Denver. The way I remember it, he was trying to comfort me and I ran off in the Suburban without so much as a goodbye. Our phone conversation afterwards had been heartbreakingly short. *Let's take a break, yada-yada. We need to heal. If it's meant to be, it will be.* We'd both been too wounded to actually deal with each other. We hadn't spoken since I sent his things back by UPS.

'I just heard that the kids are missing, Kit. All of them! A state trooper was here and told me all six of them are gone.'

There was a pause and I knew that Kit was in shock, thinking of all the horrible possibilities just as I had done. Why would the kids run away together? Why now? Where would they go? But worst of all, had someone kidnapped them?

I was completely unprepared when Kit said, 'I know, Frannie. I couldn't tell you so I'm glad the local cops came by.'

'You *what*?' I actually yelled into the phone receiver. 'You *knew* about this?'

'I couldn't tell you. I wasn't allowed to call. I was forbidden under orders from the director.'

I just *hated* it when Kit went FBI on me.

'You jerk,' I said. 'You seriously thought it was better for me to hear this from a stranger? Oh, never mind,' I said.

Then I hung up on him.

# CHAPTER FORTY-FOUR

I sat on the kitchen stool, holding a dead phone in my hand and fuming at Kit. I was really hot, *and* hurt. I stared at the Colorado State Wildlife calendar over my stove for a while. Pretty pictures, but they didn't help. I had to get out of the house or go crazy.

I took my denim Carhart jacket off the back of a chair and put it on. Then I whistled for Pip. 'You want to walk with me, little guy?' He couldn't believe his luck.

We set out on a trail that runs along the top of a ravine. Fortunately the moon was almost full, so we had plenty of light.

Pip ran up and down the gully snorting and chuffing. I could hear various four-footed beasts scurry deeper into the woods at the sounds of my footsteps on the forest floor.

Then I heard rustling in the trees overhead.

An image of a bobcat came full into my mind. I froze at the thought of a ninety-pound cat somewhere in the skinny branches right above my head. Not good. Very bad, actually.

There was more rustling up there. My knees went a little weak. Then a voice I recognized.

'Hey there, Frannie. How's life on the planet?'

First Max jumped down from the thick, overhanging branches. Then out came Matthew, Ic, Oz, and the twins. Everybody was hugging me at once. Wendy kept saying, 'Mama, Mama, it's you, Mama!' My heart was melting. Nothing I could do to stop it, not that I really wanted to.

The pack of us finally separated, and we scrambled, jogged and literally flew back to my cabin. We celebrated with hot chocolate and cookies, pineapple chunks for Wendy and Peter. I couldn't take my eyes off the little feathered wunderkinds.

I was so relieved to have them in my kitchen, each one alive and well. I mentally counted their fingers and toes. I kissed their sweet faces again and again. And I wondered, what was I going to do now?

After dessert, Max was still hungry. 'I've had a really long night,' she said, laughing. 'I could eat a rhino. But pasta with marinara will have to do.'

Max knew her way around my kitchen and insisted on doing the cooking. She took a large pot from the pegboard over the stove, filled it with water and put it on the burner. Ozymandias located a jar of red sauce in the pantry. Matthew started chopping parsley.

They were home again, home again. God, it was sweet. The best stuff on earth.

As Max and the crew cooked pasta, she told me why they had run away. With disturbing nonchalance, she described the armed men in black who'd broken into the Marshall house. She used a line from a recent movie poster: 'Same planet, different scum.'

I wasn't laughing. I was shocked, horrified, chilled to the bone. I asked Max point-blank if she knew *why* someone was after them.

She shrugged, then said, 'Because we're priceless works of art? Who knows? Let's leave it at that, Frannie.'

At about two a.m. Wendy and Peter and Matthew and Pip finally fell asleep on my bed. I put Max under a quilt on the sofa, threw blankets and pillows down on the floor for tough guy Oz. Ic tucked himself into the linen closet, which was where he felt most secure. I kissed everybody goodnight.

Once they were asleep, I knew I had to give some serious thought to the situation. Six extremely frightened kids were in my house, and they were on the run from someone who apparently wanted to harm, or possibly sell them. Who? And why, why, why?

Trooper McKenna had told me to call him, but I hadn't done it. Past experiences had taught me not to trust people just because they had badges or even positions with the government.

The FBI was involved.

*If Kit couldn't tell me about the kids, could I tell him?*

I fell asleep on that thought.

# PART FOUR

---

# YELLOW BRICK ROAD

# CHAPTER FORTY-FIVE

## The Hospital

Kristin Morgan was a senior medical technician who had one job only, but she figured that it made her an important, if small, part of medical history. In fact, her perspective on herself had given rise to her nickname, 'Cog'.

She was in charge of the Scoop, a streamlined titanium instrument with Porsche-like curves and sensitive calibrations, which, like an expensive car, needed constant fine-tuning. Cog was responsible for the Scoop's performance and maintenance, and it would be her neck if anything went wrong with this state-of-the-art technotool. And that was no joke at the Hospital.

A faint, rather sexy *hum* announced the Scoop's entrance into the operating theater and its movement along the grooved track in the ceiling.

Cog, anonymous in her cap, mask, and blue cotton scrubs, followed below the Scoop as it made the first leg of its journey.

It finally came to rest above the naked body of Raoul Ramirez, an eighteen-year-old boy from Coral Gables, Florida.

Raoul's body had been split in a long H: the incisions cut from throat to groin and across the clavicles and the pelvis. Then the gaping cavity had been clamped wide open. The ribs were spread, and the organs, severed from the connective tissues, were laid bare.

Cog reached up and took hold of the Scoop's two lateral handles, which looked like the handlebars of a bicycle. She tried not to think about the person once known as Raoul Ramirez.

*This was science*, she told herself. It was important, necessary, and it was happening all around the world, but especially in China and Japan. It was essential that the United States keep up, and, ultimately, surpass other countries, wasn't it?

The Scoop was important, and so was Cog.

She guided the hydraulic Scoop's jaw to a precise position over the youth's torso. Checking by eye and correcting by judgment, she cranked open the Scoop's jaws, then lowered and fitted the titanium teeth under Raoul's internal organs. She adjusted the jaws so that the enclosed viscera wouldn't slip or break apart. Then she locked the machine's glittering maw and flicked a switch in the stem.

With a well-oiled hum, the Scoop grabbed hold of the connected 'package' of organs and lifted them out. In medical lingo, Raoul's carcass was now a 'canoe'.

She threw another switch and followed the Scoop as it once again traveled along its track and through an opening to an adjacent room called 'the baths'.

To Cog, the baths resembled a photo-development lab. A long stainless-steel sink took up one wall, and in the center of the room was a gray metal table. On the table were three rectangular stainless-steel basins, ten inches deep, and filled with fluid.

The Scoop hummed along the track until it came to a shuddering stop over Basin 1.

Cog reached up and lowered the machine so that it was fully submerged. Satisfied with the procedure thus far, she opened the Scoop and inserted tubes into the severed ends of the two major arteries. She then opened the guillotine clamps in both the vena caval artery and the femoral artery.

Blood poured from the femoral artery and was conveyed into a waste canister, while a short-term oxygen source loaded with a plaque-cleaning enzyme flowed through the vena cava to the organs.

When the heart and lungs and other organs were shining pink from the infusion of the oxygenated solution, she clamped off the arteries again. She closed the Scoop's hungry jaws.

The Scoop lifted the organ package and repositioned it over Basin 2. This container held a different enzymatic solution, a cloudy soup biologically tailored to seek and destroy fat nodules, blood, and any stray strands of connective tissues.

She let the package soak in the cleanser. In some cases she would manually strip fat from the liver and the heart.

But Raoul had been young and his organs were lean. He'd been a beautiful specimen, actually. A real hunk of chocolate.

Cog watched the Scoop rise out of Basin 2. This time she lowered it into Basin 3. As the 'canoe' soaked in a potent solution of saline infused with neural stem cells, ultrasound stimulated the nervous system with high-frequency sound waves. The stem cells, originally harvested from fetal tissue and then cloned, attached themselves to the severed nerve bundles, invigorating the nerve endings preparatory to reconnection.

Kristin Morgan breathed out a sigh of satisfaction. The process had gone well. After 'the package' was transferred to the blue room, she would carefully dismantle and disinfect the Scoop. There could be no danger of malfunction or infection in the next procedure, which was to take place not too long from now, actually.

Cog would soon forget about Raoul Ramirez, just as she'd forgotten about all the others before him.

*Hundreds of donors.*

All of them murdered in this very room.

# CHAPTER FORTY-SIX

D awn hadn't yet broken through the thick tree cover in the woods around Bear Bluff, Colorado. The air had a bracing crisp chill.

Dr Ethan Kane leaned against a tree trunk and cursed. He had to stop to massage the bruise on his right thigh where the little bastard girl had dared kick him. He had another deep bruise on his forearm. He was sure it had gone to the marrow.

The pain served as a lesson to remind him that he had underestimated the girl. She was a superior being, wasn't she? Well, now he knew.

He sucked on a brutally refreshing Altoids as he watched Frannie O'Neill's cabin through the best of the new German-made binoculars.

He was more than two hundred yards away, but he could clearly see the veterinarian. It was as if he were standing just outside the bitch's window.

He wondered if she got up this early every morning, or if maybe she'd had a premonition that this was the day she was going to die. *It was*, Dr Kane knew. *She was a dead woman; she just didn't know it.*

He could read the time on the stove clock: 4:22.

His own watch, a Breitling Aerospace #270, read the same. Dr O'Neill was careful about keeping the precise time. Probably careful about a lot of things.

*All was quiet on the western front,* he chuckled to himself. *Soon he could get back to his important work at the Hospital.*

His two-man teams were deep in the woods, positioned to watch the doors on the north and south sides of the cabin. Each member had a Motorola handheld radio, infrared goggles, a tool with assorted blades and cutters, and a GPS locator that could pinpoint just about any spot on planet Earth.

Dr Ethan Kane mentally reviewed his game plan. The team would *not break into* the cabin because it left too much room for confusion and failure. That much he'd learned. The children were frightfully strong, fast, and clever. They seemed to combine all the best characteristics of human and avian life.

Instead, they would stay in the woods. At the ready. This time there would be no painful mistakes.

When the children eventually left the house, the teams would simply grab them.

One bird-brat at a time.

# CHAPTER FORTY-SEVEN

I think I slept for about a half-hour, but I really couldn't be sure. Maybe I was down for a whole hour. Suddenly, my eyes were wide open. And I knew there was trouble.

Nine-year-old Matthew was beside me, shaking my arm, staring at me in total horror.

'What is it, Matt?'

'There are some creepy sickos outside in the woods. Even Pip doesn't hear them. They're the ones who broke into our house in Pine Bush. Yes, *I'm sure*, Frannie. I can smell them. They smell of death. They're bad to the bone. Trust me on it.'

Terror flooded my body. If adrenaline were rocket fuel, I'd have been halfway to the moon. We were totally exposed, vulnerable! My cabin had a dozen or so windows, no curtains at all. I now knew that I had been stupid. Instead of a reunion with the kids last night, I should have called for help. *Or I should have run with them. We should have run!*

'Stay right here,' I whispered to Matthew. 'Stay here, you superscout. Don't stand up or go anywhere near the windows.'

'Do I look that *dumb*?' Matthew retorted.

'Nope. So stay *down*.'

I sat on the floor and hurriedly dressed in yesterday's clothes. Then I heard Pip's toenails click on the hardwood floor. In a second, he located me, danced around on his hind legs.

'Hush,' I admonished him. 'You blew it, bub. Some watchdog you are.'

We crawled together to the kitchen. I went directly to the wall where the cordless phone was mounted.

I walked my fingers up the Sheetrock and patted around the cradle. Then I went into denial, unwilling to believe what my fingers were telling me.

*The phone was missing!*

*The cradle was empty!*

Where the hell was the phone? Where was the damned phone? What the hell? Were they in the house right now?

I held in a scream, but a tiny moan escaped from my mouth. Then I crawled along the floor, reached up and touched the countertop with my hand.

I found the sugar bowl, but knocked over the saltshaker. *Damn it!*

Then my fingers closed on the cordless – right where I'd left it after talking with Kit. Talk about relief.

I pressed a button on the receiver.

*There was no dial tone. Nothing at all.*

Maybe the batteries were dead. It really didn't fucking matter. I was up shit creek without a paddle. Six little kids were in the badly leaking boat with me. I was in the *panic room*, wasn't I? I wasn't Jodie Foster.

*That was when I stood up in the kitchen.*

And that was when I felt a hand on my leg and nearly screamed.

'Try this.' It was Max, pressing a cell phone into my hand.

I heaved a sigh of relief. The battery light was green – a full charge. 'Thanks,' I whispered.

Another shadow crept into the kitchen. Ozymandias the Brave. Looking as if he were ready to do war.

'They're moving on us, Frannie,' he reported. 'The cowards are coming closer to the house. We can fight them! We can win, too! Don't doubt it for a nanosecond.'

'Max, get all the kids together. You too, Oz. Get your coats. Take everyone and go down to the cellar quietly. And *crawl*. Don't fly. *Do not fly.*'

Hiding in the cellar was only a stopgap. If we stayed there, we'd be rounded up. And killed? I had another idea, though. It's been said that pressure makes diamonds. If so, my idea was a real gem.

And like all good gems, the price would be dear.

# CHAPTER FORTY-EIGHT

I knew what I had to do, and I hated it more than drinking a quart of castor oil straight up and full to the brim. It made me unbelievably mad, and also inconsolably sad.

Maybe a little nuts, too.

This had to be one of the worst moments of my life, *and it hadn't even happened yet.*

I was also angry at Kit for not being here to help me. Maybe he could have come up with another, better plan. *Damn you, Kit.*

I crouched low behind the children as they filed down the stairs into the cellar. The twins were wild-eyed and hootering, distressed at being roused so suddenly from the comfort zone of sleep.

Max put her hands on each of their heads to silence them. 'Chill,' she whispered.

'I'll be right there!' I told her. 'Don't do anything crazy. I'll join you guys in a couple of minutes.'

I hoped it was a promise I could keep.

The brilliant early-morning sun was slanting through the windows. My hands were shaking some. Before sentiment could get its hooks into me, I did *the unspeakable.*

I took a really sharp carving knife to my sofa. I slashed the cushions until the frame was covered with feathers and goose down.

Next I piled the magazines from the coffee table on top of the ruined sofa. *Shit, shit, shit. This hurt. It really sucked.*

I looked around the living room, at the books and mementos of my marriage to Dr David Mekin: the model boat he'd constructed, signed and dated; our wedding photo on the mantel. I couldn't stop the flood of memories: nestbuilding, long evenings spent before the fire, love-making, and even fights that we worked through.

I pulled myself together and crawled to the hall closet. I swiftly stood and pulled down sheaves of my murdered husband David's old medical journals from the top shelf. I hadn't been allowed to throw them out while he was alive, and I hadn't wanted to throw them out after he died. David had been a medical researcher, and a good one. He had found out too much about the School a few years back, and the bastards had killed him. They did that sort of thing, and right now, someone appeared ready to pursue me and inflict mayhem. *Poor David*, I thought. *Poor kids. Poor me.*

Tears automatically welled in my eyes. I remembered seeing David's sheet-covered corpse on a stainless-steel slab. The horrible pain of his loss. After he was murdered, I'd moved out of the cabin we'd shared and into a spare room at the Inn-Patient. It was too painful to live with his artifacts and my memories. Then I discovered Max in the woods After I'd gained her trust she took me and Kit to meet the other kids. When the bastards from the School found me, they burned down my animal hospital. Nothing remained but charred timbers. I was able to rebuild with insurance money. I'd re-established tenancy of my old cabin in the woods.

Well, it looked like it was time to move again – only this time I was pretty sure Nationwide wouldn't be picking up the tab.

A dozen Duraflame logs were stacked high next to the wood-burning stove. They would do just fine.

I tossed the flammable logs on to the mountain of magazines and feathers and added a kitchen stool for good measure.

I steeled myself to do what *had to be done*.

I touched a match to the pyre. The flame sputtered innocently enough, then caught with a flash.

I watched tendrils of smoke curl up toward the peak of the

cathedral ceiling, and when the fire was burning well I took the cell phone from my pocket and made the call.

'*Please help me,*' I said, with genuine urgency. 'There's a house on fire in the woods behind the Inn-Patient animal hospital. Yes, right on Highway 34. Please hurry!'

I put on my jacket, grabbed and tucked a whimpering Pip under my arm. I was crying as I got ready to leave my burning house.

# CHAPTER FORTY-NINE

I was also mad as hell, absolutely furious, bent on revenge *somehow, some way.* There was always a way.

I ran down the steep stair slats before second thoughts could slow me. It was totally dark in the cellar.

It took me several seconds to get my bearings.

I could hear scraping and dragging, and I went toward the sound. *Scraping, scraping, scraping.*

The kids were working, lifting and moving really heavy boxes and furniture. I mean incredibly heavy stuff.

With shock, I realized there was all sorts of old junk piled up in front of the cellar doors – our exit was blocked. And it only got worse. I looked back toward the stairs and saw smoke starting to seep under the door to the cellar. I hadn't expected the fire to get here so fast.

*What a trap I'd set for us!*

*We would all die down here.*

*We'd be burned to death.*

*I had started the fire!*

I waded into the fray and helped Oz, Max, and Matthew move a bed frame and dozens of cartons of books away from the cellar door. We moved a couple of old dressers as well.

'Stronger than you look, lady,' Max said and smiled encouragement my way.

A bolt locked the door, but I was able to bang it off with a couple of blows from a sledgehammer.

*Suddenly, an alarm went off upstairs! Then another!*

*Really loud! Screeching!*

'It's just a fire, don't worry about it,' I told the kids. *I'm burning down my house.*

# CHAPTER FIFTY

I listened to the piercing wail of the smoke detector with a mixture of sadness and satisfaction. When the timbered walls caught it would create a smokescreen outside, the diversion we needed. At least I hoped so. *But God, at what cost!*

The cellar doors were of the hatch type and the hinges were rusted from the weather. We put our shoulders and backs to them and pushed. The doors creaked open. I'd forgotten how incredibly strong Max and Oz were, especially Oz, who was really impressing me in all ways.

The hatch doors lie nearly flat to the ground on the east side of the house, about fifteen yards from a ravine. The ravine averages about ten feet deep, is lined with dramatic and striated rocks dripping with moss, and under normal conditions makes a nice little nature walk.

Now I saw the ravine as a long chute to safety. That was my prayer.

There had been *no way* we would escape – but now there was. The fire, the smoke, all the distractions had worked so far. Now if we were just a little lucky . . .

Wendy was scared and crying. I couldn't blame her. I wanted to cry, too. I slowly stuck my head out of the hatch doors and looked around. I listened. No footsteps. No gunshots. I ducked back in and took Wendy in my arms and hugged her tightly.

'Mama!' she wheezed.

*Damn it. See? I was their mother. The only mother they would ever have.*

'It's okay, baby,' I whispered against Wendy's ear. 'We're going to get out of this. Somehow.'

Then, with Pip racing beside me, I sprinted to the lip of the ravine and slid down to the bottom on my butt. The children followed, Oz guiding Ic, Max shepherding Matthew and Peter.

I counted all the noses.

The kids were scared, but at least we were still together, and unharmed so far.

Now what to do, what to do?

Hot smoke clouded the cold morning air, and I thought I'd done as good a job as a girl could do under the circumstances. I'm no commando or Superwoman, *I'm a veterinarian!*

Before I could fall over from patting myself on the back, I heard a sharp pinging sound and rock fragments scattered.

There were bullets ringing out around us. *We'd been spotted again. Oh my good God, or bad God, or some kind of God, we were in such big trouble!* Then we got a little break. Not much to cheer about, but it was something. The wind shifted. The smoke from the fire gave us some cover.

'Now *fly*! Keep low. Very low. Meet me at the car. Go! Run!'

I yelled to the children and for once they didn't question me; they actually obeyed. It was probably a quarter of a mile to the road where my car was parked at the Inn-Patient lot.

At least I hoped to hell the car was still there. I didn't have a plan B!

The kids flew away, as I clambered over rocks and logs and twisted bunches of fallen branches. I kept the smoke from the fire between myself and the armed men.

Just when the ravine became too shallow to hide me, I saw a large blue shape I had always loved.

*Like a rock. The Suburban was there. And so were the kids, all of them. Thank God.*

I leaped ahead and opened the doors for the children, and Pip, who all piled in without any extra urging from me.

'Where are we going?' Max and Oz both asked as I fired up the engine.

'Strap in, everyone. Put your seatbelts on,' I said by way of an answer.

I didn't have the heart to tell them that I was clueless and frightened.

I didn't have a plan.

# CHAPTER FIFTY-ONE

In the course of the next three hundred miles or so, we drove through majestic plains and foothills, passing Pikes Peak and other scenic wonders that I would have marveled at any other time than this.

Once in a while one of the kids would wake up and I would stop for snacks and gas, but mostly they were good and stayed hidden in the car. All potty activity took place behind roadside bushes because that was the way it had to be. We weren't on vacation.

It was déjà vu all over again. We were on the run once more, and I wasn't the only one having sickening feelings as I recalled past events.

'It's just like old times, huh?' Max said, but her face showed sadness and irony rather than any hint of humor. 'I feel just like I did when Matthew and I escaped from that rotten, stinking, obscene School last year. Only back then we'd never seen the real world. Now we know.'

'I'd rather be on the run than with my bio mom,' said Ozymandias. 'She called me Oliver. Didn't have a clue about avian life.'

'You got that right!' said Matthew. 'Oliver.'

I'd been driving for about six hours when we passed an old volcanic cone near Walsenburg, east of the highway that was part of the old Santa Fe Trail. I was burning out from a high-test blend of fatigue and fear when we finally crossed Ratón Pass and the state line at noon.

That was when I spotted a sign for a motel called the Pines.

I pulled off the highway on to a smaller road just outside the town of Ratón, New Mexico, and checked in. I paid cash for one night in a bungalow, way off the road.

Then I backed the car right up to the door of number 8. I went inside and checked it out before I allowed the kids out of the Suburban.

It was a dank and cheesy place with no amenities, apart from a thirteen-inch RCA circa the mid-seventies. The carpet was dark gray, no doubt chosen for its dirt-hiding capacity. The two double beds were lumpy with blankets and covers that would never get the Good Housekeeping Seal of Approval, or mine either. The place was perfect for one of those Hollywood creepy-crawler movies.

The kids were hungry, and I told them I'd go shopping. But first, I wanted them to call their parents on the cell phone.

'The less said, the better,' I warned them. 'I'm worried about *their* safety, too. We have to keep it short and sweet. And please, be nice. They're scared too.'

We rehearsed our lines and put a thirty-second limit on the calls. One by one, they told their folks they were on a 'fly-away', that they were in no danger and would be home soon. When the kids were finished, I called Doc Monghil and told his answering machine – without explanation – that I needed him to watch over the Inn-Patient for a day or two, or maybe even three. *Or possibly for the rest of my life.*

Suddenly, I was more exhausted than I'd ever been. I was at the end of my own resources. I needed help myself.

My heart was pounding as I cleared switchboard security and also an executive assistant.

Then I heard a male voice say, 'Agent Brennan.'

'Kit,' I said, 'I'm in the middle of nowhere. Literally. I'm scared out of my mind. And I've got the kids, all six of them. I swear to God, someone's trying to kill us. I might be understating this situation a little.'

# CHAPTER FIFTY-TWO

That night the kids and I sat around a cramped fourteen-by-sixteen-foot motel room and told each other ghost stories. Real ones! A baseball game was on the TV but nobody watched it. Mets and Rockies.

For the most part, the tales were about what the kids called their 'months in captivity without torture', or 'our bio-parent period', 'the abyss', 'nightmare in the suburbs', 'I know why the caged bird sings, too'. Basically, they sounded like most other kids growing up and being forced to obey rules for the first time. They hated it, and wanted to rebel; they wanted to do what they wanted to do, when they wanted to do it.

Of course, it was more complicated than that if you happened to be – gasp! – *different* from the other kids.

'We had to go into therapy,' Matthew confessed. 'Can you imagine *therapy* in Pine Bush, Colorado, with some Dr Phil-like guru who thought *he* knew what it had been like at the School for Max and me? Because he'd been tossed out of *two schools* himself as a kid.'

'Tell us about the *cereal* commercials.' Oz looked over at the twins, who were cuddled in my lap, and thought they were safe because they were little.

'No way.' Peter sat up straight and folded his arms across his chest. 'Up yours, Ozymandias. I mean, *Oliver*.'

'We *love* to fly,' said Wendy, 'and we also *love* to start our day with a balanced breakfast of Wingdingers. That's how the cereal commercial went.'

'That's *wrong*,' Peter interrupted. 'We love to start our day with a balanced breakfast *including* Wingdingers.'

'We're in test,' Wendy said proudly. 'Bridgeport, Connecticut and Columbus, Ohio.'

'Oohh,' said Matthew. 'I'm impressed Or is it depressed?'

'C'mon, give me a break,' I finally edged in as referee. 'Anybody want to talk about the here and now? What we do next? Or should we start our careers in TV and cinema. Like Ic's appearance in *Touched By An Angel*?'

'Don't *anybody* go there,' Ic warned and put up his fists as if to box somebody's ears, even mine. 'Yeah, what *are* we going to do next? And who are the hunters?'

Suddenly everybody was looking at Max.

She threw up her hands. 'Not me, guys. I don't know who they are or what they want. I'm in the scary dark just like everyone else. Pinky swear.'

As I looked around the motel room at the others, I could tell that none of them really believed her, but they were afraid to challenge Max's leadership. Nobody took up the pinky swear invitation.

'Hey,' said Max and grinned. 'How 'bout those Mets?'

Nobody laughed.

# CHAPTER FIFTY-THREE

## The Hospital

E than Kane stood tall and very imperial-looking over a patient named Andrew Mellon McKay in the operating room. His mind was running fast on two tracks. On one, he prepared to do a miraculous arthoplasty for a $200,000 fee, and on the other he considered the disaster that had happened out in Colorado.

Max and the other bird-brats had disappeared off the radar screen. So had Dr Frannie O'Neill. And darling Max knew too much for her own, or anybody else's, good.

'We're just about ready, Dr Kane,' said one of the OR nurses.

'I'm aware of that,' Kane snapped.

She inserted a foley catheter into the patient's urethra to monitor hydration and kidney function. Dr Kane sighed and began.

He examined the draped knee joint on the operating table before he made an incision across the patella with his scalpel. He pulled back the skin and began separating the muscles and ligaments to expose the knee capsule, the tough gristle surrounding the joint.

Immediately he could see that the patella, or kneecap, had deteriorated beyond reasonable repair and it would be both quicker and better to remove it entirely. He had suspected as much.

Dr Kane selected a tool with a fine saw and a soft rasping sound. He sawed off the end of the patient's right femur and tibia, dropping the fragments and scrapings and the entire patella into a basin.

Then he chose a particularly fine-tooled drill, essentially a milling machine. It was three inches long and made of space-age metals and plastics. The holes it made were accurate to within a millimeter, perfectly calibrated to the dimensions of the pin ends of the artificial knee.

*This perfect fit would make a difference of months in healing time. And when a patient was already eighty-three, months could matter.*

Within seconds, the drilling was complete. He applied a medical glue to the pins before fitting them into the newly drilled holes. Satisfied with the perfect fit, Kane stepped back. Another doctor was waiting to attach the ligaments and muscles. He flexed his fingers absentmindedly, then moved to the other side of the table and the second draped knee.

'I've received unfortunate news,' Ethan Kane said to the team as they worked. 'The experiment named Maximum is still unaccounted for, still missing. So are the others. They're running. We don't know where any of them are at this time.'

Kane thought about Max, her unquenchable curiosity and her fearlessness. And in that moment, he fumbled.

The scalpel spun at the ends of his fingers. The instrument dropped and clattered to the floor.

He stared at the knife lying on the brown-speckled linoleum, and his scalp prickled.

*What the hell was going on?*

*This was unheard of.*

*Ethan Kane didn't make mistakes.*

# CHAPTER FIFTY-FOUR

$M$ ax's heart skipped as she watched through a narrow gap in the nearly closed grayish-blue curtains of the motel window. *What was this?*

A dusty black Jeep had backed into the parking slot in front of the cabin next to theirs. Who was here at Bungalow 8? Then Kit got out.

'*Oh God, hooray, hooray,*' Max whispered to herself. 'Now things get really interesting.'

She watched Kit stretch his long limbs, then shake himself like a big dog. He was dressed all in blue: blue denim shirt, blue jeans, and a navy-blue blazer that set off the shining gold of his hair. Max's heart lifted, and a sudden smile eclipsed her terrible, horsespit mood.

'Frannie, he's here,' Max said in a whispery voice. 'It's Kit. The cavalry has arrived.'

Frannie's expression changed in a second from bone-tired and sad to bright and hopeful.

Max felt another surge of happiness – and it was *for Frannie*. Kit was here! And the question in her mind was, why had they been apart? How could two smart people be so dumb? They belonged together. Anybody could see that, and feel it too. Except, obviously, Kit and Frannie themselves.

Frannie pulled open the bungalow door and walked hurriedly to Kit's car. She was *so* cute sometimes. They reached out for each other, hesitant at first, then they hugged hard and swayed together.

Without completely knowing why, Max's eyes brimmed with tears. She got it then. *She loved the way they were with each other. She just loved it!*

The two grown-ups, 'Mom and Dad', finally let go of each other and started toward Bungalow 8. Kit was smiling.

Frannie entered first. 'Kids,' she said. 'Look who's here. Rumpelstiltskin!'

There was an explosion of excited laughter and yelling as the children flocked to hug Kit. He didn't have enough arms to hold them. From where she stood off to one side of the room, Max watched him greet each child in turn.

Then he sought her out.

'Hey, Maxie,' he said, walking over to her. 'How's my best girl in the world? Still playing hard to get, I see.'

'Why not? It always works,' said Max.

Kit was the only person who called her Maxie, and Max just loved that. He held out his arms to her and she wrapped herself around his waist and just held on. She was home. This *was* home – the eight of them together.

'I missed you, Kit,' she whispered. 'Corny but true.' For the briefest moment, she had the feeling that everything just might turn out right.

But in her heart, Max didn't really believe in happy endings.

She knew too much about the way the big bad world really worked. She knew more than Kit and Frannie.

*Max knew that she and the other kids would never be allowed to live.* Sad but true.

It just wasn't in the cards.

*A tragedy, that.*

# CHAPTER FIFTY-FIVE

This was so unexpectedly sweet. I was in Kit's arms again, both of us fully dressed – decent, maybe a little too decent – but definitely cozy.

We had kissed a couple of times and hugged, but too much water had flowed under the bridge since we'd last been together. Passionate embraces would have felt weird and inappropriate.

Or so I told myself.

Right now I had some control. Not much, I'll admit, but some. It's a scientific fact that when a woman makes love to a man a hormone called oxytocin is released in her brain which makes her bond to the guy like Krazy Glue. Accent on 'crazy'. If that wasn't enough, I still remembered how good it was to be with Kit. Like it says in the song, 'Nobody Does it Better'. Nope, if Kit and I made love I'd be handing him the keys to my heart, and I wasn't about to surrender mine in this creepy bungalow motel.

*Not here, not now, not yet.*

*Nuh-uh. Not me.*

*Not that he'd asked!*

It was such a good thing to be held again, after going so long without. Kit and I didn't talk at first, just breathed together quietly. Then out of pure nervousness, I suppose, I started to jabber about the situation at hand.

'I've got a lot to tell you,' I said.

'I'm here. I've got all night, Frances Jane,' he said. He always called me that when he was trying to calm me down. It was a little patronizing, but so what?

I told Kit how the kids had scared me silly by dropping out of the trees when I went for a walk in the woods. Then I told him why they had flown the coop. How I'd outsmarted the killers by setting fire to the only thing I owned in the world, my house. Kit looked at me fondly, a smile twitching at his lips as I described our steeplechase down the ravine, and when I caught him up on the four-hundred-mile dash to the Pines Motel, he laughed out loud.

'Jeez,' he said with a wide grin. 'You're actually better than Scully.'

'I am, aren't I?'

I loved it when Kit smiled like that. Hard not to! I grinned back at him and maybe I touched his long blond hair for a minute. I love his hair. *Don't lose control, Frannie. Just keep playing Scully.*

'The kids are maturing,' he said. 'Oz is a man and a half. He show you his tattoos?'

I nodded. 'Living out in the world has been good for them. Ic knows three languages already and he's making up a new one. Oz is our resident ornithologist. I think that his reading up on every kind of bird in the world is his version of *Roots*.'

'And Max? What's her story?'

'Um, she's still in charge, the mother-surrogate. Maybe she'll be a teacher some day. A professor.'

Kit was smiling at me, again. 'What I meant to say was, did Max tell you what's going on? I assume that she knows. Max always seems to know more than she lets on.'

I shook my head *no*. 'Max isn't talking. So, now *what?*'

Kit's face took on a serious mien. 'First things first,' he said. 'I think we need to set some priorities.'

'Like what?'

'Like we order out for three or four pizzas and all the fixings.'

I nodded. 'And then?'

'And then I'll have a private talk with Max.'

# CHAPTER FIFTY-SIX

That was exactly what they did.

Veggie pizzas – then a heart-to-heart.

Max sat next to Kit on a low branch of a big old spruce tree in the nearby woods. The waistband of her jeans was pleasantly tight from the food she'd just packed away. She was treasuring the one-on-one with Kit.

She told him about living in Pine Bush, or 'Bush League', as Oz and Matthew called it, and how hard it was getting along with the 'regular folks'. She knew over fifty names the kids had made up and used behind her back. Max said she'd also been hurt by the lies told in several news stories. 'I just wanted to fit in, y'know,' she said. 'Is that too much to ask?' Kit seemed to understand. He almost always did.

'You've got a lot to deal with, kiddo,' he said. 'You're doing great. I'm really proud of you. So is Frannie.'

Max nodded. But she hadn't told Kit *half* of what was on her mind. She hadn't told him that she was on 24/7 red alert, listening and watching for anything out of place, or that she was certain she and the other kids were going to be abducted, maybe killed, and probably sooner rather than later.

Max had visualized their current location topographically. A quick flyover had given her a sense of the scale of the hillside and the height of the trees, as well as the wind speed and temperature in the forest microclimate. Actually, the area reminded her of the mountains around the Lake House. She and Kit had talked about that, too. Until Max finally said, 'Enough nostalgia, Kit. It's dumb.'

Now Max's ears registered a tightly woven symphony of traffic and forest sounds, and she could even hear Frannie running the shower in the bungalow.

She could have counted the whiskers sprouting in Kit's shaved face if she'd wanted to do it. No bug on a branch, no puff of pollen could escape her notice.

But Kit was there, and it made her feel a little more secure. Being with Kit was as close to feeling taken care of as Max had ever felt.

*Dad. Dear old Dad. Except Kit wasn't so old. He sure didn't act old. He and Frannie were just about the coolest adults ever.*

Max sighed and looked out on the totally gorgeous evening. The sun had just dropped below the horizon and the sky was red where it met the earth, fading upwards to a greenish-gold band, then a luminous cobalt-blue ceiling sprinkled with stars.

The other kids were playing, laughing and shouting in the woods behind the bungalow, and it was almost possible to believe the lie they'd all told their parents today.

*It's just a fly-away, a harmless little run-away from home. No harm done. We'll be home soon. La-di-dah, la-di-dah.*

'Maxie,' Kit said, 'we've got a real tough situation here. I think you know that.' Kit's expression had gone grave, and Max felt a pang. 'We're going to have to leave this motel soon. Then what?'

'You'll think of something,' Max said. 'You always do. Am I right?'

'Your confidence in Frannie and me is flattering. But it's not enough. I need to know what's really going on. Max? Who's after you? Why are they after you? Tell me what's going on, Maxie. I need your help.'

Max shook her head in the universal sign for *no way, absolutely no way.*

'Don't do that,' Kit said with an edge in his voice. 'Don't shut me out. I'm not Superman. I can't begin to protect you guys if you don't tell me *who* is after you, and what they want. You *know*, don't you, Maxie?'

'See, this's why Frannie hates it when you "go FBI" on her,' Max said, and shook her head from side to side again. Her ears and cheeks were hot from a rush of blood.

Then, before she could say anything worse, Max pushed off the branch, and with a loud rustle of wings she flew away from Kit and his probing questions.

She kept going up, up, up, until she was at least a half-mile high. Talk about the great escape! God, it was totally gorgeous up here!

Except for one terrible thing – flying away didn't change what was going on down below.

She knew things, horrible secrets, and they could all die because of that. It sounded crazy, but it was true. All eight of them could be murdered because of what she knew about the Hospital.

*You know, don't you, Maxie?*

*Oh yeah, she sure did. She knew a lot more than she wanted to.*

God, she felt so alone.

*That* was what she truly hated about Pine Bush – the loneliness.

She thought about the Lake House again – the one place where she hadn't been lonely, not for a single minute. The best place on earth. God, she'd loved it there. They all had. *Stop it, Max. Just let it go. The Lake House was too good to last. It's gone now.*

Then Max heard someone whistle and call her name. Was it possible? Yeah, it was.

'Hey, Max. *Ollie-ollie-oxen-freeeee.*'

It was Ozymandias.

# CHAPTER FIFTY-SEVEN

It was Oz, and she was unbelievably happy to see him. He was flying, hovering actually, in the clouds above her – and then he dived right past her.

Max followed close behind.'Watch your butt, bub,' she hollered.'I'm on it!'

She spotted Oz bouncing on a tree limb down below, and since she could see every particle of movement, it seemed as if he were bouncing in slow motion.

She landed on the same slow-moving branch.'Hey,' she said.'I was just thinking about you.'

'Likewise, I'm sure.'

Ozymandias reached out his arm to steady Max, touching her at the sensitive place between her wings and shoulder blades.

A kind of electrical jolt went through her, an amazing shock of pleasure that made her a little dizzy. *Hey! What was that all about?*

She uttered an entirely involuntary whistle:'Whooooooh.'

'You're flushed,' Oz said, concerned.'You okay? Max?'

Max felt her face and her cheeks. They were warm.'I had a fight with Kit,' she said.'It's nothing. No biggie.'

'I heard.'

'We'll get over it,' she said. 'I can't stay mad at Kit for very long. Nobody can.'

'Come on, Max. Why are you keeping big bad secrets? From *everybody*.'

'Can we forget it right now?' Max said, and turned away from Oz. 'Just forget it.'

'Okay, okay.'

He plucked a spruce branchlet and stripped away the needles. He looked contemplative. Also, he looked incredibly beautiful, handsome, whatever. 'I'm glad to be away from home. I hated it there. My mother was always selling interviews and appearances. She played the saint, the martyr, but she wasn't.' He looked Max full in the eyes. 'I've been thinking about you a lot. Just about every day. Every minute.'

Max caught her breath. *So it wasn't just her thinking about Oz. Picturing him in her mind. Hearing his voice all the time.*

As they looked at each other, she felt the same dizzying feeling she'd had when she'd been with him at the raptor center. Oz's pupils dilated and contracted rapidly. His stare was superintense.

Max furtively grabbed the trunk of the tree and held on tight. *Oh boy. What now?*

'I'm feeling kind of crazy,' Oz told her. 'But I think I like it.'

'You *think* you do?'

'I *know* I like it. And I know I like you an awful lot, Max. I always have. Almost since we were babies.'

Max could barely contain the wild emotions she was feeling. She wanted to laugh out loud only she didn't think that would be the right thing to do.

But what was the right thing? What was she expected to do now? She was supposed to be so damn smart. Well, how did this work?

She wanted to touch Oz, to kiss him on his sweet mouth. And just about everywhere else.

She wanted to hold him so bad, and to be held.

*If he felt it too, he would reach out for me.* Max concentrated on that simple thought.

*Do it, Ozymandias. Reach out and touch me. Do it now. Plee-ease.*

*Please kiss me, Oz. Then I'll know I'm not crazy. Or at least that we both are.*

'I want to show you something,' Oz whispered. 'My secret.' He unzipped the hood he was wearing and lifted up his T-shirt.

'The eagle, I know. You showed me last time.'

'No, there's more to it than that. Look closely,' said Oz. 'Come closer, Max. Please. Don't be afraid to get close to me.'

Max did. She cozied up next to Ozymandias, feeling his warmth, smelling him, loving it. And there on the tattooed eagle's breast was a small red heart.

Inside it there were three inked letters in curling script: *MAX*.

Max gasped. 'Is that a tattoo? Like, it's permanent?'

'It's a little rough,' Oz said. 'But I did it myself. And you know, I was writing upside down.'

'Thank you. I love that you did that,' Max said softly. 'I mean – I *love* it.'

Max lifted her eyes to look at Oz. She searched the strong lines and planes of his face, the gentle slope of his nose, the curves of his mouth, the thin white scar across his right eyebrow, the curling lashes around his deep brown eyes. Frannie said that he looked eighteen. In bird-human years he might even be older than that.

She leaned over and kissed Oz on the cheek. Her lips lingered. The smell of his skin went straight to her brain and she was instantly overcome by feelings she couldn't begin to name.

*Kiss me back, Oz. God, he is so handsome; he is gorgeous. A real-life prince.*

Oz's face flushed with pleasure.

'Hey,' Max said then. 'Let's go for a fly, you and me. Let's go where no one's ever gone before.'

# CHAPTER FIFTY-EIGHT

Without waiting for Oz's answer, Max assumed an athletic crouch and shoved off the branch, into the air.

'Whoo-eeee!' she yelled at the top of her voice. 'I say – whoo-eeee!'

She beat her wings rapidly, climbing fast and high, pointing her hands straight up, aiming for the moon. She was still feeling a little dizzy on account of Ozymandias being there with her.

*Shake it off, girl, shake it off.*

She turned her head when she heard a disturbance in the air. Then she smiled. Oz was right there again. She watched him. His flight pattern was beautiful, a work of art.

'Chee-rup-te-rup-te-rup,' she messaged, as she flew in a long, undulating upward flight path.

Oz followed, duplicating her movements exactly. She figured it had to be just about the most mindblowing game of follow-the-leader anyone had ever played. A couple of Air Force jets couldn't do it any better.

She peeled off, rolling to the left, again with Oz tailing only a few feet behind.

She couldn't lose him. *Kind of, well, sexy,* she thought. Whatever was going on, she liked it a lot.

Who wouldn't?

Then she dived straight toward the ground, pulling out of the dive just a hundred feet above the forest floor.

*You still with me, Oz?*

*You keeping up? You on my tail?*

When she saw that Oz, too, had pulled up right beside her, she shot him a smile, and winked outrageously; and did a 'talon drop' until they were a dozen feet above the treetops.

They were facing each other as they dropped. Max reached out for Oz and he did the same. Their hands touched briefly – *electrifying.*

They were doing an intricate dance and somehow both Max and Ozymandias seemed to know all the steps.

*God, what does it mean? What is happening to us? Does Oz feel it, too? He must!*

The moon was at its zenith, the light soft on his feathers, turning them platinum white. She had never seen anything more beautiful in her life. Nothing even came close.

'Chee,' Max said softly, tenderly, a sound just for Oz. The two of them beat their wings in unison, flying above the woodlands again.

This time, Oz fluttered just above her. Maybe a foot and a half. No more than that. This was so great, so cool. Their movements were synchronized. Oz was so close that the air warmed her back. It was as if he had covered her with a cashmere blanket.

He called her name softly. 'Max, Max, sweet Max.'

Max called out his, the sound magical to her ears. 'Ozymandias.'

*What is happening to us?*

*Why do I love it so much?*

# CHAPTER FIFTY-NINE

There was a picturesque clearing below them, like a deep bowl filled with moonlight. Max and Oz dropped toward the spot as if it had been placed there just for them.

*Maybe it has been*, Max thought. *Maybe God is watching out for us after all.*

Their feet touched down on thick layers of pine needles. Suddenly, their arms encircled each other. They were face to face. So close. Ozymandias kissed Max for the very first time. A *real* kiss. She had the notion that she had been dreaming about this kiss for a long while. Only it was even better, so much better and sweeter and sexier than she'd imagined it could ever be.

She felt a rush of heat flow through her body. As soon as the magical kiss had ended, she wanted to do it again. She couldn't stop kissing Ozymandias, couldn't get enough of his mouth. She'd never felt anything like it before, couldn't have imagined that it existed, whatever *it* was.

They clung fiercely together. Both of them were on fire; *their hearts and minds and bodies.* Then they lost their balance, fell head over wings over heels.

'Timber!' Oz called.

Laughing, they fell to the ground, which felt like a soft bed made with pine needles. *God must have taken care of this, too.*

The laughter stopped as suddenly as it had begun. Oz gently folded

Max into his arms. She couldn't resist him. She didn't want to.

She blocked out the surrounding *buzz* and *whistle* and *whirr* of the forest. She was aware of their ragged breathing as they kissed again. A little voice in her head was saying, *This is so good. My God, I love this. It has to be right. I am so happy right now. I was never happy before. I didn't understand happiness.*

Oz touched her cheek, her lips, her neck, her shoulders, the small of her back. Everywhere he placed his hands was warmed under his touch.

*Rapture*, Max thought.

That is the right word. *This* is what it means.

Max began to unfasten her jeans with badly trembling fingers. God, she was shaking all over. Ozymandias pulled at his pants, his shoes, his shirt. Soon their clothes were in loose piles on the forest floor.

Max whispered, 'My prince. Oh my sweet prince. Ozymandias.'

He said, 'Princess.'

She smiled. 'No, just Mad Max.'

The feeling of their naked skin rubbing together was delicious, and Max's fear of the unknown spun out of her mind. It was replaced by incredible longing, need, love for someone other than herself. There was a brief moment when maybe she could have said no. But as she gazed into Oz's eyes and felt the intensity and honesty of his love for her, she returned the feelings. Then there was no turning back.

*Rapture.*

Max opened herself to Ozymandias. She trusted him completely. He fitted himself perfectly to her body. They rocked and they rolled and they waltzed. For a brief moment they fluttered their wings and rose a few feet above the forest floor. Oz sighed deeply and Max held him with her arms and legs, and, most important, her whole heart.

A warm feeling rippled through Max and left her tingling in its wake. She knew a truth had emerged from this, their first time. She thought, *We were meant to do this, Oz and I.*

*We were made for this.*

# CHAPTER SIXTY

$M$ ax clung to Oz, and as their breathing slowed, she knew that her whole world had suddenly changed.

She'd been shy with Oz before, but that feeling was completely gone. It just was. Gone. She knew him now; she knew Oz as a natural being in the universe; she was one with him. And he knew her in a way that no one else had ever known her, and in a way that no one else ever would. She silently promised that to herself. Max felt a deep bonding with Oz. She was sure that Oz, her dearest friend, her lover, felt it too.

*They were mated for life.*

*That was what birds did.*

They lay together on the pine needles, shivering slightly as their skin began to cool.

Innocent.

Pure.

Yet more experienced.

And wiser.

They used their wings to cover each other, keeping their damp chests pressed tightly together, their arms and legs and hips still entwined.

Max loved just lying there with him, listening to the subtle, very slow quieting of their heartbeats. She cooed in his ear, and blew softly on his pin feathers.

Then Oz spoke.

'Max?'

She lifted her eyes lovingly to his face.

'Hmmm? What is it, Ozymandias?'

'Did you hear that? A car stopped by the highway. Listen. I hear footsteps. Someone's coming fast. Someone's coming this way!'

# CHAPTER SIXTY-ONE

'Just a SEC-ond,' I yelled to whoever was knocking like a crazy person on the bungalow door. I had a skimpy towel wrapped around my hair and another around my bod, so it took me a minute to dress before I could open up and stop the blasted racket.

It was Kit, and he had a disappointed look on his face.

'What happened with you and Max?' I asked. 'Are you all right? Is Max okay?'

'Sure,' he answered brusquely as he pushed past me and into the room. 'She's just fine. She's Max.'

'How'd it go? Really? The third degree.'

Kit pulled a face. 'Not well.'

'She stonewalled you, didn't she?'

'Yeah, well, she's awfully good at it,' Kit said. 'She's hiding something, Frannie. I'm sure of it. Something scares her, and that scares me.'

'Any ideas at all?'

Kit shook his head. 'Not a one. It's driving me crazy. What could she be hiding? Why hide it from us?'

I felt him watching me towel-dry my hair as I walked back and forth between the bathroom and the bedroom. I switched on the TV, got a fuzzy version of Oprah and Brad Pitt on her talk show. I stood in front of the set for a few seconds. Then I started stuffing empty pizza boxes into a tiny trash can.

'Why don't you sit, Frannie? You're twitching like a cat in a box,' Kit said finally.

'Yeah? I'm worried about the kids. I'm worried about you, me, everything. I'm worried about what Max won't tell us. She's hiding her secret because she thinks the information could hurt us. Has to be that.'

'Come sit over here. Please. I'll rub your back some. You look like you need it. Just a back rub.'

I looked into his big blues for one electrifying second and felt his gaze grabbing on to me like that tractor beam in *Star Trek*.

'Thanks, no,' I said. 'Thanks anyway. Really.'

Kit breathed an exaggerated and comical sigh. 'The two of you,' he said. 'You and Max are the most stubborn women I've ever known.'

I laughed because I didn't know how else to react. Well, actually I did. I wanted to go over to the bed. I wanted to lock the door, close the curtains, peel off every stitch I was wearing, and make love to Kit for the first time in months.

Okay, let me be honest here.

I was still very much in love with Kit, but what if he didn't feel that way? What if he just had, you know, an itch? Whoever said ''Tis better to have loved and lost than never to have loved at all' must've never loved and lost as hard as I'd done, because I didn't think I had the flexibility to withstand emotional whiplash again.

So back rubs were out until I got a better sense of Kit's true feelings. And yeah, I probably needed to hear those three little words.

Kit must have been reading my mind. He can do that sometimes. 'I know we've been apart,' he started to say. 'I got spooked. First I lost my family. Then the kids. Frannie, I still—'

*Still? Still what? Say it!*

But Kit was staring at something *behind* me. What? I slowly turned and saw that the front door had blown open. Max and Oz were peering at us, stricken and ashen-faced, looking as if they'd just survived a tornado.

'The woods are crawling with hunters,' Oz said.

# CHAPTER SIXTY-TWO

*This couldn't be happening again – but damn it, it was!*

Kit didn't hesitate for more than a couple of seconds. He drew his scary automatic weapon, or semi-automatic, or whatever in hell it was, and bolted out of the bungalow at a gallop, moving on the ground as Oz and Max took to the air.

Kit didn't have their raw speed, but he was quick and agile on his feet. Pip and I were running behind him, trying to keep up, not doing such a great job of it to tell the truth.

There was a rough trail running through the woods and Kit stayed on it. Suddenly, he looked back and saw us coming.

'Goddamn it, Frannie,' he whispered loudly as he ducked behind a tree. 'Get down,' he hissed. 'Please get down. Now! I *mean* it, Frannie!'

I did as told. There was a lot of movement in the dark and overgrown woodland, so it took me a few seconds to understand that the rapid mothlike flapping at the bend in the trail was Matthew.

Jesus God! He was flying swooping circles over the four or five men dressed in black. He was swinging and kicking at their guns and their faces.

*Matthew was attacking the gunmen! Dear God in heaven, he was nine years old! But he was so fast. And furious. And fearless, even if he had no right to be.*

Then I noticed another small figure doing the same thing.

'Kit, look! Oh my God! Stop him!'

It was Peter! Four-year-old little Peter was imitating Matthew, fearlessly dive-bombing and attempting to create confusion with his hooting and hollering and kick-boxing.

The only problem was, Kit couldn't fire safely at the men in black. Peter was in the way.

There was no way to get off a clear shot.

It was frustrating, maddening, crazy. And I wasn't the one with the gun.

Just when I didn't think I could feel more helpless, Oz came out of nowhere and furiously threw himself into the action. He was like a missile, targeting one of the gunmen, who fired off a series of *rat-a-tats*, each deadly sound illustrated by an orange flameburst.

But the shooter *missed*. It almost seemed that he'd missed *on purpose*. What was going on here? Who were the hunters? What were their orders? Who was in control of them?

Oz knocked the gunman out cold with one swipe of his powerful wings. Talk about your winged avengers. I almost couldn't believe my eyes.

I was screaming at the kids to get away. So was Kit. Even Max was yelling. They might be super, but they weren't bulletproof.

Oz kick-boxed one of the shooters from behind. The bastard went down hard, and Oz gave him a good stomp to the head. I saw another gunman making a grab for a small dark shape as it fluttered past him.

*Wendy! He had Wendy!*

'Okay,' the gunman yelled out, and seemed really angry. 'Everyone back off. Drop the gun. Kick it toward me.'

The entire forest seemed frozen in time and space. I saw Kit's face as he weighed his limited options – drop the gun or shoot – when the silence was broken.

A shrill caw! Oz rose from the ground and slapped aside the shooter's gun. It was only a glancing blow, and the gunman turned fiercely against Oz. He backhanded him with his pistol.

The crack to Oz's head made a horrifying sound.

But Kit finally had a clear shot. He fired! The man was hit

somewhere high in his chest. He staggered and fell down hard, holding his ribcage tightly with both arms, bleeding all over himself, probably dying before our eyes.

The other men were either down or in retreat. Wendy had managed to get away. She shouted in triumph. Then she darted into my arms, screeching, 'Mama, Mama! We won the war!'

# CHAPTER SIXTY-THREE

I doubted it! I sincerely doubted it!

I was panting hard, nearly in shock, as I watched Kit holster his gun. Even though it had saved us, I still hated the weapon, despised what it could do, aware of its awful potential for deadly violence. And one other thing bothered me a lot. Why hadn't the gunmen fired right away? What had stopped them from shooting all of us? They certainly could have. *What was going on? Why weren't we all dead?*

'Okay, everyone,' Kit called out, still trying to catch his breath. 'Gather around so I can see you. Is anybody hurt?'

One by one, the children enveloped us. Oz got up from the ground and wiggled into the embrace. Kit kept talking them in. 'It's okay, everyone. It's okay for now.'

'Is anybody hurt? Yeah, *they* sure are,' Matthew finally piped up. 'We kicked some proper ass.'

'We were lucky,' Kit said.

'And we were good,' retorted Oz, and shook a fist over his head. 'I'm proud to go to war with you guys!'

'Yeah, right,' little Peter piped up. 'Bet your butt.'

I checked each of the kids for injuries. Oz had taken the worst of it. There was a darkening bruise on one side of his face.

Miraculously, bruises and scrapes were the only damage we'd sustained.

But Kit was right – we were lucky. Damned lucky! Or maybe it was more than just luck. *Of course it was more than luck.*

The battle we'd just been through had happened and ended quickly. It left me breathless. A five-minute assault, during which any one of us could have been killed! We hugged in pairs and then we hugged in a big pile. I was still breathless from all the excitement. Some of the kids started to whimper and shiver. Finally, reality was setting in.

I saw Kit walk Max away from the group and I followed them. Kit stooped down and took Max by the shoulders.

'This was too close, Maxie. I take responsibility. I should have kept everyone under lock and key until I could get us to safety. We have to get out of here. Now. But we have a problem, don't we? We still don't know what's going on.'

'They don't want us hurt. Not yet. They prefer capturing us,' she said. 'That's *obvious*, isn't it? What do they want? *What?*'

Max had scratches on her face and her eyes were as huge as saucers. I saw her shudder, and then make her decision.

She spoke softly, so faintly that Kit and I had to strain to hear.

'It's in Maryland,' she whispered. 'It's like another School, like the shit-awful place we were kept. Only I think it's even worse. They've taken this biotech madness even farther. They've gone to the limit this time. Maybe past the limit. Yeah, *way* past.'

'How do you know this, Max?' I asked. 'What is the limit?'

She shook her head, then stared at the ground. 'At the School they made me file and do other scut work on the computer. At first it was just to keep me out of their hair. But then they realized I did the job of three of their drones in less than half the time.

'So I filed their records and important communications. But I also *read*, and I remember it all. There's another experimental lab. In Maryland. Not too far from Washington, DC, where Kit lives. The doctor who runs it is supposed to be a genius, but personally, I think he's totally whacked. I know he is. He visited the School once, but I didn't get to see him. Not a good look anyway. They locked us away in our cages. I know that the doctors there were in awe of this guy, and whatever he was working on. They were also scared shitless of him. And *yes*, there are people in the government who *know* about the outlaw lab.'

Max looked into Kit's eyes, then into mine. She shook her head. 'You talk,' she said, 'you die. Looks like I die.'

# CHAPTER SIXTY-FOUR

M ax's confession changed everything.

That evening, around the golden hour, she and Ozymandias took the kids for a short flight with Frannie's permission. They were in tight formation, gorgeous to watch as they sailed toward the setting sun. She was thinking they were more like a squadron of jet fighters than a flock that night.

Icarus called out and Max turned to him. His sightless eyes were closed against the wind. 'Where are we going, guys? Tell all! What am I missing on the way?'

'Great sunset, Ic. Burnt orange against powder blue. Beautiful pine forests and mountains that seem to go on for ever,' Max called back. 'We're going up into the woods. Primeval forests. We're not coming back, little buddy. It's too dangerous for Frannie and Kit.'

'Oh, so we're the only ones who die?' Ic asked, his little voice thick with irony.

'Yeah. I'm afraid so, Icarus. This is our fight.'

He shrugged his small shoulders. 'I can live with that.'

It was Oz's plan, actually, and the first part was that the flock would have enough time to find safe shelter before darkness fell in the mountains. Oz had thought everything through. He was sure of it, and of himself. They would build temporary shelters high in trees, using branches and wild vines to weave sleeping baskets. The baskets could be lined with ferns and loose leaves.

Max approved. Basically. Actually, it sounded kind of comfy the way Oz described it, and everybody had confidence in him, especially since she did.

If they didn't want to be too ambitious at first, they could raid a nearby farm for food. Root vegetables and gourds, such as pumpkins and squash, were in season. Carrots, maybe peas, tomatoes, melons might also be available.

Plus, there would be sunflower seeds, which they all loved anyway. Oz explained that the delicious seeds were packed in flat discs at the center of every flower head.

'What if there are no farms?' Wendy asked. 'You ever think about that, guys?'

'No problem,' said Oz. 'There'll be plenty of nuts and seeds and roots. Pig nuts are pretty good. Burdock roots are sensational. And . . . turn over any log and you'll find fat white grubs. A great source of protein!'

Max looked around again. The kids made faces at the grub mention, but they seemed to be keeping their sense of adventure, and humor, as they flew into the mountains.

'Burdock roots and white grubs! Burdock roots and white grubs!' they chanted.

They were on their own.

Maybe back where they belonged.

It will be like the Lake House.

Well, almost, but never as good.

# CHAPTER SIXTY-FIVE

Oz and Max had decided they would share the watch. For the first night anyway.

They sat huddled together on a rocky ledge that was maybe fifty feet above the trees where the children slept. There was no way human hunters could sneak up on them, but Oz was especially nervous about mountain cats, which could be incredibly fast and vicious, tear you apart in about thirty seconds.

'Was this part of your studies in ornithology?' Max asked. 'How to survive in the wilderness? How to fight mountain lions?'

Oz smiled. 'Our instincts will kick in and keep us safe – the way it was for a while at the lake. It's the truth. Don't forget – burdock roots and white grubs.'

'You're so *sure* about things, Ozymandias. Be careful of too much pride. You could eat grubs?'

'I'm sure about some things. Grubs, *maybe*. I'm sure I want to be with you, y'know, even though you're a girl.'

'It's not just some kind of dumb infatuation? Are you sure about that?'

Oz laughed. 'I went through being infatuated with you when I was much younger, when we were both at the School. I used to go to sleep every night thinking about you. True tale. Every night.'

Max laughed. 'I had no idea.'

'Of course you didn't. You were too hung up on yourself. I was petrified around you. Whenever I had to talk to you I got the shimmy-shimmy-shakes.'

'Hold my hand,' Max said in a softer voice. 'Hug me for a little while, then I'll take first watch.'

Oz cuddled Max gently. 'Whenever I hold you, I never want to let go,' he said. 'I guess that could be dangerous tonight.'

'Oh, Oz, Oz, Oz,' Max sighed, then whispered against his cheek. She was starting to cry, and she almost never cried.

He felt her warm tears and pulled away sharply. 'What's the matter? Please don't cry. It's the one thing that could make me lose my nerve.'

She looked deeply into his beautiful, magnificent eyes. 'Oh, Oz, everything that could go wrong is going that way in a hurry. We're on our own with a little blind boy, two darling babies, and my kid brother, who's still pissed because of you and me. We had pine and pig nuts for supper. Humans are trying to capture or kill us and probably will. And you know what?'

Oz hugged her even harder. 'What, Max? Tell me what?'

'I have never been happier in my entire life. It's all because of you, tattoo-boy. I love you, Oz.'

'I love you, Max. Always have, always will. Now I'll take the first watch.'

Max grinned. 'I already knew that, sweet patooie. You're such a *guy*.'

# CHAPTER SIXTY-SIX

This was not good!

Kit and I rode in the Suburban on a dirt road as far as it would take us, and fast. The damn trail just dead-ended into the mountain face. We were in the middle of nowhere. Smack dab.

Staring at a cold, hard rock face.

Not good at all.

'You could say that this is the end of the road,' Kit quipped from his place behind the steering wheel. 'Damn it. Damn Max.'

I immediately started to cry a little, and Kit slid over, put his arms around me, started kissing my tears away. I still liked being held by him, no use denying or fighting it any more.

'The kids'll be all right. For now anyway,' he said. 'I'm sure they just need to hash things through. Max was seriously programmed not to talk about anything she learned back at the School. She and Oz will do the right thing. They do act like grown-ups now.'

'They're all geniuses, Kit. Off the charts, remember? They know it, too.'

'So maybe they won't come back. But they'll be all right.'

'Don't say that.'

'Let's go back to the hacienda. Maybe the kids are already there waiting for us. Besides, we don't have any other choice.'

It took us a good half-hour to get to the Pines, in Ratón, New Mexico's finest. Neither Kit nor I saw signs of trouble. Nor did we see the kids.

We waited up for them – the kids. But there was also the awful possibility that more gunmen might show up. *Hunters.*

'I felt safer when the kids were around,' I said to Kit, who was putting another log on our fire. 'They could spot an intruder coming a long way off.'

Kit spread a wool blanket not too far from the fire. He *patted* the floor by his side.

'Woof! Woof!' I barked.

'That's not how I meant it. I'm just recommending a cozy spot by the fire here. Please, Frannie, *please*. See? I'm begging.'

I brought a couple of borderline-comfy pillows from the bed.

'That's all this is?' I asked Kit. 'Sit by the fire together? Warm our toes?'

'I didn't say that either.'

I finally lay down beside Kit and he took me in his strong arms. 'I missed you every day, every hour, every minute, Frannie,' he whispered.

I rolled my eyes. 'That's a little thick.'

'You're tough,' Kit said and grinned. 'I missed you every day we were apart.'

'How about every day *and* most every hour?'

'That's about right. I did.'

'Me too. So, uhm, why did we stay apart?'

'Too much loss, too much awful pain, way too much chaos and confusion. My family dies, then we lose the kids in that courthouse fiasco in Denver. I thought you might bolt on me next, Frannie. I swear I did.'

'Kiss me,' I whispered. 'Shush up and kiss.'

He did. A whole lot of times. Tender, sweet, strong Kit kisses. Just like always. Kisses so true that I had to believe him about why he'd stayed away. Then Kit was touching me everywhere I wanted to be touched, which was everywhere. God, how I loved his touch, too.

First he thoroughly explored my face; and I explored his. Then he covered my neck and shoulders with touches and kisses. He unbuttoned my flannel shirt and I returned the favor by unbuttoning his. He did my belt, my trousers; and I did his. Only when we were finally naked did I completely understand how much I had missed Kit, and maybe how much I loved him, which was with all my heart and soul, and, obviously, my body as well.

And for once he said exactly the right thing. 'I love you, Frannie. Simple as that. I really love you, Frances Jane. In fact, I adore you.'

And I whispered back, 'I love you, Thomas.'

Eventually, after a good long while, and some rather spectacular shenanigans, which I won't go into in a story that will be heard by old and young, we fell asleep on the blankets in front of the fire.

The first time I woke in the morning I was cold, and quickly stole my share of the covers. Maybe more than my share, but isn't that what love is all about?

I fell asleep again immediately. In the cocoon of Kit's arms. Safe and sound and blissful. Swaddled in blankets. Perfectly content.

The second time I woke, buttery sunlight was streaming through all the windows.

Something else was at the windows, too.

The kids! They had come back. My God, they were gawking at Kit and me.

'Get away from those windows, you little Peeping Toms,' Kit hollered at them.

'Nothing we haven't seen before,' said Icarus, blind poet that he is. 'You guys want some burdock roots?'

# PART FIVE

# THE HOSPITAL

# CHAPTER SIXTY-SEVEN

## The Hospital

D r Ethan Kane was humming the Eagles' golden oldie 'Hotel California' and doing a lot of heavy thinking about Resurrection. It was almost here. His reverie was interrupted by an important phone call. It was long-distance from Los Angeles, and Kane had been expecting it for most of the day.

The California folk were attempting to play with his head, which was a very bad idea.

The voice on the other end was clipped and businesslike, probably a transplanted New Yorker. 'Dr Kane, this is Anthony Depino calling.'

Dr Kane's tone of voice was the opposite of Depino's. It sounded jovial and unconcerned. 'Anthony, so good to hear from you. I'm afraid you caught me working late in my office. It's after nine. How are my friends the Stevensons?'

'They're *old*,' said the lawyer, and left it at that. Depino wasn't having any of the idle chitchat. Well, fine. He was one of the most powerful attorneys in Los Angeles, and had handled the Stevensons' private affairs for the last few years. Also, he seemed to believe that his shit didn't stink.

'Well, since they're not getting any younger, let's get down to business, Anthony,' said Ethan Kane.

'Splendid, Dr Kane. I might as well start by informing you that the figure you quoted for the procedures is totally unacceptable to us,' said the lawyer. 'The price for Resurrection is just too much, even for Roger Stevenson. You'll have to do better.'

'I understand perfectly,' said Ethan Kane. Then he hung up the phone on the snot-nosed lawyer.

He grinned, then scooped out a handful of M&Ms, candy-covered peanuts, one of his few serious vices. He put three different-colored candies in his mouth, and then the phone rang again.

'Some fucking negotiator,' Kane mumbled and smiled thinly.

He let it ring a few times before he picked up, put the receiver to his mouth, and bit down into the crunchy M&Ms. *Take that, Mr Depino from the City of the Angels, that second-rate dumping ground for second-raters.*

'Let me ask you a simple, but somewhat profound question.' Dr Kane spoke before being spoken to. 'What is one more day on Earth worth to Roger Stevenson? Do you have a *final* number in mind? Does he? Have you actually consulted him on a number?'

'It's certainly not a hundred million dollars,' said Depino.

'Goodbye, sir. I have many others in line for the final spot in Resurrection.'

'Wait! Roger is just being cautious,' said the lawyer. 'So am I, on his behalf.'

'Mr Depino, I have other worthy candidates, but I happen to like Roger a great deal. And Roger was a great leader once, after all. The price is firm at one hundred million. To be perfectly honest, I could get *double* or *triple* that for the final spot in Resurrection. Now give me an answer. No more dilly-dallying. Is Roger Stevenson in or out?'

'We will pay your price,' said the lawyer.

'You won't regret it. Roger Stevenson will outlive you, Anthony. A hundred million is a pittance for this scientific miracle. We're going to make history. We're going to make the world a better place, and maybe even save it.'

# CHAPTER SIXTY-EIGHT

The kids had decided, voted actually, to entrust their fates to us. I just hoped we were worthy of the task, and of their trust.

We certainly started out badly. We had made a small deal with the FBI. Kit hitched a ride for us to Washington, which just happens to be very close to Maryland. Exactly what we had to give back to the FBI wasn't clear yet. But I was sure they wanted *something*.

We all hung on to our armrests as the Beech King slammed down at Dulles International and bounced along the runway. The brakes squealed, the plane slewed to the left and then stopped a little hard, jerking us in our seatbelts.

We discovered that the wind was blowing fiercely as we disembarked and clung to the railing of the metal staircase that had been rolled up to the side of the plane.

Feathers ruffled, hair whipped across our faces, and dust scurried across the moonlit airfield.

*First stop, Washington, DC.*

*Second stop, hell.*

My arms prickled with goose bumps, and not just because of the chill wind. Three men in dark suits waited for us as Peter proceeded to get sick on the tarmac. Then they escorted us toward a freestanding aluminum utility shed that stood alongside the terminal building. I didn't like this. They had no right. But we'd made a deal.

The oldest of the three men, a lanky guy with a beakish nose, small dark eyes, and a receding hairline, introduced himself as Senior Agent Eric Breem. He nodded at the children and me, then swept Kit aside and engaged him in an intense conversation.

Man to man, of course. Very private. I was completely excluded from all this.

They were soon arguing about something, and Kit was clearly furious with Breem. I heard him exclaim, 'In a pig's ass you will. That's not gonna happen.'

Moments later we were assembled in the shed, and the door was shut and locked with a loud metallic clang. I guessed the place was used to detain illegal aliens or inspect contraband, because the furnishings were sparse: a long table and a stack of folding chairs leaned against one wall.

Now what?

A dark-haired, broad-shouldered agent with huge hands opened the metal chairs and the wary children sat down in a fidgety row – except for Max, who stood. 'Just a formality,' he said.

'Me no likee,' commented Peter, and his little joke seemed dead-on. None of us was very comfortable with this. The FBI can be really weird. They need a make-over. Trust me on this.

Another agent, blond and slight, wearing a bright yellow tie to enliven his charcoal-gray suit, addressed Kit. He introduced himself as Adam Warshaw. 'We'd like to question the children one at a time. It won't take very long. It's important. *Essential.*'

Kit shook his head. 'Sorry, that's not happening. It's past midnight and they've had a long day.'

'Okay, Brennan, it *is* going to happen. But we'll make it brief,' said Agent Warshaw. He turned his gaze toward Max, who was standing watchfully on the sidelines, as she tended to do.

'Max? You *are* Max?' Warshaw said. He had a pen and notepad in his hand.

Max stared at him, but didn't answer. She looked a little pale and shaky, but she stuck out her chin in a defiant gesture I thought of as 'Max's brave front'.

'Of course I'm Max,' she finally said. 'What of it?'

'Well, the way I understand it, some men broke into your parents' house with guns. Is that right?'

'Yes. Except for the parents' part. Frannie and Kit are our parents. We chose them as our parents. Write that down in your little notepad.'

'Max, do you have any idea why these men were trying to harm you and your brother? What did they want? What *do* they want?'

I read the distress on Max's face. 'No idea at all.'

'I'm sorry. I'm afraid I don't believe that,' said Warshaw.

Kit spoke up. 'Breem, this has to *stop*. You have no legal right to question these kids, so don't. I'll come into the office tomorrow. I'll tell you everything I know and everything the kids know. If that's not good enough, I'm instructing them not to speak to anyone without their parents and *attorneys* present at all times. Is that clear?' Kit looked over at me. 'Was that clear, Frannie?'

'I think that was amazingly clear, and also concise. Only a complete moron couldn't follow it. Right, Agents Breem and Warshaw?'

There was a tense silence as Kit faced off with Breem and Warshaw. Meanwhile, the wind rattled the aluminum walls, making a drumming sound like spoons beating on tin pie pans.

At last, Breem nodded. What else could he do? Then he showed some teeth. His idea of a smile, I guess. 'It has been a long day. Tomorrow morning, then, Brennan. Let's get you all someplace comfortable. We've made temporary arrangements in—'

'They're staying with me,' Kit said. 'We've taken good care of them before. We'll do it tonight. Let's go, kids, Frannie.'

Little Peter stood up tall and straight. 'Me likee,' he said. 'Let's get out of here.'

I grabbed on to Kit's arm and whispered, 'Your place?'

Kit's answer was chilling. 'If they wanted to kill us, we'd already be dead. Let's go, Frances Jane. Let's vamanos, kids.'

'Vamanos!' they chorused.

# CHAPTER SIXTY-NINE

Two anonymous-looking black town cars sped down a wide-open avenue in our nation's capital late at night. I was so overtired that I distrusted everything, even my own feelings about staying in Kit's apartment. I wasn't so sure it was such a good place for us to go right now. On the other hand, I didn't have any better ideas, and I definitely distrusted the Federal Bureau of Investigation so far, especially Agents Breem and Warshaw.

There was a sudden, infectious burst of giggling in the back seat of the car I was riding in. I craned my head to see what had so amused the twins. *Oz had put his arm around Max!* What was this? Oz and Max?

I was still pondering the shiny new paradigm shift when the sedan pulled to a stop in front of Kit's apartment.

The apartment was in a residential neighborhood near Dupont Circle, a relatively short distance from the White House and also from several important monuments and federal buildings. Kit told us that the small apartment building had once been a single-family Victorian house.

When he opened the heavy old front door we thundered up four flights of stairs to the top floor. Kit's. A few of us *flew*.

'It's not much, but it's home,' Kit said as we stepped inside. His apartment was decorated with country furniture, Persian rugs, a piano, and crammed bookshelves. Very, very nice, actually. Homey. Kit-like.

'Watch your wings,' I hollered to the kids who were zooming

around in a potentially destructive manner.

'Watch my *stuff*,' bellowed Kit. 'Have mercy. There are a lot of memories in here.'

Icarus found the piano and sat right down. He immediately launched into a spirited rendition of 'Fly Me to the Moon', both singing and playing. The kid was a born mimic and his linguistic skills were amazing. He sounded exactly like Frank Sinatra, down to the minutest detail of the song's phrasing.

My gaze snagged on some simple silver frames sitting on the piano top.

In one was a snapshot of a slender, pretty blonde woman with two handsome young boys who were spitting images of Kit.

I flashed on some others: Kit hugging his sons, teaching them to ride bikes, and playing ball. They told me how Kit had watched them as they grew. A wave of sadness washed over me and I felt a chill. Kit caught me looking at the grouping of photos.

'Beautiful,' I said. 'Your place is.'

'Thanks,' he murmured. 'It was a great time, Frannie, great time. But so is this.'

Then he walked me away from the piano, and toward the kitchen. I could tell he didn't want to talk about his family right now. I couldn't blame him.

The fridge was nearly full, and we were starving. Kit pulled bread and crackers out of a cabinet. Cheese and raw vegetables and cold cuts soon appeared on the oak dining table along with the remains of a roasted chicken. Pip was awarded the poultry, and the kids made short work of the rest. Kit poured me a glass of pinot grigio and I needed it. But after a few swallows, I found that I still couldn't relax. Reality was setting in:

I was homeless.

I'd seen a man in death throes a short while before. I'd narrowly missed getting shot at the same time.

I felt responsible for keeping six kids safe and sound, but I had no real idea how to do it.

Something truly horrifying might be taking place nearby in Maryland.

Nothing, and I mean *nothing,* was under my control at the moment. Other than that, no problems.

I was so exhausted I think I could have slept standing up. So my jaw dropped when Ic announced, 'I've got energy to burn.'

'Me three,' shouted the twins.

'No, don't!' I shouted, too late. Oz had already opened a window and Ic had climbed out on to the ledge.

There was no stopping them now. With a few 'byes' and 'be back soons', the kids shot out of the windows. I managed to snag Wendy by the waistband of her jeans. She turned to me with a hurt look and a pitiful cry.

'Frannie, please. Everybody's going. It's a night flight! Pleeeeeeease? I have to. Like we used to at the lake! Pleeeeeeease?'

I cast a questioning look at Kit and he shrugged, so I turned the little girl loose. She spread her wings and darted up to join the others. She was so cute I couldn't stand it.

Kit came over and put his arm around me and we watched the children fly across the broad, beaming face of the moon. This was a sight that never failed to fill me with awe – until now.

'I feel the earth shifting under my feet,' I said. 'I don't feel safe anywhere. Not even here.'

'I was having the same thought,' he said. 'Unfortunately.'

'We're just paranoid, aren't we? We're paranoid, right?'

Kit sighed.

'That was the wrong answer,' I said.

# CHAPTER SEVENTY

The children were taking a night flight above Washington, DC. Icarus was singing 'Fly Me to the Moon' again. It was kind of close to perfect, actually. The kid could *croon.* 'Just don't call me Ole Blue Eyes!' he warned.

As always, Max thrilled to the powerful upward pull of the air on her wings as the winds gusted forcefully around her. It was like being on an amusement-park ride, and it was about a hundred times better. The other kids whooped with joy as the air lifted and dropped them. And lifted them yet again.

Max still had the best aerial dexterity, though Oz was faster and a bit stronger. She closed her wings a few degrees and used the wind as a chute or air flume to carry her in a long, breathtaking swoop.

But just when she was beginning to fully enjoy herself, she remembered.

*People might be dying nearby in Maryland. No, people were definitely dying! In her opinion, modern science was spiraling out of control.*

*Everyone she cared about was in terrible danger.*

'Mind a little company?' Oz asked. He glided to Max's right side. 'Or do you want to be alone?'

'I'd like some company.'

Max turned her face and smiled at the sight of him. She flew closer and touched his hurt cheek with her fingers. 'That's a very impressive bruise.'

'It's a war wound,' Oz said proudly. 'From the Battle of the Pines.'

'Sure is,' Max agreed. *And I'm afraid the war has just begun, Ozymandias. Only just begun.*

Oz did a somersault in the air, then looped back. He guided blind Icarus to Max's side as they crossed the moon-silvered Potomac River.

'Max, are you wearing *perfume*?' Ic asked. 'You are, aren't you? *Interesting*.'

'So you can follow me easier,' Max said, and laughed.

'What a city! Okay, listen up, everyone,' Oz called out so all could hear. 'Welcome to the nation's capital. I'm Ozymandias, and I'll be your tour guide tonight. On your right is the John F. Kennedy Center, and there, just below us, is the famous Iwo Jima statue. And that,' Oz said dramatically, 'is an American Airlines 747 coming straight at us. Let's get outta here before somebody calls in jet fighters to shoot us down!'

The kids screamed loudly with pleasure. Then their yells were drowned out by the incredible roar of the American jet passing overhead.

The flock, now in formation, flew almost directly over the Lincoln Memorial.

Oz continued his guided tour, pointing out the Vietnam Veterans Memorial and numerous traffic circles with avenues radiating out from them like spokes on a wheel. 'Isn't that the most amazing building?' Oz shouted as they flew over the Capitol.

'The dome-capped rotunda on the Capitol building is the biggest of its kind in America. *That's* Pennsylvania Avenue,' he said. 'Look straight down and you can see the White House where the President and his family live. And the Hoover building's down there somewhere close. The Federal Bureau of Investigation.

'C'mon, Ic. *Cawwww-roll!*' Oz shouted. He and Ic then barrel-rolled to the left, and the whole flock followed.

They flew very close to the ground, finally dipping their feathers in the reflecting pool, then, with a *chee-rupppp*, they rose and circled the amazing Capitol dome.

'Do you think the President knows what's happening out in the real world?' Oz asked as he came close to Max again. 'Like in Maryland? Like among us common folk? Like that people are trying to kill us?'

Her eyes shut, then opened slowly. 'I sincerely doubt it. Maybe we can tell him some time. Or *show* him. Now hold my hand, please. I need my hand held.'

Ozymandias did even better. He glided over Max, and then let her snuggle underneath. Magical! They flew like that all the way home to Kit's apartment.

# CHAPTER SEVENTY-ONE

I t was the crack of dawn, although in my current mood I preferred to think of it as the crack of doom. Kit and I had already started driving south on Route 1 toward the FBI's Critical Incident Response Group in Stafford, Virginia. It was something we had to do. Lives could be at stake, including ours and the kids.

We'd left the kids in Kit's apartment with a video game that had a play time of *700 hours*, I swear to God; a freezer full of frozen pizza; and strict orders not to fly under any circumstances.

We were headed straight for the nightmare that had haunted Max for so long, all of her life, actually. *You talk, you die.* Kit's apartment seemed to be the safest place for the kids. For the time being anyway.

I sucked on the sippin' lid of my coffee container, hopelessly trying to calm my nerves. Less than an hour after leaving DC, I caught sight of our destination.

There was no sign out front, no discernible address. Just two plain two-story red-brick office buildings connected by a concrete walkway.

'Looks innocent enough,' Kit said, 'but don't be fooled, Frances Jane. Not for a minute.'

'Don't worry, I'm not going to be taken in by any fast-talking FBI dudes,' I said, and winked at him. 'Been there, done that.'

The Critical Incident Response Group had been formed in 1994, post-Waco and Ruby Ridge. It had been housed at the FBI Academy at Quantico for five years, but it had recently been moved to a location about eight miles away. The unit's objective, Kit told me, was to 'provide emergency response to a variety of crises, including terrorist activities, hostage takings, and barricaded subject situations'.

*Okay, that should cover just about everything. But then again, maybe not.*

About three hundred people worked here, according to Kit, and the parking lot was mostly full when we pulled in. Kit parked and locked his Subaru Outback. Then we walked up a poured concrete path and through the glass doors to a vestibule that was empty except for a single elevator.

'Are they going to believe us? And are they going to help?' I finally asked Kit.

'I sincerely doubt it,' Kit said and frowned.

'I sincerely question why we're here. *Why are we here, Kit?*'

He ran his hand back over his blond hair. 'We're here because they might help us – inadvertently. They might know something important, and just not know that they know it. It happens more than you'd imagine inside the Bureau.'

'Oh. So we're here to interrogate them, not the other way around?'

Kit winked. 'That's the plan anyway. We'll soon find out. Besides, I promised I'd come.'

The door slid open and Kit and I took the elevator to the second-floor reception area. It was protected from the world by a thick pane of bulletproof glass. Kit presented his ID, and speaking into a grille in the bulletproof partition asked to see Special Agent Breem.

A female agent at the front desk smiled pleasantly and buzzed us in. 'Take a left and keep walking,' she said. 'Agent Breem is expecting you. We all are. We were hoping you'd bring the whiz-kids.'

# CHAPTER SEVENTY-TWO

We followed the agent's instructions, our footsteps echoing eerily down the linoleum-tiled corridor. My anxiety level was rising pretty fast now. Visits with the FBI can do that to you, I guess. I'd had bad experiences with them before. Ironically, so had Kit. They're good people, mostly, but something got screwed up along the way. I guess that's what happens when Herbert Hoover is your daddy. Talk about the road to perdition.

There were pods of offices alongside both sides of the hallway, most of them brimming with agents, some in suits and ties, others in jeans and T-shirts. A surprisingly motley crew. Not as uptight as I'd imagined they would be.

At the end of the hall a slender, blond man in a blue suit was waiting for us. Agent Warshaw, from last night.

*Prick. Jerk. Insensitive asshole. And yes, that was how I really felt about him.*

'Dr O'Neill, Brennan. Come in. Please.'

'How could we refuse such an offer?' I said.

'What did I do to her?' Warshaw asked Kit, who merely shrugged.

First there was the de rigueur offer of coffee, that Kit and I turned down, followed by inane commentary about our drive down, the weather, and the Washington Redskins. Just to establish that we were all on the same side.

I wasn't buying it. We weren't. An old cartoon character called Pogo had once said, 'We have met the enemy and he is us.' That pretty much matched my feelings.

'Where's Breem?' Kit asked as Warshaw unfurled a cloth wall map of Maryland.

'He said he'll join us if he can,' Warshaw said, basically dismissing Kit's question. 'Now, suppose you tell me what you're looking for.'

'You already know what we're looking for. Help. Information. Max knows something that's pretty scary. It has to do with an unlawful experimental project,' Kit said. 'Illegal experiments may be going on somewhere in Maryland. Location *fuzzy*, name *unknown*. People, *unnamed*, are possibly being killed as we get ready to stick pins or whatever in your map. It's pretty much what happened at the School in Colorado.

'You *know* all this. *It's in the report I filed*. The problem is – nobody believes Max. Or me,' Kit said, the tension rising in his voice.

'You're here, aren't you?' said Warshaw. 'We're helping you.'

'Only because I have a little juice left in Washington. Very little. Because nobody is really taking this very seriously.'

'All right, then, do I understand this much correctly?' Warshaw asked. 'Someone connected with so-called biotech experiments wants to shut Max up so bad, they're willing to kill all of the children to do it.'

'Something like that,' Kit said. 'Actually, I think they're trying to capture the kids. Murder might be a backup option. The children are valuable. I don't know why these people want them so badly. It's driving me crazy.'

'Come on,' Warshaw said derisively. '*Listen* to yourself. You have no real evidence, no documentation, nothing but the half-formed musings of a twelve-year-old who is probably under an awful lot of stress anyway.'

'I tend to agree with Warshaw,' said Agent Breem, just now entering the office. 'Why don't you tell us what you know, Agent Brennan. We need to hear it all firsthand. And Dr O'Neill, you feel free to contribute too.'

'Oh, thanks,' I said.

Kit could be as compelling as hell when he wanted to be. For the next hour, he filled Special Agent Breen in on *some* of Max's scary information. But only *some*. Seemed that Kit didn't completely trust Breem either.

Breem listened without questioning a single point. Then he tapped out several numbers on Warshaw's desk phone, relayed some information, paused, and said, 'Get back to me as soon as possible.'

No more than fifteen minutes had passed when a blonde woman appeared and handed an accordion file to Breem. He looked carefully at the contents.

I read the label upside down. *Liberty General Hospital*. What is this?

Breem said, 'You do still have a few friends in the Hoover building. They want you to have assistance from us, so assistance is what you get. Liberty would seem to be a facility around here that *could* be the site the girl is referring to.

'Having said that, you can probably rule Liberty out. It's a first-class teaching hospital. Hell, Liberty is where the President and Vice President go for their checkups these days. It's the best hospital facility anywhere near DC. Better than Walter Reed.'

Kit nodded affirmatively as he flipped through the documents inside the file.

'Unlike some children her age, Max doesn't confabulate and she doesn't lie. She says there's an outlaw lab in Maryland. Wherever it is, they're conducting experiments. On humans.'

'*Maybe* there are illegal experiments being conducted somewhere, but I doubt it would be at Liberty,' said Breem.

I saw Kit tense, and a muscle in his cheek was doing the cha-cha. 'I understand,' he said. 'Thanks for the file anyway. We'll be going now.'

'I really don't like him,' I said when Kit and I were heading back to the car. 'I hate how he talked down to you. Same for Warshaw. Do you trust them?'

Kit looked right at me. 'At this point I trust you and the kids. Nobody else. I figure that everybody else is trying to kill us.'

I stared at him. 'That sounds like something Max would say.'

'She did.'

# CHAPTER SEVENTY-THREE

*Everybody else is trying to kill us.* What a concept. Chilling, and possibly true.

It was late afternoon when we arrived back at Kit's place in Washington. I was anxious, hyper, and flat-out scared. So were the children. We spent the rest of the day nervously peering out of Kit's windows, watching office workers and tourists browse the toney galleries and restaurants around Dupont Circle.

But as the saying goes, *It isn't paranoia if people really are after you.*

When the offices and shops closed for the night and the street darkened, we made our break.

One by one, the children slipped out of the bathroom window that faced away from the street.

Six times, the flurry of their wingbeats echoed against the brick and concrete of the back courtyard. I held my breath and thanked God that there were no gunshots, no screams. I was beginning to think like Kit about this whole scary nightmare. At this point I trusted him and the kids, nobody else.

'I'm shaking some,' I finally admitted once the last of the kids was gone.

'Don't worry, it will probably get worse. *No,* we're okay. So far anyway.'

Kit and I waited half an hour before we left the building, then we walked to the corner of Massachusetts Avenue and caught a taxicab. I

felt as if we were characters in a movie, a really scary one, the kind I
don't go to.

We rode in silence as the cab took us south on Massachusetts
Avenue for a couple of blocks, past several small embassies and the
like. Then Kit hopped out at a red light and disappeared.

I stayed in the taxi as it turned right on to Sixteenth Street at Scott's
Circle and continued on to P Street, where I got out. Real spy stuff.

The Subaru was still parked where we'd left it earlier. After a few
minutes Kit came ambling up with the car keys.

He gave me a hug. 'You okay?'

'Hugs help. But *nope*.'

We took off to the west, looping and turning, passing right by his
apartment again, then heading out toward the zoo. We collected the
children from their hiding place behind a Safeway, four blocks north-
east of Kalorama Park, and quickly loaded them into the car.

Mission accomplished. So far, so good.

'Buckle up,' Kit said. 'I mean it.'

He carried on with his expert driving maneuvers for losing a tail –
just in case there was one. This thrilled the kids no end, but scared me
half to death. We zipped around cars at racetrack speed, backtracked,
got off ramps and on to other ones. By the time we had finally eased
off the main roads and checked into an idyllic and rustic motel called
Alma's Valley Rest, in the backwoods of Maryland, we'd surely shaken
anyone who might've been following us.

Or so I prayed.

Alma's was another funky, bungalow-type motel. We had our own
four-hundred-square-foot cabin in the woods, and it was actually
much nicer than our bungalow at the Pines. There were two double
beds covered with matching powder-blue spreads, plus some folding
cots, and a cable-powered TV.

To top it off there was a little brook out back shaded by the
spreading branches of several elm trees. What more could a girl ask
for?

I was even starting to like sleeping with all of us in one room. It was crowded, but very *nest-y,* and as sweet as a spoonful of molasses.

Then daybreak arrived and my storybook fantasy of Princess Frannie, her handsome Prince Kit, and six magical children burned off with the morning fog.

The *hunters* were out there somewhere. There was no doubt about it.

Somehow, we had to stop them, before they stopped us.

But *how?*

# CHAPTER SEVENTY-FOUR

In the end, it was simple really – we had to hunt the hunters. We had to get them before they got us. There was no other way out of this.

Kit had managed to cast a spell over the FBI. Maybe he did have connections in the Hoover building. Anyway, *somebody* was instrumental in getting us an interview at the Hauer Institute inside Liberty General Hospital.

Half the kids were fast asleep and the others were watching the Cartoon Network while drinking milk and digging into a heaping pile of Krispy Kreme donuts when Kit and I left for Liberty Hospital, which we already knew was *beyond reproach*.

Once we were on the road Kit said, 'Man, this is one beautiful day,' and it *was* gorgeous, all golden yellows and soft blues.

October breezes puffed at the fluffy clouds, sounds of the sixties be-bopped from the radio, and Kit sang along with Bobby Darin's 'Dream Lover'.

Kit has a pretty good singing voice and was giving Walden Robert Cassotto a real run for his money. We were remembering how much we liked each other and forgetting for a little while that this wasn't the first day of summer vacation.

Unfortunately, we were headed straight into Max's nightmare. If not at Liberty Hospital, then somewhere else out here in rural Maryland.

I couldn't begin to imagine what these experiments might be like, but if they were anything like what I'd seen at the School in Colorado, maybe I didn't want to.

The very 'well-respected' Liberty General Hospital was in Carroll County, about thirty-three miles northwest of Baltimore, not far from the Liberty Reservoir. The hospital was so well hidden in a cleft between the gently rolling hills of Maryland that we overshot it at first.

On the second pass, I spotted the discreet bronze sign that directed us off the main road to a narrow lane, then to a wide gravel drive that wound through mature plantings and beautifully manicured grounds.

'It almost looks too good to be true,' I said to Kit. 'Maybe your pals at the Bureau are right for a change.'

'I don't have any pals at the Bureau. Not any more. They all think I'm Mulder, remember?'

The hospital appeared to be made up of two wings set at sixty-degree angles to each other, like the halves of an opened book standing on end. The three-story-high buildings were made of white stone and had lots of wide windows opening out to a magnificent view.

I had to admit, it looked totally benign.

*So why did my hackles rise at the first sight of the place?*

# CHAPTER SEVENTY-FIVE

*A*nd *why did my hackles stay up? Why did every instinct tell me to run from this place as if I was at the gates of eternal damnation? And why didn't I run?*

Kit lightly touched the small of my back as we walked through the automatic sliding doors that led to a large open reception area. I needed to be touched right then, to be reassured.

'I'm okay,' I turned and whispered. *Liar. Big fat liar.*

'I'm not,' he said. 'I get funny around places where they might be doing experiments on humans.'

'*Not* at Liberty Hospital,' I said. 'The *President* and *Vice President* come here for their checkups.'

'You think this is the place that Max found out about? The Hospital? The Unholy of Holies?'

'For some totally crazy reason,' I said, 'I do. It's just a feeling, Kit.'

'*Now* I'm scared,' he said.

Morning sunlight blazed across the terrazzo floor and seemed to light the way to a circular granite information desk. There, an extremely helpful and nice elderly man pointed us to a bank of elevators marked 'The Hauer Institute', where we would have our interview. He had our names and seemed genuinely impressed that we were there to see Dr Ethan Kane.

The elevator took us down to an underground level and opened on to a small, very tasty-looking reception room. It was thickly carpeted in deep blue and furnished with matching upholstered chairs.

There was a coffee table covered with crisp copies of daily news-papers foreign and domestic, and magazines. Coffee brewed on a nearby mahogany sideboard. Vivaldi's *Four Seasons* played from hidden speakers. Perfect, too perfect.

But the metallic smell of disinfectant broke the spell for me. We were still in a hospital. No doubt about it.

'You ever read *Coma* by Robin Cook?' Kit asked me. 'Gruesome stuff.'

'Stop it,' I said, but at least he'd made me smile.

'Listen, Kit, I know your FBI buddies set up this meeting, but why do you think the people here are willing to talk to us?'

Kit allowed himself a slight smile. 'Because if they refused, then we'd get *really* suspicious.'

'Too late. I'm already there.'

Kit presented his creds and a letter of introduction to the blue suit seated behind a small antique desk. The officious young man made a phone call to a Ms Analise Miller.

'Analise will be right out,' said the receptionist, and it was as good as done.

Ms Miller was a thin, prim woman in her late twenties. Her dark hair was tightly pulled back in a long ponytail. She was wearing a taupe pants suit that looked *très chic* and businesslike at the same time. Her smile was vivid, but in my opinion feigned, as if her light green eyes had failed to convey the message her mouth was sending.

She enthusiastically extended her slender hand. 'I've never met someone from the FBI before,' she said. I glanced over at Kit. Yeah, sure. Like this was such a big treat for her.

We were led to a different elevator bank. The elevator that responded to our call was vast, with doors on both sides. It had a composition-rubber floor and brushed-metal walls.

The car dropped like a shot to a floor that I suspected was at least twenty or thirty feet underground.

'Forty-four feet,' said Analise. I *believed* she could read minds.

The elevator door opened on to a gray, rubber-tiled corridor, where medical personnel in blue scrubs and white nurses' uniforms walked quickly in both directions.

'This is the research area at Liberty. The Hauer Institute is dedicated to carrying on the work of the famous team of Clara and Harold Hauer,' Ms Miller told us. 'They were killed in a tragic car accident outside Boston, as you probably know.'

I did know about the Hauers. 'Sad,' I said.

We paused in front of a glass-fronted room filled with floor-to-ceiling metal racks. Each held hundreds of cages resembling plastic shoeboxes.

The cages were alive with dark, rounded shapes. They were lab mice.

My hackles were hackling again.

'Our so-called fuzzy test tubes,' the PR lady said brightly. 'We do a huge amount of animal testing here – as you can well imagine.'

Her words triggered a flood of bad memories. Really bad ones.

I remembered a similar room at the School, that horrific place where Max and the other kids had *lived* for most of their young lives. There had actually been a 'Mouse Room' like the one I was staring at now, and also a 'Nursery' of horribly deformed children who had been left to die. I would never forget the first time I saw Peter and Oz and Ic and Wendy – the children were cowering in cages and covered with excrement.

I shook my head to banish the disturbing images. This *wasn't* the School, I reminded myself. The *President* came here for physicals.

Our escort didn't see these pictures in my mind, fortunately. Maybe Analise had some of her own. She led us briskly away from the fuzzy test tubes and down some corridors. We saw rooms filled with technicians sitting at computers. They were probably feeding DNA information into the center's database.

We took the elevator down another level and stepped out. The third subterranean floor had laboratory after laboratory filled with shining, modern medical equipment and signs pointing to *Operating Rooms One Through Six*.

'The Hauers were pioneers in the field of stem-cell research,' proclaimed Ms Miller. 'As I'm sure you know, Dr O'Neill, stem cells are fresh primary, unassigned cells, harvested from fetuses or from bone marrow. When injected into the body, these cells have the ability to become whatever type of organ cells are required by the body. The cells seem to know where an injury has occurred, and they go to the site of the injury and repair it.'

'This is all terrific. Really helpful,' Kit said without a trace of cynicism; in fact, he was wearing his most winning smile. 'Now,' he said, 'take us to your leader.'

'Dr Ethan Kane is just around this corner,' said Analise. 'As usual, he's operating today. The man never stops, never seems to rest.'

# CHAPTER SEVENTY-SIX

The killer named Marco Vincenti wasn't all that surprised when he got the call to go to Maryland and was told to get there pronto. He had sensed earlier that these particular employers were reluctant to hire too many outsiders, even when they desperately needed a specialist of his caliber, pun intended.

They had tried it the other way, though.

*Catching the kids.*

But they had failed.

So now it was time for other options. As he had prophesied on the rooftop of the building in Denver, *'Catch you next time, kid.'*

Vincenti's specialty: a long-distance sniper. Before he'd gone into business for himself, he'd been in the US Army. Nowadays the jobs were less frequent, but the pay was so much higher.

Marco had decided to drive from his house in Hempstead, Long Island, down to western Maryland, where the six freak-show kids were supposed to be hanging out. His job, specifically, was to kill only one of the kids – the older girl, Max. But there were other potential bonuses, and he planned to go home with as much money as he possibly could.

Marco listened to a 'Best of Mozart' tape all the way down from New York. The music didn't calm his nerves – he didn't need that – but he enjoyed the brilliance and, most of all, the precision of the compositions.

This job had a code name known only to him and to his secretive employer.

*SKEET.*

He liked that one.

Shooting targets that didn't, couldn't, shoot back.

# CHAPTER SEVENTY-SEVEN

K it and I finally got to meet Dr Ethan Kane.

Analise Miller led us up to a man 'scrubbing' at a wide metal sink outside one of the operating rooms. We watched him take a towel from a nurse, who then helped him out of his operating gown. Analise Miller reminded him that the FBI had set up our visit. He smiled at the woman, then nodded her away. Then he introduced himself, offering up strong, soap-smelling handshakes and twenty-twenty eye contact as Kit told him our names.

Dr Kane was incredibly handsome, I'll give him that much. He had a square, seamless face, thick salt-and-blond hair, broad shoulders and a narrow waist. His eyes were a luminous blue and his smile was as warm as a Gerber baby's.

'Call me Ethan,' he said. 'I prefer that. It's very good to meet you. What is this about again? The Federal Bureau might be interested in using our hospital from time to time? You don't know how much that pleases me. This is a great research facility, perhaps the best in the United States. Have you got time to talk? I have a few minutes if you do.'

'That's very kind of you, Doctor,' Kit said in a gentle, mellifluous voice. I had never seen this very smooth, diplomatic side of him before. As we followed Dr Kane, Kit turned to me and whispered, 'Don't blow my nice-guy act. And don't laugh either.'

We knew from the PR document Analise Miller had given us that

Dr Kane was the winner of the American Society of Transplant Surgeons' Pioneer Award and that he was doing 'breakthrough work with stem-cell therapies'. We followed him through a labyrinth of corridors to his office, an unimposing, very cozy space crowded with books that were stacked almost desk high on the floor. There were also pictures of Dr Kane with a few well-chosen political leaders, movie stars, and a financial wiz or three.

'Sorry about the *face*-dropping.' He waved dismissively at the photographs. 'It helps with our fund-raising. You can't imagine. Ours is the celebrity age, isn't it?'

There was also a large family portrait on the credenza. In the imposing picture, Dr Kane stood on the front steps of a gracious Greek Revival-style farmhouse. His arms were around a dark-haired woman, who had a Jackie Kennedy look about her, and two gorgeous children: a teenaged boy and girl; and a third child, a girl of about four, who was clowning at their feet.

'Sissy is our so-called change-of-life baby,' he told us, pointing to the little one. 'And boy, did she change our lives. What a little pistol she is.' He smiled and put a bowl of M&Ms within our reach. 'I'm addicted.' He winked. 'There are worse things, I suppose.'

He cleared papers from two side chairs and asked us to make ourselves comfortable. He sat back in his desk chair, wadded up a piece of notepaper and tossed it through a miniature basketball hoop that hung just above a wastebasket. 'Two points,' he said, then rocked back in his chair, self-satisfied as an LA Lakers fan.

'To be honest, I'm awfully glad Washington takes an active interest in us,' Kane said. 'The more public awareness, the better. We need funds. Let me tell you about our pet project, which is incredible.

'Our singular mission is to extend human life, and to that end we're working on two tracks simultaneously,' he explained. Suddenly, he leaned forward, his chair making a springy squeak, and made a gesture with his hands, each pointing in opposite directions. He spoke of divergent paths.

'We're working with stem cells on one track – organ transplant on the other. As it should be, it's illegal to use human fetal material, so we're limited to clones of fetal cells taken prior to the ruling, and we're using stem cells from bone marrow. Of course, the work is slow going. But that's prudent, don't you agree? It's also the right thing to do.'

He tossed back a handful of M&Ms, and crunched them while we waited for him to continue. I could tell that he wasn't interested in our opinions, or interruptions.

'As for transplantation,' Dr Kane went on, 'the use of animal organs has been banned for good and bad reasons, so we're doing the best we can with available human organs. Human organs are in tremendous demand, and, historically, when we could get them, there was a really high rate of failure after transplantation.

'But we've had a couple of real breakthroughs in the last couple of years,' he said, a smile lighting his handsome face. 'We've learned that transplanting several organs in a system makes for better success than transplanting individual organs. So when we have a matching donor, we use the entire organ system.

'I want you to see this,' he said. He reached behind him and opened the doors of the credenza. He pulled out a chart and spread it open on the desk in front of us. We looked at the colored bars showing the number of multiorgan transplants and the success rate.

'We're up to eighty per cent success in the last six months. Can you imagine that? Five years ago, I wouldn't have believed it. Three years ago I wouldn't have!'

Dr Kane seemed completely caught up in the personal side of the work he was doing; he told us of a half-dozen case histories of young people who would have died but for organ transplantation, and of older people who'd been given a new lease on life.

I must admit, his confidence was bracing, his enthusiasm infectious.

'I can hardly sleep at night I'm so excited by some of this work,' he said. 'We're closer than ever to being able to keep people alive for a long, long time. I have hopes that soon the two tracks will merge. When that happens, we'll have so many choices. To either replace organs or use stem-cell technology to repair tissue. Or to use both methods simultaneously. I think we can bank on it, Frannie and Kit. We're all going to live to benefit from these most incredible advances. Isn't that glorious? Imagine it. In our lifetime. Now let me tell you about the rest of our hospital. I'll make it short but very sweet.'

Kit and I were a little dazzled as we left the facility. It was the opposite of what we'd seen and felt at the terrible School in Colorado. The evidence was compelling that this was an exceptional medical complex. The Hauer Institute was advanced, famous for good works, well run, possibly the best research center in America. Dr Ethan Kane was clearly brilliant, and he had a great reputation.

'I don't get it,' said Kit.

I did.

My hackles were still up.

# CHAPTER SEVENTY-EIGHT

D r Ethan Kane smiled as FBI Agent Brennan and Dr O'Neill finally
left his office. What incredible fools they were. He knew exactly
what they wanted here, and although he was disappointed that the
Hospital was under suspicion, there wasn't much that he could do
about it, was there? Besides, he was almost certain that those two
imbeciles had believed his bullshit. He'd been so patient and ingrati-
ating with them. Just thinking about the smarmy interview made him
ill.

Ethan Kane left his office and boarded the private elevator down to
the basement. He had an important meeting to attend.

He got out at B3 and hurried along a lengthy corridor to a
conference room.

He would've loved to show Brennan and Dr O'Neill *this* on their
guided tour of the Hospital. Blow their little minds.

Ethan Kane used a special pass-key to let himself into the conference room. Three men sat around a glass and metal table.

Even Dr Kane had to admit that they were extraordinary specimens,
miracles, if you took the trouble to think about it.

Each of the three looked exactly like him.

They almost *were* him. But it was more like – they were the arms
and legs, and he was the head. And, of course, the head ruled.

'Doctors Kane,' he addressed the three lookalikes, 'we have a lot of
work to do, and not much time to do it. Resurrection is close, but

there's something else on my mind right now. I want those children! I especially want the one called Maximum. I have seen the future, and Resurrection is only the beginning.'

# CHAPTER SEVENTY-NINE

Ozymandias couldn't get the thought out of his head that he was happier than he'd ever been in his life.

*By a lot! By miles and miles! By light years!*

Of course, he'd been mostly totally miserable before this. It was a weekday, and the woods were empty of human life but filled with other familiar and reassuring sounds. Brooks rippled musically over mossy rocks, and the air was filled with birdsong and squirrel chatter.

And best of all, he and Max were alone. The sweet, unbearably beautiful golden-haired girl was right beside him as they soared over the woodland, literally skimming the treetops with the tips of their wings.

As he glided on the soft, fresh-smelling air, Oz considered a profound thought: *how angry he'd been his entire life*.

Sad but true. And undeniable.

He'd raged and fought against his keepers at the School in Colorado, and ever since he'd been returned to his so-called biological mother, he'd been furious at the world. But in the last few days that hot red flame had almost completely gone out of him.

Max was the whole reason. He wanted her to feel as tremendous as he did, and thought he'd die if she didn't. He flashed her a conspiratorial look, then zoomed straight up into the air, disappearing into the blue as if he were a fighter jet trying to escape from a sneak missile attack.

Then he swooped down on Max, hugging her from behind. He kissed her on the nape of her neck as the two of them fell toward the earth.

This was glorious. Everybody should try it at least once. When it was almost too late to come out of the dive, Max said, 'Oz, let go! *Now!*'

He did! And they spread their beautiful wings wide, *beating, beating, beating* back against the air, stopping their fall in a move that would have brought a Cirque du Soleil crowd to its feet.

'You,' said Max laughing, 'could be dangerous!'

'But you like it, right? Right? You're not terribly tired of me already, are you?'

'No, Ozymandias, I love you to pieces. I've never felt like this before and I don't want it to end. We're, well, we're Romeo and Juliet.'

'Let's skip the suicide part if you don't mind.'

'I'm not the suicide type,' Max grinned.

She took long rowing strokes of air and pulled herself skyward in a ninety-degree trajectory. At the top of the climb, she folded her wings and swept down on Oz. She caressed his cheek with her fingers as she fell past him. God, she did love him.

'Catch me. If you can,' she called out.

'That's not a problem. Consider yourself as good as caught.'

'What a guy.'

The race was on.

Max shot over a gorgeous copse of ash trees, then dropped below their canopy, exhibiting a serpentine flight path between the trunks. Definitely a ten out of ten on the judges' scorecards.

Oz rushed right behind her, breathlessly beating his wings, which were a blur. They swooped past tree trunk after tree trunk, an incredible feat of daring and skill.

Then Max landed.

So did Oz.

They were wrapped in each other's arms even before their feet touched ground. Their trembling lips met. Their excited breathing seemed the loudest sound in the forest.

Oz raked back Max's golden hair with his fingers and gently held her head by the knot he made at the nape of her neck. He kissed her, and she sighed under him. Suddenly he became very hard and she laughed. *'What* a guy,' she whispered.

'And what a girl,' said Oz. 'What a *woman* you are, Max.'

'You really think so?' she whispered breathlessly.

'I know it.'

Their bodies rose and fell, rose and fell, under the dappled light cast by gently tossing branches of ash trees. They were completely lost in each other. They were one with everything in the woods. There was something about their complicated genetic makeup that made this beyond compare. After quite a long time, they finally broke apart, the sweat shining on their perfect bodies.

Max was already thinking ahead to the next moments – when they would do it all over again. She didn't feel an ounce of guilt. She felt beautiful, pure. *We were made for this. It's so right.*

She and Oz lay together quietly for several breathless moments, gathering strength. Then Oz felt Max's fingers begin a slow dance, tracing the proud eagle on his chest, lingering as they brushed across his flat belly.

Oz took her hands, rolled over on to his stomach, and pinned her wings flat behind her. He looked deeply into her eyes. He lowered his face so that he could feel her sweet breath on his cheeks.

'You mean everything in the universe to me, Max,' he said. 'It will always be this way.'

'Even if we have to live on pig nuts someday?'

'Even if it comes to slugs.'

'I do love you,' she breathed. 'What we have is better than just human love. I don't think anyone has ever felt this way before. Isn't science wonderful? Occasionally, anyway.'

'Remember, they think we're a *mistake.'*

Max was still feeling lightheaded, so when she heard the sound of cracking branches it caught her off guard. She pushed away from Oz. Her whole body tensed.

*She and Oz weren't alone.*

Oz sprang to his feet, her warrior protector. He spread out his wings to their full ten feet across and assumed an eagle's crouch to shield her.

As he shifted on his haunches, a scream of rage exploded through the forest!

They both saw who it was – and it couldn't have been worse.

# CHAPTER EIGHTY

I t was Matthew.

He was totally freaked out by what he had just seen in the woods. Max . . . and Ozymandias? They were doing the dirty deed. His sister was making whoopie with Oz. Gross. He was totally grossed-out.

'What the hell is going on?' he yelled at them. 'What are you two doing together? Stop it right now. Get away from her, Oz. I'm warning you. Jeez, Max. Oh man, oh man.'

It was dead quiet for a second, then Ozymandias spread his wings and shrieked. Matthew shivered and started to cry as Max quickly got dressed. He didn't turn around to look at his sister even when Max told him it was all right.

'I'm telling what you did,' he sobbed. 'I'm telling Frannie and Kit. I'm telling everybody.'

'Matty, come talk to me. Come here, you.'

'Matty, I wasn't hurting Max,' Oz said. He didn't look angry now. Maybe just embarrassed, and perhaps sensitive to Matthew's feelings. 'This is how it is with our kind. You'll see when you get a little older, buddy.'

He walked over to Matthew and took him by the shoulders, the better to see into his face. 'I love Max. I love you, too.'

But Matthew roughly pushed Oz away. 'Go fuck yourself, *buddy*. You too, Max. Oh, wait, it's too late for that! It already happened.'

Matthew ran blindly through the woods, and when he felt the air pull on his opened wings, he leaped upward and flew higher than he ever had before. Then Matthew screamed like a banshee into the heavens.

And Marco Vincenti had the little bird twerp right in his sights, in the crosshairs.

All he had to do was *pull*.

And down would come baby.

# CHAPTER EIGHTY-ONE

K it and I had just turned into the parking spot at the ever dee-lightful Alma's Valley Rest when I heard one of the kids crying.

Which one? What was going on now?

I ran behind the cabin to the small clearing leading into the woods. Matthew came running toward me and blasted into my arms. *Matthew? He never cried.*

'Frannie!' he whined. 'Fran-neeee!'

'What is it? What happened, sweetie? What's the matter with you?' I asked as I hugged him tightly.

'They were naked in the woods! I swear to God, Frannie. I'm not making it up. I'm not.'

'Who, Matthew? What are you talking about?'

He turned and pointed. Max and Oz were walking out of the woods toward the motel. My heart sank. I think I might have gasped. I'm not exactly sure what I did. But I know that I felt what any other mother would have felt. Fear, disappointment, anger, *more* fear.

I kissed Matthew's face and then the top of his head. 'Matthew, please go to the car and help Kit with the presents we bought. Yeah, that's right, go on,' I said. 'Go.'

He stumbled off toward the car, and I turned back to Max and Oz with their rumpled clothes and leaf-bedecked hair.

'*What* is going on?' I asked. 'What happened in the woods? What is Matthew talking about?'

'Matty snuck up on us and I didn't know it was him. I got kind of fierce,' Oz said, trying to explain. 'I guess I scared him.'

'That's another matter,' I said, struggling to keep my own feelings very much under control. 'Part of this is that he snuck up, and part of it is what you were doing in the woods.'

I let silence rule for a second as I tried to figure out my role here. There was a voice in my head that belonged to a snooty lawyer lady who'd once said, '*You've never been a mother, have you, Dr O'Neill?*'

The uncomfortable silence dragged on, and Max and Oz weren't helping one bit. Their faces glowed, but they also looked strangely calm.

'Listen,' Max said reasonably. 'Please don't worry so much about us, Frannie. We know exactly what we're doing. This is natural. It's good. It's the right thing.'

'Oh, Max, Max, listen to yourself. What are you saying? How can you be so sure?'

'Because it's second nature for us,' Oz said, as if reading my thoughts. 'It just is. Besides, we don't exactly need your permission, Frannie.'

'Max, you are very young!' I said. 'And you too, Oz.'

'In *human* years, Frannie. But we're more than human,' Max said. 'We're special, remember? And we're also in love. Deeply, passionately, wonderfully in love.'

She combed her hair with her fingers and tied it up into a loose knot. 'Our bird genes make us mature for our age. In fact, I think we're probably about *your* age,' she added, her eyes twinkling irresistibly. 'You're old enough to mate, aren't you?'

She had me there.

# CHAPTER EIGHTY-TWO

**M**ax sat *cooing* in a big, comfy blue armchair by the cabin's front window. She held Matthew in her lap and gently smoothed his silky blond hair. They had made up. Mostly anyway. As much as they were going to right now.

'I'm sorry, Matty, but don't hate me for ever,' she cooed affectionately. 'Okay? Coo. Coo. Please? Matty-poo? Coo, coo, coo.'

'Stop manipulating,' was all he said to her. 'Stop that stupid cooing.'

Kit and Frannie had gone to gas up the car and pick up food for dinner. Hopefully they'd be going back to DC soon. Max couldn't wait to leave this ratty motel and be as far from here as possible. Apparently, the awful experiments weren't being conducted at Liberty General Hospital. But they were happening *somewhere* near here. She was sure of that.

The hunters were near too. She sensed them in the air. She just *knew*.

'I will too hate you for ever, ' Matty said. 'You probably scarred me for life. Do you know that?'

That was when Pip started barking his little fool butt off.

Max parted the curtain and saw an SUV, a Dodge Durango, approaching the cabin. Her heart sank about a million and a half miles. Deep, deep, deeper into the abyss.

The Dodge stopped and three men climbed out and positioned themselves in front. The men were wearing ordinary clothes: jeans, khakis, dark shirts. They had guns, though. Big death-dealing weapons.

'Oh holy shii . . . iit,' Max groaned. 'Matthew, go in the bedroom. Right now.'

Matthew's eyes popped. 'Are *we* going to do it?'

'Just go! Right now! *Everybody!* In the bedroom.'

One of the men wore a black windbreaker over his shirt and a long-billed cap pulled down over his eyes. He was clean-cut and good-looking. He looked *right at Max* and spoke in a pleasant, singsong voice.

'Hey there, Maximum. I see you. My name is Ethan, and I need you to come outside with your friends. No one will be hurt if you do as I say. I know how valuable you are. Believe me, I know. I'm in awe of you children. I'm a fan.'

Max's senses prickled at the sound of his voice. She didn't know why, but she had the thought: *he's a doctor.* And he's a really bad person. The worst she'd ever met. Then she felt the little feathers on the back of her neck lift and a chill coursed through her body.

They were in terrible danger and there was only one exit – the front goddamn door. Right where they were standing with their guns.

The bathroom window was so small even Wendy wouldn't be able to squeeze through. Max shot to her feet and bolted the lock on the door.

'Our parents will be back any minute,' she called out.

'I don't think so,' *Ethan* said. 'Actually, they were spotted going to the market in Kit's car. That's how we found you this time. They're *still* at the market, Max. But a little earlier today they came to visit me at the Hospital. Wonder how that happened, hmmm? Do *you* know, Max?'

He leveled his gun at the window.

Then the son of a bitch fired!

A warning shot!

The plate-glass window tinkled, splintered, and scattered all over the floor. By instinct, the children dropped down low.

Oz screamed ferociously and puffed out his chest.
Pip let out a furious round of barking.
*But it was all just fear.*
They were trapped.
Like lab rats.
And the *rat fuckers* were right outside the front door.

# CHAPTER EIGHTY-THREE

'Come out right now, children. Max! The rest of you! This is your last chance. I'm a busy man. You have no idea what trouble you're causing me. Come out right now or you all die!'

Oz, Max, Peter and Wendy, Icarus, Matthew, the six of them slowly filed out to the creaky wooden plank porch of the cabin.

Six kids.

Very, very special ones.

Priceless.

'We're not going to hurt you, Max,' said Ethan. 'Perish the thought. Not going to happen. *Unless* you run.'

She nodded. 'No. We're way too valuable to you, right? We're big money to you. A lot of people want a piece of us. What *else* do you want, you jerk?'

'Don't believe a word he says,' Oz whispered at her side. 'Look at his eyes. He's a total piece of shit. He's lying.'

'I know he's lying. Just be cool. We have to make the best of a terrible situation, Oz.'

'Don't whisper, and don't do anything foolish.' Ethan spoke in the calmest, yet most authoritative voice.

*Doctor? Scientist? A very bad dude. George Clooney's evil twin,* Max thought. *And he wants us for some kind of collection, doesn't he? He's a collector, right? He's the one who runs the outlaw lab in Maryland. Has to be. He has the eyes of a stone-cold killer.*

'Oh, we won't do anything foolish,' said Oz. 'We aren't stupid.'

'No, you're anything but that,' said Ethan. 'You're all geniuses. I know that. I've seen your test scores.'

'Whatever I do, you do the opposite,' Oz whispered again. 'I love you, Max.'

Suddenly Max couldn't breathe. 'Oz, no.'

'I said no whispering and I mean it. Come down off the porch, children. Right now. That's an order. Do you hear me?'

'All right, all right.' Max spoke. 'We're doing exactly what you say.' *Dr Creep-Me-Out.*

'We won't do anything foolish,' Oz repeated. 'You know, like trust you for a second. *Go, Max!*' he screamed.

Oz took off like a bolt of lightning to the left. Max and the others veered right.

The woods on the right were closer. Oz was the one who would be exposed for the longest time, but he was the fastest, the strongest, the alpha male.

Dr Ethan Kane shook his head, cursed under his breath, then yelled, '*Pull!*'

Suddenly, gunfire erupted from at least two guns, maybe more. Max hadn't made it into the trees yet. She and the young ones were exposed.

So Oz made a decision and shot right over the gunmen's heads. He thought he saw goddamn Ethan smile. Then the doctor pointed to the south. *What?* Oz looked that way. *Oh shit.*

A rifleman in camouflage was perched on a hillside. He was perfectly still. His rifle had a long black scope. The barrel was aimed directly at Oz's eyes.

Pull!

# CHAPTER EIGHTY-FOUR

He couldn't miss. He just had to decide which of the children to take out. *The little freaks were valuable. The head doctor wanted them alive, if possible, although no one had told Marco Vincenti why.* He knew the drill. If they couldn't be caught, one of them would be killed. Then another. And if necessary, all of them.

*Like shooting skeet.*

Marco Vincenti played a little mind-game with himself to make the slaughter easier. He thought of them as disgusting, godless freaks of nature.

*Yeah, that helped a lot. And it was true, wasn't it?*

Though in truth, they were stunningly beautiful, as striking as a Michelangelo sculpture. And the littlest ones were drop-dead cute. No—

*Freaks!*

*Mutants!*

*Mistakes!*

*Monstrosities!*

*Just take 'em out. Do the world a favor.*

He sighted on the girl – Max . . . Maximum. He'd heard she was worth tens of millions and wondered who the hell would *buy* her. Europeans? The Japanese? Ragheads? What the hell would they do with her? Take her apart and put her back together again? *Why did Kane really want her? It was more than just the money, wasn't it?*

He moved his scope to the little ones, the smallest targets – Wendy and Peter.

Named after what? Characters in *Peter Pan*?

He thought he could easily do a one-two . . . Max and her brother, Matthew?

Or Max and Oz? Obviously, they were the leaders of the flock.

That would probably produce the most disharmony and chaos, and get the others to give up.

He had watched them talk to Dr Kane on the porch . . . and then the six of them *exploded* into the air. A little trickery. Okay. If that was the way they wanted to play it.

They split up. Beautiful timing. Perfect. He admired that. Then—

Bingo! The target was so obvious to Marco that it was a done deal.

The powerful-looking male was coming right at him. Had he spotted Marco and his rifle? Probably had. The kids' eyesight was supposed to be extraordinary, something else.

*Freaks of nature, right! Come and get it, bird-boy.*

Though Jesus God, this kid was flying right at him, looming incredibly large in his rifle sight. Coming on like a guided missile.

*So dead on, it wasn't even funny.*

*Dead on the wing!*

Marco's body was frozen still. So still, he could feel his own heartbeat, the pulse throbbing in his throat.

The aiming port of the rifle was floating on the bridge of the male's nose.

No, make that the right eye . . . make it *the center of the eyeball.*

His finger gently squeezed.

Something in Marco's peripheral vision was coming fast. From his left! How could that be?

*Oh Jesus, no. Oh fuck! He'd made a mistake. Bad one.*

The shot cracked loudly, and the noise almost seemed to follow the bullet's flight. Smoke rose gently above the rifle barrel.

And something went terribly wrong, so wrong.

One of the little freaks, the boy Peter, was coming at him.

He was barreling in from the side . . . a little bullet himself, a second guided missile.

No time to get out of the way.

Or even blink.

The boy hit Marco Vincenti at full speed with an outstretched arm. He clotheslined the sniper.

Something – a *rock* – was in his small hand.

*Snap!* It broke Marco's neck, just like that.

He was dead before he even hit the ground.

*Zero ability to fly.*

# CHAPTER EIGHTY-FIVE

Max screamed, '*Noooooooooooooooo. Nooooo! Noooooo!*'

She watched horror-stricken as Oz crashed through the trees, dropping toward the ground like a heavy rock in freefall.

There was only one thing for her to do. She had no other choice in the universe.

She had to go to him. Now! No matter what the risk to herself. Go! Now!

Her world narrowed to exclude everything but Ozymandias. She saw his dark form sprawled on the ground below her; his strong limbs splayed at crooked, at impossible angles, his wings obscenely twisted under him from the steep fall.

And yet his face seemed untouched, unhurt. Was it possible that he had survived? It had to be.

*Oh, Ozymandias, I love you.*

Her heart hammered almost to bursting as she dropped to the woodland floor. She ran and threw herself beside Oz. She waved her fingers in front of his unblinking eyes. She muttered his name over and over.

Max pushed a branch away from his chest and placed her face against his ribcage.

*She heard no heartbeat, felt no rise and fall of his chest. Oh, Oz. Why?*

'It's me, it's Max. Talk to me, Oz. Talk to me, damn you!'

She pinched his nose and cleared his air passage. She breathed into his mouth, her hair spilling softly around his face. She put pressure on his chest. She kept breathing air into him, mouth to mouth, again and again. She listened to his chest again.

Still no sound. So weird, so awful. Impossible. This couldn't have happened.

'Oz, *please breathe*,' she whispered, holding back tears with all of her strength. 'Remember what you said? Remember, Oz? We're together for ever.'

Max ripped open Oz's shirt, the buttons spinning into the dust and pine needles. That was when she saw the awful, ragged, absolutely obscene wound. It was an oozing hole, two fingers wide.

'Noooooooooo.'

The wound went through the heart of the eagle tattooed on Oz's chest, right where *Max* had been inscribed.

*Oz can't be gone! This can't be happening.*

He had been so alive just seconds ago. So strong, so beautiful. She could almost see him flying, his wings beating like an engine. She could still hear him calling out to her.

'No! No! No! I won't accept this!' she screamed, covering him with her body and wings. Peter and Matthew had gathered around her, their pitiful cries blending into undulating howls. The entire universe was a single howl now.

'Talk to me, Oz. Talk to me, talk to me. Please. I *know* you can hear me . . . Oz,' she whispered, 'at least say goodbye. At least that. Oh, Ozymandias, why?'

She never saw the shadows of the men, but she felt the heavy 'big bird' nets fall on top of her. Just as she'd thought – they wanted her alive, if possible. What a joke! Didn't they realize she was dead. *Inside.* Where it mattered.

Max's mind separated from her body. As if from a great distance, she felt someone lift her roughly and toss her over his shoulder. She writhed and struggled fiercely, screaming at the top of her voice, 'Put me down! I'll kill you. I swear I'll kill you!'

'I warned you,' said Ethan Kane, 'and now look what's happened. He was worth millions.'

An old image flickered into her mind. So strange. She'd seen a neighbor's tabby cat take a sparrow down from a feeder. The cat had trotted across the yard with the bird in its teeth and the bird was still, *but alive*.

Max felt like that now. Still fighting them with all her might, she began to keen.

She and Ozymandias were supposed to be for ever.

*We were made for each other.*

This couldn't be the end.

It just couldn't happen.

Could it?

*Could it?*

# PART SIX

# A BRAND NEW DAY

# CHAPTER EIGHTY-SIX

Clouds hung heavily over the small private airfield to the south of the Hospital. The tarmac was empty except for a small flock of mourning doves pecking for bugs on the heat-retentive runway.

Dr Ethan Kane shot the right cuff of his black Burberry windbreaker and looked impatiently at his Baume and Mercier watch.

It was seven past three in the afternoon.

The plane was thirty-seven minutes late. Everything was ready. Damn it! Where were they?

He hated inefficiency. His precious time and energy were being wasted. It wasn't acceptable.

Ethan Kane wasn't alone at the airfield either. Six members of his medical team had been pulled from their jobs, still wearing their scrubs, and they waited restlessly for the flight to arrive. Kane clamped down on his rage at this *criminal* waste of time. It was inexcusable! Someone would pay.

He had pressing business at the Hospital, but leading this welcoming committee was also critically important. Within hours, the resources of the Hauer Institute would be stretched as never before.

It was going to be a trial just to process the incoming shipment. Dr Kane was mentally running through a plan to 'warehouse the overage' when he was distracted by the low drone of an incoming aircraft.

'It's about goddamn time,' he snapped. 'Do you realize who you've kept waiting, you imbeciles?'

The sound grew louder, then an Embraer ERJ135 dropped from the cloud cover. Its gorgeous, streamlined shape seemed to magically materialize above the long, flat runway.

The landing was as slick as a cat's whisker. There was a discreet squeal of brakes, the rush of air against the flaps, and then the pristine white airplane rolled to a stop less than a hundred feet from the hangar.

Men in blue jumpsuits ran out from the maintenance shed and sprinted toward the plane. A staircase was wheeled up to the cabin door and Dr Kane's mood lifted.

*Live from New York – his wonderful new shipment had finally arrived.*

He watched intently as the passengers stepped one by one from the aircraft.

Thirty young men between the ages of seventeen and twenty-three. Each optimistic and brave, each disease-free. They filed down the staircase and on to the tarmac, looking like a professional sports team.

Dr Kane smiled as his eyes caressed the young faces. They looked perfect, and only perfection would do.

He knew the specimens better than they knew themselves. He knew their blood types and hematocrits. He knew their heights and weights and bone lengths. He knew their ethnic and racial origins, their allergies and genetic predispositions. He also knew their names but not their faces, and he tried to guess which was *Charles*, *Tyrell*, *Bandy*, and *Sean*. Who was the prince in the tight black T-shirt? Was the massive young black in cords and green sweater Tyrell?

But it didn't really matter who was who, did it?

Only the parts mattered – not the whole. They would all be *shucked* soon.

Then his real work could begin.

*Resurrection.*

The time was here. Finally.

One of the most important moments in world history. And it was coming none too soon for the welfare of their pitiful civilization.

These thirty fine specimens were key to the special day which was so close now.

These thirty – and most of all, the thirty beneficiaries.

Dr Kane walked briskly toward the group with outstretched arms. 'Welcome,' he said, calling the group to attention. 'Welcome, welcome. What a great pleasure to see you . . . in the flesh. I can't tell you how happy this makes me.

'I'm Dr Ethan Kane, director of the Hauer Institute. My senior medical staff join me in welcoming all of you to Maryland and to Liberty General Hospital.

'Think of it! You've been chosen to take an extraordinary journey with us. You'll be making medical history, making some very good money as well, and this will be the best experience you've ever had. I guarantee it!

'Young men, today is your lucky day. You are essential to the future of America! And the rest of the world for that matter.'

Resurrection was right on schedule.

The *donors* were marched inside.

The *beneficiaries* would all be here by nightfall.

# CHAPTER EIGHTY-SEVEN

I wanted to be strong but I was getting pretty close to losing it, something I almost never did until lately. Well, until that night when I first met Max in the Colorado woods anyway.

*Oh God, poor sweet Oz was already dead. What had we gotten into? Who else might die before this was over? How could we stop the madness? How could we turn it off?*

I was in the front seat of Kit's car, speeding along Route 194 east toward the Liberty Hospital. A gathering storm was blowing in from the north. I shivered as seamless thunderheads dimmed the late-afternoon sun.

The children, the ones who were still alive, were being held at the Hospital, or somewhere nearby. Kit and I knew that much. Just enough to scare us half to death. To give us the willies.

'Maybe I should have taken the kids to the Lake House when we ran,' I said.

'Don't beat yourself up, Frannie. They would have found them no matter where you went. I'd rather take this fight to them. I don't see another way. I wish I did, but I don't.'

We had gotten a message just an hour ago: *Come and talk. Tell no one, or the children will die. Hurry!*

*We have eyes and ears with the local police. And the FBI! We don't want to harm the children . . . But we will.*

Pip lay curled up at my feet as Kit drove as fast as he could go on

---

these narrow, twisting country roads. I thought of poor sweet Oz again and again. I could still hear him telling me that he loved Max, still see the incredible happiness in his face, especially in his eyes. And in hers. It was unthinkably cruel that he should die so young. None other than Emily Dickinson had written, *'Dying is a wild night and a new road.'* No, I didn't think so. Sorry, Miss Emily. *Dying usually sucks the big one. That is what you should have written. What you did write sounds cool, but it's bullshit.*

It was less than an hour's drive to the Hospital, but I had lost all sense of time, and even place. Whenever I looked over at Kit, I saw the terrible strain in his face. *Come and talk . . . We don't want to harm the children.*

I finally muttered Kit's name and he reached for me, held my hand tightly, almost too tightly.

A quarter of a mile later, I pointed to the discreet bronze sign, and Kit veered off the main road and on to the unlit narrow lane. Just seeing the name *Liberty General Hospital* again was unsettling and turned my stomach.

Soon the wide gravel drive appeared and Kit drove slowly up it. Crushed stone cracked under our wheels.

We were about to loop around to the entranceway when a couple of bulky guys wearing hooded yellow rain slickers blocked our path.

'How thoughtful of them. A welcoming committee,' Kit said.

'Should we feel honored?' I said.

'Sure. I'll bet the goon squad is here just for us.'

'You haven't told anyone, Kit? Not even a few close friends at the Bureau?' I asked.

He didn't speak, didn't answer my question. Had he told someone in the FBI? Was that his plan?

One of the men in yellow pointed toward a service ramp, and we headed there in the misty gloom. The ramp terminated at the base of a concrete loading dock. God, this was eerie. I almost couldn't stand it.

Kit braked to a stop but left the car engine running.

'This is it. End of the line,' one of the yellow slickers said. How droll of him. Rubbing it in.

He opened Kit's door, the other bastard opened mine. 'Madam,' my bastard intoned deeply. 'This way, please. You're expected.'

From that point on, everything got a little fuzzy. Well, actually a lot fuzzy.

I remember Pip lifting his leg against the wall. '*Good boy*,' I whispered.

I remember being ordered to place my hands on the platform of the loading dock as the cold rain soaked right through my clothes.

I remember being felt up. Top and bottom. Wanting to punch somebody in the face, but holding back. I remember the sharp stab of a needle in my right bicep.

I remember the blur of faces as I swung my head around and saw the mirthless looks of our slickered captors.

I don't remember anything after that.

Until I woke up.

*In a cage.*

# CHAPTER EIGHTY-EIGHT

Ozymandias came up close – so wonderfully close – and kissed Max on the mouth. His taste was always so clean and sweet and good. Then he whispered, 'Goodbye for now, my darling girl.'

'No! No!' Max started to scream. 'Please come back, Oz! Don't leave me again. *Ozymandias!*'

She burst out of the drugged sleep as if she were being pulled up from the depths of the ocean. She resisted consciousness, thinking instead of Oz, holding on to him. Pictures floated before her eyes; she heard his laughter. She imagined flying with him, soaring above the clouds, caressing him.

*But that was all such fake bullshit. Ozymandias was dead. This was no fairy tale with a happy ending.*

*This was the world – as humans saw it, as they wished it to be. So sad, such a waste of potential, such a shame.*

Max snapped open her eyes and took stock of her awful, hateful surroundings.

She was in a stuffy, foul-smelling, darkened, windowless room at the Hospital. Prison! Worse than prison. Hell! No, this was worse than the fantasies man called hell.

There was a stainless-steel sink and some cabinets across from her, and a big white-faced clock. It read 4:36, but she honestly didn't know if it was morning or afternoon or even what day it was.

She was in a horrible, locked cage. She gauged the dimensions precisely: five feet long, three feet high, two feet deep. Just about right if you were a medium-sized dog.

There were other cages against the adjacent walls. She could make out two dispirited chimps, three beagles, a shelf full of caged rabbits and white rats.

She was a lab animal again.

Max's eyes continued to search the room until she located Peter and Wendy. My God! Their small forms were enclosed in cages too. How unbelievably sad. The twins were unconscious, but they seemed to be breathing.

Were they?

*And where was Matthew?*

*Ic?*

*Frannie and Kit?*

Max noted the shredded newspaper bedding on the floor of her cage. She'd also been given two chocolate-peanut power bars and a bottle of water. Thanks for nothing. She wasn't hungry or thirsty. She wanted to die. She couldn't stand captivity – not after being free.

The paper gown crackled as she shifted, seeking a position that didn't hurt. But that was impossible, wasn't it?

*She hurt everywhere.*

The lab door opened, jolting her. Someone entered the semidarkness and closed the door. It was fricking Kane, the man she despised. The leader of the inhumans. She had been hearing about him since her days at the School – and now here he was, the monster of monsters.

'Hello, Max,' he said, walking up to her cage. 'I've got your latest test results back. Your intelligence is off the chart. That's fabulous. We can't even measure your IQ. Why, aren't we just full of surprises?'

'Why, aren't we just full of shit?' she barked at him.

'Now, now. You really knock my socks off. You're even funny.'

'Yeah, you're a scream too. They ought to get you to host *Saturday Night Live*. Are you letting us go? Of course you're not!'

'Well, no. I'm not. But I just wanted to tell you that you are one smart kid. It's too bad your internal systems are so, how shall I put this, unusual? But I do have a surprise for you.'

Max fricking *hated* surprises. They were always, always bad. She closed her eyes. Looked away.

'C'mon, Max, give me a nice smile. You're going to like this.'

She opened her eyes and turned them on her mortal enemy. 'What is it?'

'*Look*,' said Ethan Kane. He turned up the lights to reveal the rear of the room. 'Your friends are here. Frannie, Kit, everybody. Except Ozymandias, of course.' Kane smiled again. What a scream he was, what a joker.

If she possibly could, if she ever got the chance, she would break his neck.

*Break.*

*His.*

*Neck.*

# CHAPTER EIGHTY-NINE

Resurrection was beginning, and nothing would ever be the same again, and that was mostly because the fools of the world *just couldn't see it coming*. Science was about to change the ethics governing life and death. It would change the way the human race perceived life in virtually every country around the globe. The medical breakthroughs would hit like meteors crashing to earth, and it would have the same explosive impact as a meteor storm.

Patricia Stevenson held tightly to her husband's hand as their Lear jet approached the small, unimposing airport in the rolling hills of Maryland.

Patricia's clear gray eyes were full of compassion for her Roger, who kept fading in and out of sleep. His cancer was so far advanced that no one could, or would, perform any more surgeries; the cancer had metastasized, from his colon into his lungs and spread to his liver.

Roger Stevenson, her hugely talented, wonderfully generous husband, had only days to live. If that. He needed to be here . . . because the world couldn't afford to lose him. Patricia genuinely believed that. And so, apparently, did the people at the Hospital.

When the captain announced that they would be landing momentarily, the eighty-year-old woman reached over and tightened her husband's seatbelt. She kissed him on the cheek, then adjusted the jade-green leather seat so that he would be in an upright position.

She smoothed his baby-blue cashmere lap throw. At this touch, his eyes opened, and he seemed a little disoriented.

'Patty? Is that you?'

'Yes, darling. I'm right here. I'll always be right here. We made it, Roger. We actually made it.'

She and Roger were both wearing the best clothing money could buy: cashmere and Harris tweed and three-thousand-dollar handmade shoes. The jet had cost seven million and it was their own, as were the houses in Dallas, Palm Beach, and Dah Bead. It had repeatedly been said that money couldn't buy happiness, but whoever said it was wrong. Money might not always bring happiness, but it certainly could.

Patricia stroked the mottled skin on Roger's hands and gazed fondly at his face. She knew every line and wrinkle, the part in his hair, the way his fingers quivered now, all of his appetites and aversions, and stories oft told. Patty had known Roger nearly her whole life. They had been lovers since their early twenties and married for fifty-seven years. Patty Jo Clark Stevenson, originally from Lake Forest, Illinois, candy heiress, Vassar graduate, director of the Dallas Symphony Foundation, philanthropist, mother of five, grandmother of fourteen, felt the tug on her stomach as the airplane began its descent.

She glanced briefly at the runway below before closing her eyes. She prayed to God that this was the right thing to do – that this was His will. Of course it was! Roger was so important, not just to her but to the whole world. A brilliant engineer by training, he had gone on to found not one, but two, Fortune 500 companies; he'd been the president for one term; then a close adviser to two other presidents. Of course he had to live! He of all people.

The landing was soft, the Lear jet kissing the tarmac and swiftly rolling to a halt. The overly polite young captain came back to the passenger compartment and made certain that the Stevensons were all right. Then he personally escorted them off the plane.

As they walked very slowly down the steps, Patty saw the one man she trusted. Dr Ethan Kane was standing at the foot of the staircase.

He had a wheelchair for Roger. He smiled brilliantly and she lifted her hand in greeting.

'Look, Roger. It's Ethan! Oh God, everything is going to be all right now.'

Stretched out on the airfield directly behind Dr Kane were several other private planes, twenty-three in all. Two more were just now landing. Yet another was waiting to land.

Everyone scheduled for Resurrection was here.

*The chosen ones.*

# CHAPTER NINETY

They were in their fifties, sixties, seventies, and a few in their eighties.

All leaders of industry, science, and government from around the world. Powerbrokers, masters of the universe, legends in their own time.

*All males, every one.*

*The chosen ones.*

They wore expensive business suits, mostly in dark colors; all but a few disabled ones had proud, straight bearings as they deplaned. They were accustomed to being in command, in full control of the lives around them.

Ethan Kane watched the men come toward him, and even he was struck by the eeriness of the scene. Actually, the irony of it. That these *few men* should be saved.

He and his surgeons were the receiving line, and they greeted each powerful man with the required deference and respect. They were used to it, expected nothing less, even here, where they came like beggars to a king.

Dr Kane lightly took the hand of the current President of the United States, but then hurried him along, effectively dismissing the man.

Behind the President was someone much more important, more powerful, infinitely more worthy of salvation, the most pre-eminent scientist from Germany. A genius who was almost on a level with Kane himself.

And behind him, someone more important still – from mainland China.

Ethan Kane found it easy to make small talk with each one, and especially to smile at the thirty men. They had been *chosen* – and so had he.

They were the last best hope of the world.

# CHAPTER NINETY-ONE

A loud groan, or possibly a snore, woke me from the deepest and probably creepiest sleep of my life.

It took me a few seconds to realize that I was the one making the godawful noise. The *good* news – I was still alive.

I was visually and aurally disoriented, hardly knew which way to look. Where was I? Then I heard Kit calling softly. He was alive too. We both were. At the Hospital.

But *why?* I wondered. Were we to be used as bargaining leverage? Was that it? It had to be. Kit and I were alive because we might be needed to influence the children in the next few hours. What part were they supposed to play in Resurrection? *Why were they so important?* The question was driving me crazy.

'Kit?' I mumbled. 'That really you? Or am I dreaming again?'

'Frannie,' he said. 'Frances Jane, it's me. In the flesh, such as it is. Misery sure loves company.'

I turned on to my side and I felt as if I were rolling under water. *Oh God!* I saw Max first and I lazily waggled my fingers at her. Then I turned back to Kit, who was in a cage catercorner to mine.

'Where are we?' I asked.

'Liberty Hospital,' he whispered. 'We couldn't get a private room.'

Right. *In steel cages used for lab animals. Waiting for Resurrection, whatever that was.*

And I was also coming out of a morphine stupor.

'You okay?' Kit asked me. 'Within reason?'

'I don't know,' I said languidly. 'My head feels like it weighs a hundred pounds. You?'

'Nothing I couldn't remedy with one clear shot at Dr Ethan Kane. Something's going on out there. That's why they're not paying attention to us for the moment.'

Max called out to us from across the room. She was in a rage. 'I have to get out of here. I'm going to go break Dr Kane's neck. That's a promise I made to Ozymandias.'

'Calm down, Max,' I called to her. Then I rattled my bars for the hell of it.

We were in KennelPal cages, a brand I used myself, and I was quite familiar with this type of closure. To open it, you had to pinch two spring-loaded prongs together and that would cause a bolt to slide out of its sleeve. There was a heavy metal plate behind the latch, so it was impossible to squeeze the prongs from inside the cage. No one could do it. Thus the guards *outside* rather than in here with us. We were trapped.

I watched Max work quickly through all the possibilities mentally. She was frustrated, livid. But she wasn't giving up.

'Frannie, you ever read *The Adventures of Kavalier and Klay*? There was a character called "The Escapist",' she called from her cage.

'Max, what are you talking about?' I asked.

'Getting the hell out of here. *Trying*, anyway.'

I almost couldn't believe what I saw next. This was Max at her best.

I watched her spread the bars of her cage wide enough for her hand to go through. She had incredible strength. *Off the charts.* Sometimes I forgot about that.

She pinched the prongs together. The bolt instantly sprang loose from its metal sleeve and Max swung the door free.

'I'm a strong girl and my IQ is off the charts,' she said with a note of defiance that made my heart sing.

There were footsteps out in the hall and it sounded like people were coming our way. In a hurry.

'Let me take care of this,' said Max. 'It'll be a pleasure.' She started toward the steel-framed door.

'*Max*, come back here!' I yelled. 'Don't go out there.'

'Don't worry about me,' Max said.

Then she yanked open the door and disappeared outside.

There were three shots and my heart sank. Max screamed. Then nothing. Not a sound for several seconds.

The door to the outside finally flew open. Several doctors rushed into the room where we were being held.

'What happened to Max?' I screamed. 'Where is she? Where is Max? Is she hurt?'

In answer, one of the doctors jabbed a needle into my arm. I saw another doctor stick Kit with a needle in his thigh.

And then the lights went out again, but not before I whispered or cried, 'Max, dear Max.'

# CHAPTER NINETY-TWO

K it woke with an unbearable pressure at the back of his head, such a really bad feeling, like nothing he'd ever experienced before, or even thought possible. An old Doors song was playing over and over in his head, 'This is the End . . . the End, my friend.' He'd also been moved to another room in the Hospital. Frannie, the kids, Max, were nowhere to be seen.

*Unreality.*

*Was.*

*Taking.*

*Over.*

Very slowly, tentatively, he tried to look around. He needed to orient himself. He could almost *hear* his eyes move from side to side.

It took a few seconds for Kit to realize that he was lashed to a wheelchair and that all he could move was his head. Still, he could see the entire room from this position.

More than he wanted to see.

There were corpses all around. Young, naked, very dead. *Recently* dead. All males. Lying on gurneys parked casually at odd angles, like nobody cared, and obviously, they didn't.

*These are murder victims,* he thought. *This is a slaughterhouse. I'm in a slaughterhouse.*

The bodies had been precisely and thoroughly carved up.

Why? And why all male victims? What in the name of God was

Resurrection? Who was supposed to rise from the dead? Not these poor devils on the gurneys.

'Jesus God Almighty,' Kit whispered. 'Help us.'

The horrors just wouldn't stop coming and he had a terrible feeling that he was next on the chopping block.

Unreality.

Had.

Taken.

Over.

# CHAPTER NINETY-THREE

*God, it was so damn cold in here,* Kit was thinking.

*What was this place? A meat freezer? A hospital morgue? What?*

*Let it be some kind of high-tech medical morgue. Let the bodies be cadavers for legitimate research.*

But the bodies were all too uniformly young. In their teens and early twenties. Just kids, really.

*Am I next? To be disemboweled?*

Kit's fear for the kids and Frannie finally overcame his terror for himself. Horrific guilt swamped him, but he couldn't even afford the luxury of despair. He had to get out of here. *But what a total crock that was!* How could he get away?

*But how could he not try?*

He had to find out what had happened to Max. Had she been murdered? And Frannie? Where were they? And why was he the only one in the meat locker?

He reared back against his tight restraints and the chair finally rocked back. Then it fell over!

Kit landed on his shoulder, and it hurt like hell. *Neat move, swiftie. You're so sharp sometimes.*

Just then, the door to the room creaked open. Dr Ethan Kane stepped inside. He seemed to be everywhere; totally hands-on.

'Hey, hey,' he said to Kit. 'Trying to escape? Hope springs eternal, doesn't it? Looks like you had a little accident here. No problem,' he said. 'We'll fix you right up.'

Then he kicked Kit hard in the ribs. *Jesus, that hurt! That really, really hurt! Who was this guy – Mengele?*

Kit wouldn't give up. Wanted to. But he wouldn't surrender. It wasn't his nature.

'Dr Kane. Now that I'm awake, let's talk. The kids will be missed. I'm going to be missed eventually.'

'Not as much as you'd think. I've taken care of all that. I'm sorry I can't stop and chat,' Kane said. 'I'm sure you have all sorts of fascinating questions and insights, but we're overbooked at the inn right now.'

'Listen to me!' Kit raged. He just couldn't *move*. Not an inch.

And Ethan Kane was walking away, not listening at all. Kit felt completely helpless; a bug caught in a spider's web. No way was Kane going to let them survive.

He watched the doctor walk to a wall of cabinets over a sink and remove a syringe and a small bottle. What was Dr Death doing now?

He screwed the needle on to the syringe, plunged the point into the rubber stopper at the top of the bottle, and retracted it.

He advanced on Kit again.

'Just tell me what you want,' Kit said. 'I'll tell you the truth. Everything I know.'

Ethan Kane laughed softly. 'This will pinch,' he said.

# CHAPTER NINETY-FOUR

E verything was so unbelievably confusing. So chaotic. So hopeless. I came out of my drugged stupor in Ethan Kane's office.

I was carefully, *artfully* positioned so that I was looking at about a two-gallon jug filled with a solution and dozens of dark floating objects.

I tried to focus my eyes.

*What were those reddish gobs?* Then I knew what the floating shapes were: *fetal hearts . . . The hearts of pre-born children!*

I whispered, 'My God, my God, why have You forsaken me? Why *now*?'

It got worse. I was bound to a wheelchair. And Dr Kane was working at his desk, calm as could be. 'I want to talk to you about the children,' he said without looking up from whatever he was writing. 'You can be of some help. I need to know everything I can about the work that was done on them at the School. I know you examined the children thoroughly.'

'*Where* are the kids? Where's Max?' I asked as soon as I could manage a few words.

'Oh, they're fine.' His eyes narrowed. 'And as for Max, don't worry, she'll never escape me. Fuck the kids though. I want to spend some quality time with *you*, Dr O'Neill. I have a feeling that you may understand my work more than you think you do. You were there at the School. And you certainly have useful information about the bird-children, don't you? You're a veterinarian. I'm not. You can help me with my work. If you so choose.'

'I wouldn't choose to help you if you were choking on a chicken bone,' I spat out.

Kane's face turned cold. 'Good one. For a trailer-park cretin like yourself. Now listen to me closely, Frannie. Don't say another word or I'll cut out your tongue.

*'Don't you understand the value of improving and extending human life?* You must! Last month, we "resurrected" a mathematical genius from London. The world desperately *needs* this man's brilliance. One can only imagine what his mind will produce in the coming decades! Do you comprehend what I'm saying? Maybe *a little*? Can you get past your own pitifully outmoded system of ethics?

'You may speak now. Frannie? You did tests on Maximum. Tell me exactly what you found. Strengths and weaknesses.'

'Absolutely not!' I shouted at him. 'What's going on here? What is Resurrection?'

Kane rose from behind his desk. 'What is Resurrection? Where to start? OK, I'll let you in on a little secret. Our secret. I'm one of the first beneficiaries,' he said. 'New organs, and in my case, a new body and head!'

I felt as if the earth had come to a stop as I tried to absorb what I'd just heard. I looked at his smooth pink skin, his bright blue eyes, his full, thick head of hair.

He showed off his brilliant smile again. He *knew* that he'd just blown my mind.

'My name is Dr Harold Hauer. *The* Harold Hauer. I didn't die in a car accident outside Boston eleven years ago. I've been *resurrected*. I look pretty damn good for ninety-four, don't you think?'

# CHAPTER NINETY-FIVE

D r Harold Hauer was alive and he looked like he was in his mid-forties. I was still reeling with amazement and shock as Ethan Kane began to push my wheelchair out of his office. Fast! We were going somewhere.

'Ninety-four years old and my current life expectancy is unlimited. I'm smarter than I was, too. Wish I could say the same for you, Dr O'Neill. You obviously *won't* help me, so what good are you? To keep the kids in line? Maybe. So tell me the similarities and differences between Max and the birds she physically resembles. Where does her strength come from? Her intelligence?'

'I will not,' I said.

'Fine then. I can control the little bastards without you. So much for small minds like yours. My wife is smarter – and she's a *robot*.'

My wheelchair was pushed into an eggshell-white-painted ward full of sleeping patients. There must have been a dozen people in there, each with IV lines dripping from TPNs.

All of the patients wore metal helmets hooked up to monitors positioned over their heads. Each monitor showed a different film. The films seemed to be free-flowing dramas, romances, even nature documentaries.

'What are these movies?' I asked. 'What are they for?'

Kane/Hauer was standing at the foot of one bed, gazing up at a monitor, no longer paying attention to me.

'Oh, *this* is delightful,' he said of underwater cinematography of spectacular fish, the likes of which I'd never seen. He looked over at me. 'This is the Dream Room and what you're seeing is Simulated Reality – a kind of human-and-machine collaboration. See, there are electrodes in the helmet that stimulate areas of the patient's brain. We manipulate them, then the patient thinks or imagines or remembers, and the story that's created is more real to him than reality itself,' he said. 'You're looking at the patients' *dreams.*'

I didn't want to be, but I was dazzled. I turned from one monitor to another, taking in the vivid images: sailboats, passionate kisses, intercourse, ballet, abstract art, raw speed, a bordello, a palace.

Then something truly obscene caught my eye. My heart began to *thump* so hard it caused a pain in my chest.

I watched a small form in one of the beds, a girl of no more than four or five. A doe and its mother were nuzzling gently on her screen. *That was her dream, wasn't it?*

I strained to see the girl's face a little better. But I knew I'd seen it before. Photographs in his office.

'That's *Sissy,*' I said. 'It's your own daughter. My God, what have you done to her?'

There was an embarrassed chuckle from Dr Ghoul. 'Well, yes, it is the child I called Sissy. But she's not actually my daughter. This little girl has very special organs, and I'm keeping her here for a recipient in Germany.'

The monster saw my look of horror and disgust. 'Don't judge me, *you cow.* You're starting to really piss me off.'

The Q-and-A period was apparently over. Dr Kane/Hauer rolled my wheelchair down to the end of the nearest row of patients.

Another shock! Honestly, my heart couldn't take any more of this.

There, up to his armpits in crisp white sheets, was someone I hadn't been sure I would ever see again.

*Kit.*

A Simulated Reality helmet was strapped over his head. He had a soft, dreamy look on his face. A doctor was working on him, his back to the door.

On the screen a baseball game was in progress. It was Kit's beloved Yankee Stadium, and I was watching from the vantage point of home plate. A ball was coming in hard and fast . . .

'What are you doing to him?' I screamed.

'Giving him the time of his life,' said Kane/Hauer. 'And we've saved a bed for you, Frannie. Sweet dreams. Oh, and by the way, Frannie, watch this. Watch closely. *Oh, Doctor?*' he yelled across the room.

The physician working on Kit turned to us. I nearly fainted. I don't know why I didn't.

The doctor standing next to Kit was another Dr Ethan Kane. An exact fricking replica.

'Don't be alarmed.' The duplicate Kane spoke to me. 'I'm nobody. I'm just a clone.'

# CHAPTER NINETY-SIX

I was lost in wild, dizzying thoughts about what was happening. The Hospital. Kane/Hauer. His robot-clone. Max. Was she alive? *And what was Resurrection? Who was being resurrected?*

Suddenly I heard the very loud buzzing of an electric gadget, followed by cold metal raking across my scalp.

Then something soft and loose was falling on my shoulders. I realized it was my own hair.

*They'd cut off all my hair. I was bald.*

An orderly slashed the duct tape holding me to the wheelchair with a box cutter and I was roughly transferred to a stainless-steel gurney. I punched out at him, but he merely laughed.

'Relax,' he said. 'This is the fun part. Fun for me anyway.' He jabbed me with another needle.

*Boom! I was out like a light.*

And the bastard had lied to me.

No Simulated Reality trip for me. No helmet, no comfy bed in the Dream Room. The needle went into my arm and that was it: *death, down and dirty.*

I rose up from the bed, or at least my 'spirit' or 'soul' or 'astral body' did.

I floated up to the corner of the room and hung there, face down, while the orderly drew the sheet over my face.

I'd been done in. Just like that.

I couldn't process my shock quickly enough. I had been alive seconds ago. Now I was dead. I hadn't said goodbye to anyone, hadn't truly prepared for this moment. *I'm only thirty-four*, I thought, and tears came into my eyes.

Before I could carry on like this any longer, I was drawn up through the ceiling. I felt as if there were a hand at the back of my neck, a cord in the middle of my back, attached to some winch high in the sky.

I passed upward through the floor above, just the way I'd seen it done in the movies about ghosts.

I was there, but not there.

No one saw me and nothing obstructed my passing as I materialized up through the reception area, where I'd been with Kit the day before. As I moved through the floors of the Hospital, I felt my anguish evaporate, replaced by a peacefulness I'd never experienced before.

I'm not overly religious, but I do believe in God. Something or someone was pulling me now, taking me away from my earthly life and concerns. I was conscious of a lack of control, and I felt relieved to float away from my responsibilities and grief.

I still loved Kit, Max and the kids, but I couldn't take care of anyone any more. I realized that now.

My body cleared the top floor of the Hospital and I was surprised to see it was daytime. Last night's thunderstorm had drenched the landscape and moisture on the treetops sparkled like diamonds.

I kept moving effortlessly upward, and suddenly I could see the winding country roads Kit and I had driven along so recently. The hills looked gorgeous to me, like a rumpled calico quilt spread out below. I felt the sun gently warming my back, and it was supernaturally calming.

A flock of birds flew beneath me, and I could see the details of their feathers with astonishing clarity.

I stretched out my arms and saw the same denim shirt I'd been wearing for days – my torn nails – these were my hands, all right.

I rubbed my hand over my bald head and liked how that felt.

I tried to alter my course, but there was no jet propulsion with this astral body. I moved only in one direction and that was up.

As I rose I saw the whole of the Liberty Reservoir, and *there*, the city of Baltimore, its rivers leading to the Chesapeake Bay. I guessed I was at ten thousand feet and rising. The landscape was in miniature, the cars teeny, the houses and other buildings dotting the countryside with toylike precision.

I was bathed in soft mist, and it felt like a blessing.

I was cleansed.

Refreshed.

Redeemed.

The cloud cover seemed to last for a very long time, and when it cleared, I saw that I was high out over the Atlantic Ocean.

The water was aquamarine near the coastline, turning to dark navy blue, flecked with white, all of it astonishingly beautiful and real. I could see the eastern coast of the United States! *God bless America.*

The only sound was the brush of the wind on my ears.

I thought about my life and I could remember it all: a bake sale at a church, my first kiss in Dad's barn, the deer with a broken back that I'd put to sleep. I put my arms behind my head and looked into Kit's loving eyes. I saw Max running through the woods as I'd seen her the first time. The images came and went, each with newly minted crystal clarity. I could see all of the people I'd known and loved and feel their thoughts as well as mine. It was as if I were standing there with them, and in this way I got to say my goodbyes. But I soon tired of Frannie's life-retrospective and said goodbye to myself, to my life as a woman.

Earth was growing below me. Not like the satellite pictures we've all seen – this Earth filled the sky and was in sharp topographical focus. I could see the mountain ridges and the running rivers and the cities and the shifting seas. *Dear God, the magnificence of our planet defied description.*

As for me, the former Frances Jane O'Neill, I was a tiny speck of human consciousness. I didn't know if I was falling out of the sky or going straight to heaven.

Either way was okay.

I knew I was going home.

# CHAPTER NINETY-SEVEN

These had been the most intoxicating, heady days of his life, even more incredible than the time when he'd faked his own death – *and also murdered his first wife* – in an automobile crash outside Boston.

Resurrection was almost finished – at least the first stage, and hopefully the first of many to come.

Thirty 'new' beings had been created.

*His* creations.

And now they would go out and run the world properly for the next thirty to fifty years, or possibly even longer.

*His* world, in a manner of speaking.

The chosen ones – all males – had been recuperating for two days and every one of them was in good shape. Thank God, none had died during surgery. Of course, he could have brought them back to life. He was a miracle-maker.

They were ready to go back to their home cities now, and to do the specific jobs they had been chosen for. The world needed continuity and stabilization before third-world morons took the whole thing over, or possibly blew it up. These men, *all men*, were the best hope to maintain order and progress; they were the last hope.

Dr Kane/Hauer believed that. Several practical problems would have to be overcome eventually – like explaining how the thirty men were able to live so long – but the masses could be prepared for that, and all the scientific wonders of a brave new world. Those were small problems for small thinkers to worry about.

'God, I feel so good!' he exclaimed.

But something was missing, wasn't it?

Imagine that!

His day of days – and something was still missing. Well, he supposed that it went with the territory – being a perfectionist.

He took a handful of M&Ms into his mouth, and while good for what they were, the chocolate candies didn't do the trick.

He looked over at the couch in his office. The lovely Juliette sat there in an expensive blue pin-striped suit, creamy white blouse, heels. As always, his wife was stunningly perfect. She was at the Hospital to assist him in saying goodbye to some of the chosen. The more family-oriented ones liked that he had a loving wife. It made them comfortable.

He went over and turned on the lovely and talented Juliette.

'It's a glorious day for you, isn't it?' She spoke almost immediately. 'You're amazing, darling. I adore you.'

'So *do* me,' he said in a thick whisper. 'Right here, right now.'

Looking incredibly proper in her pin-striped business suit, Juliette knelt before the doctor. She used her perfect white teeth to pull down his zipper.

'It would be an honor,' she said, and did the work she had been created for.

# CHAPTER NINETY-EIGHT

A saying, a truism, played in Max's head: *fear is not the answer. Fear is not the answer.*

She woke up and realized she'd been knocked out cold for a while – maybe as much as half a day.

But then she knew it had to be longer than that. Maybe even a couple of days. Man! What had she missed? Her body seemed almost repaired from the gunshot wound suffered when she'd escaped.

Her left leg stung like crazy, but her anger had reduced the pain to something manageable. The bullet had caught her thigh. She'd wrapped a strip from her shirt around it to stop the bleeding.

She studied it now. The wound seemed okay.

*This is nothing,* she kept telling herself, compared to what happened to Ozymandias.

*Get a move on, Max. Time is wasting. Go.*

She had quite a struggle working her way through the air ducts, crawling on her elbows and knees. After a few minutes, she shimmied down a chute to the third floor, pushed out an air vent and dropped into a five-sided room.

The room was like an aquarium. *For people.*

It actually had glass walls, which looked like they were hurricane strength.

Behind the glass was a long, dimly lit room with rows of people who seemed to be . . . sleeping? Maybe thirty of them.

Max jumped as doors swung open on the far side of the dimly lit room. Her wings rustled. Then two female nurses entered, chatting in whispers.

The nurses calmly read the monitors at the sides of the beds, and checked several of the patients' vitals.

Who were these men on the beds? What had happened to them? If she'd been knocked out for a day or so in the air-conditioning chutes, how long had they been here? More important – where were the other kids? And Frannie, Kit?

One of the men began to stir. Max could hear clearly through a speaker in the ceiling.

'Thirsty,' he whispered in a raspy voice. 'Please. A little water?'

One of the nurses went right to him. She poured liquid into a cup, then tilted his head so that he could drink comfortably.

'There you are,' she said, 'Mr President.'

*Oh.*

*My.*

*God.*

With his head tilted like that, Max could see the man's face. It wasn't the current US president – it was the one two back.

She shook her head and almost started to gasp. He had to be close to eighty now, but he looked no older than fifty. How could that be?

None of the men in the room looked older than that.

*Is this Resurrection? What is it?*

Then more doctors and nurses began to enter the room. They were waking the patients.

Something was going on.

Something important.

Something very bad.

'Wake up, Prime Minister . . .'

'Wake up, Mr Chairman . . .'

'Wake up, Your Excellency . . .'

'It's a brand new day. You look fantastic. All of you do. Congratulations.'

# CHAPTER NINETY-NINE

*G et help get help get help get help get help.*
   *Get out get out get out get out.*

It was an alarm going off in her head. Blood roared in her ears.

*The important men in here are being given their wake-up calls. But what are they waking up to? Or are they resurrecting? Who are they?*

Near the entrance to the room was a peculiar set of sliding doors that looked like doors to an elevator. Max rushed to them.

Panting with anxiety, she pressed the call button. *C'mon c'mon c'mon.* The doors finally slid open. No one was inside. *Score one for the good guys!*

Now what? Now where? Max ducked inside and rode the car up one story to the second floor. If she remembered correctly, the Animal Room was there. Hopefully, the other kids were too. Maybe Kit and Frannie.

She got off and saw no one in the hallway. Then she heard voices, someone coming. She needed to get out of there.

Max spotted the Animal Room straight ahead. She raced to the door, pulled it open. She could have a heart attack any second now. That was exactly how she felt.

She heard someone inside the room! *Busted!*

'*Max!* You're back!' Wendy called out. Then there were more familiar voices calling her name, welcoming her and asking questions at the same time.

'Shhhh. Shhhh. Quiet down now. I said *quiet*! All hell is breaking loose outside. Something gigantic is going on. And it's bad.'

Max hurried to open the latches on the cages. She took a few seconds to hug them all: Peter, Matthew, Wendy and Ic. All except Ozymandias, of course.

'Where *were* you, Max?' Matthew wanted to know.

'In the air ducts. Getting better. I got shot. Enough questions for now.'

'What's going on outside?'

'*Stop* with the questions, Matty!'

The kids looked terrible – dirty, anxious, afraid – but especially poor Icarus who pushed her away as she tried to carry him out of his cage. 'Go away,' he hissed. 'Let me be, Max. Let me die here.'

'Ic, it's time to go, and you're *going*!'

'Leave me, please. I can't take it any more. Leave the blind boy. I can't go on like this.'

'We need you, Ic. Now shape up, little buddy. SHAPE UP *NOW*.' Max finally had to raise her voice.

Icarus looked startled, but then he grinned. '*That's* the Max I know and love.'

Damn right it was. She was in charge again. Without a map, without a weapon, without a real plan. And without Kit and Frannie. She had to hurry and find them.

'Matthew, you help out Ic. Peter and Wendy, stay with me,' she said. 'Stay close, you two.'

'I'm letting the lab animals out,' Matthew said. 'No arguments. I *have* to do it, Max. They're as scared as we are. They're our pals now.'

'Yeah! Release the skitters,' said Peter. 'Release the hounds!'

Max rolled her eyes, but she had to say yes. She couldn't bear to leave them in the cages either. 'Let'm out. The extra confusion might help.'

The two younger boys opened the chimp cages first, clowning and jabbering as if they had all the time in the world. Then Wendy let Pip out of his cage, and the beagles too.

Max opened the outside door and peered up and down the hallway. This was fricking crazy; it was the worst yet. Cold white fluorescent light illuminated every corner.

Soon the hallway filled with monkeys, rabbits, lab rats, and hounds. Maybe the chaos *would* be helpful! The hounds' vocal cords had been severed, but their harsh, breathy bays were still audible as, noses to the ground, they seemed to pursue some mystical quarry.

*It was total chaos. What a mess. Insanity.*

But that mess was probably the best chance they were going to get right now.

Max heard high-pitched female squeals as the rodents and monkeys arrived at the nurses' station. She stopped searching for Frannie and Kit for the moment and quickly herded the kids into the elevator. It was a tight squeeze and Pip seemed dead set against it, barking and yipping.

'Shape up, dog!' Max commanded, and the annoying barking stopped instantly.

There were half a dozen illuminated buttons on the panel. 'Damn this place. I *hate* everything about it.'

She pressed the button marked 'U' and the elevator started to ascend, thank God.

'Up is good,' said little Peter.

'Up is always good,' said Max.

# CHAPTER ONE HUNDRED

'**U**' *must stand for 'unbelievably lucky'*, Max thought, but kept the notion to herself. She had other preoccupations right now. Frannie and Kit. The mystery men down in the recovery room. Getting out of this snake pit alive. At least getting up out of the basement where Dr Kane did all his nasty work.

She reminded herself: *fear is not the answer. Not ever!*

The elevator doors opened into a long underground tunnel, concrete on all four sides, an exit door at one end, lighting strips along the sides of the ceiling.

It was a damp, cold, fetid place, and Max didn't know where the tunnel went, but this was what she'd chosen. Or had it been chosen for her by fate?

It *could* be an escape route.

'Let's go!' she yelled. 'I said – move it or lose it, guys! Hustle your buns. *Now!*'

The kids and one small, yapping terrier ran toward the far doorway, the only direction that seemed to make any sense.

She had to get the kids out first, then she'd go look for Frannie and Kit, and tell them about what she'd seen – an ex-president and twenty or so of his closest friends in a *postoperative* state.

'Please stay together and keep up! Once we're outside and I give the order, you fly as fast as your wings will take you! Fly to safety. You hear me?'

'Yeah,' shouted Peter. 'We fly to safety!'

She heard the distinctive hum of the elevator moving downward, stop, but then the hum began again. It was coming back to their floor. *Shit. Who was inside the elevator?*

'Faster, faster,' she yelled as they hurried down the tunnel. 'Don't fly – yet!'

Max lunged for the EXIT door. *Please, open.*

The door swung out into the blinding daylight, and it seemed like so long since Max had seen the sun! A day? Two days? There was a gray galvanized metal building off to their right – an airplane hangar – and tarmac leading to a runway.

An awful lot of private planes were down there.

Max sought her bearings. That way was Washington, DC. Maybe they could get help there. Maybe, maybe not. Who were the good guys in this hopeless mess? And how could she know for sure? She *needed* Frannie and Kit. *Right now, right this instant. All right, you two guys, show your faces!*

But it didn't happen. No Frannie and Kit.

Her bewildering thoughts were interrupted by the sputtering sound of an engine starting outside the airplane hangar. As she watched, a small cream-colored airplane with a red stripe along its side rolled forward, sending a flock of doves airborne.

The airplane stopped and two men in blue jumpsuits rolled a staircase up to the plane. A couple of the other small planes were being started up, too. A flurry of activity.

Off to the left, a tunnel door opened and two doctors came out, pushing a patient in a wheelchair. Then came bodyguards. Who was the patient?

Two more mysterious patients in wheelchairs were pushed out of another door. Then two more.

All in wheelchairs.

All males.

Was this what the wake-up call was all about? Time to go home? To do what?

One of the guards spotted Max. 'Hey!' he yelled. 'On the roof!' Then he was talking into his headset.

The doctors stared at her briefly, then one of them helped his important patient on to the staircase leading to his jet. The patient looked familiar. *Where had she seen him?* The guard drew his gun – and the bastard fired at her! At all of them!

'Get down!' Max ordered. *Goddamn them to hell. They shoot children, the cowardly bastards.*

Max peered over the edge and watched as the two doctors followed their patient into the plane. The door swung closed and the jet began to taxi.

Max was furious. At the guards, the doctors, the patients, Dr Ethan Kane, the whole goddamn shitty world that she and the other kids – *all kids*, actually – had been thrown into.

*They would not get away with Resurrection, whatever it was.*

*They would not! Would not!*

She couldn't let them get away. She wouldn't. Not even one stinking plane should get airborne.

'Get ready to fly out of here,' she told the kids. 'Those planes aren't going *up*! We own the sky.'

Then it hit her. She knew who the important patient was. Miguel Hijueras!

He was supposedly one of the richest men in the world. He owned communications companies all over Central and South America. He was supposed to be a real prick, too. An awful, awful bastard.

He was the patient.

One of them.

Who were all the rest – and what had been done to them in the operating rooms downstairs?

# CHAPTER ONE HUNDRED
# AND ONE

M ax realized she was beyond coherent rational thought at the
present time. Her fury and outrage about the death of Oz, his
*murder*, was making up for the lack of food; her anger filled her with a
kind of heady bravery.

Or stupidity.

She stretched out her magnificent wings as far as they would go.
Ten feet four inches. The wind passed over the leading edges and
pulled her upward.

Max flew, and so did the others. They followed her – *anywhere*. No
matter what side you were on, devil or angel, it was a beautiful,
amazing thing to see.

'The flock!' Peter and Wendy howled.

'Pay attention!' Max yelled at them.

She beat her wings furiously and rose even as Mr Hijueras's private
airplane still taxied on the ground. It had to travel along a runway
before turning south and beginning its takeoff in the direction of
Washington. What had happened to Hijueras at the Hospital? Why
had all of these important men come here?

Some of the other private planes were being boarded now. *More
famous patients?* For sure! What the hell had happened to them?

Max had a bit of a head start. The wind gusted suddenly, so when
the airplane's nose lifted she was there ahead of it.

She whipped across, right in front of the cockpit. She saw a pair of totally surprised pilots. The small plane tipped back on to its left landing wheel, then quickly righted itself.

*Get down!* she signaled to the pilots. *Down!*

She heard yells behind her; the other kids were cheering her on, cheering for themselves as well.

Then they were in a tight formation of five, with Max in the lead.

Matthew was on her left; he assumed poor murdered Oz's position, calling out directions and commands to Ic. Wendy and Peter flew to her right. None of them were afraid – not any more.

They dropped down near the plane, swooping and crisscrossing in front of the cockpit. Now the pilot and co-pilot looked scared. Their eyes bulged.

Max signaled again for them to put the plane down.

'Get down, you bastards! Don't try to take this plane up!' she yelled into the wind.

Max looped over and back. She saw the pilot struggle to keep the plane's nose in the air. He was speaking into his radio. Then she heard spits of gunfire from behind.

'Look out! Look out! Break formation!' she screamed at the kids.

Down on the ground armed guards had burst out of the hangar and on to the small airfield. They were shooting at them! Rifles.

Her keen eyesight picked out a few of the bastards who'd been chasing them since Colorado. What kind of secrets were they guarding here? What horrors? *These rich bastards sure weren't here for their six-month physicals.*

'Keep the plane between us and the ground,' Max shouted. 'Follow me, guys. Keep it tight.'

The small plane was gathering speed and gaining altitude. Bursts of semi-automatic gunfire creased the air and then – something went wrong! Something even Max hadn't expected. Something unthinkable.

'Oh God, Max – look!' Matthew shrieked. 'They're hit! It's bad!'

'Who's hit?' Max moaned and turned to check the flock.

But it wasn't one of the kids. Bullets had pierced the right wing. Red and orange flames and black smoke spewed from the damaged plane. There was a loud *bang*, an explosion, and the engine was on fire. The cream-white plane seemed to hang in place for a sliver of a second. Then it started to plummet toward the tarmac.

'Oh, be careful. Be careful,' Max called out. 'Level off! Level off! Oh Jeez, don't crash.'

She saw the pilot talking frantically into his headset, but the plane was nosing down.

Too fast! Way too fast! Then it smashed down on the airstrip. The right wing ripped entirely from the slender body, the plane shrieking like a dying animal. It cartwheeled four times, rolling over and over, parts flying in all directions, then came to rest belly-up.

Suddenly it burst into flames! Black, oily smoke billowed from the mangled plane. A second bright explosion bloomed.

Max could feel the searing heat of the fire high up in the sky. Oh God, what had she done! Mr Hijueras and his doctors had to be dead, blown up or cooked.

She and the other children dropped closer to the ground and watched as a bright orange truck sped out from a maintenance shed.

Almost simultaneously, doors opened from the south wing of the Hospital. Personnel streamed toward the fallen aircraft from the other private planes.

*Matthew saw him first and pointed.* 'There! Max, over there!'

Dr Ethan Kane stood alone behind the crowd, staring at the catastrophe. He wore a black windbreaker over a white shirt. And a long-billed baseball hat with the words 'Pebble Beach' on the front – the same one he'd had on when he'd abducted them from Alma's Valley Rest.

It was the first time Max had seen the prideful doctor without his nasty smile of superiority. He was shaking his head in disbelief.

'I'm still gonna break your neck,' Max muttered. 'That's a promise, you murdering bastard.'

# CHAPTER ONE HUNDRED
# AND TWO

Max exploded down toward the wretched excuse for a human being, much less a doctor, but even as she did, she couldn't help thinking about Oz. This was how he had died. *Reckless and ego-driven.*

She knew better. She'd already seen how this movie ended. *Badly. Horribly!*

So she waved off the other kids, and shouted, 'That's an order! Get*out*of*here*!' And they split away from her like the good kids they were. That wasn't the only reason. The fire in her voice scared them.

Max continued on alone. A dive-bomber focused on a target.

Kamikaze. Suicidal? Well, maybe. After all, she wanted to join Ozymandias more than anything.

Dr Kane saw her coming – and he waved her on. *Yes, c'mon, Max. Let's have a go at it. Let's end this right here.*

He was reckless and ego-driven too.

Apparently unafraid of the heat-seeking missile roaring down the runway at him.

*I want to break his neck so badly,* Max thought.

And she'd promised Oz.

But she pulled up hard and fast; she landed just a dozen yards or so from Ethan Kane. She was breathless. 'So what happened to your great goddamn Resurrection?' she panted. 'Is this it? Those pathetic men? What's so special about them?'

'They are indeed special!' Kane's voice was a low growl into the wind. 'They're what's needed to see us through this century. And now they'll live for most of it, and the world will be a better place. It might even survive. I've seen to that. I *did* it. But more to the point, Max, I know a secret about you. It's really juicy, want me to tell you?'

'I don't want *anything* from you!' Max looked at the old white men near their company-expense planes. The so-called *special* ones. Some were in wheelchairs, some lay on gurneys, recuperating, but most were up and walking. They glared at her as if they knew what she represented, the threat that she could be. 'Kill her now!' one of them shouted and shook his fist over his head. 'Get rid of her!'

Max looked at Ethan Kane and shook her head. '*They're* not the future,' she said. 'It would be too awful.'

She flapped her wings and flew straight at Ethan Kane again, screaming at the top of her voice, '*You killed Ozymandias!*'

Kane pulled out a gun, almost got it in shooting position, but he was an instant too late.

Max went for his head, his precious head, and hit it full force with an outstretched wing. She clotheslined the creepy bastard. Blasted him with all her speed and strength.

He was still standing, and Max thought: *That's not right. That's definitely wrong!* She tried to figure out what had just happened. Couldn't.

And then Max saw something that seemed impossible. Kane's head hung down sideways on one shoulder, as if his neck were broken. It was so weird. He was *still talking*.

'You can't stop this – or me,' Kane told her. 'Do you understand? Do you get it, Maximum?'

She hit him again. *Maximum* force.

Finally, Kane crumpled to the ground. But he was still *talking*. 'You can't stop what's going to happen, you little freak. You can't stop the future.'

And with those words, Dr Kane fell over dead.

Max stared at the crumpled body in disbelief. 'Talk about *freaks*,' she muttered.

# CHAPTER ONE HUNDRED AND THREE

A silent scream was inside me.
*NO, no, no!*

*Turn the glorious stars back on. Turn them on! My God, the sun is so bright, so magnificent.*

Suddenly, overhead lights just about blinded me. Two or three nurses were patting and shaking me all over. An oxygen mask was rudely slapped on my face.

Shit. I was still alive. I wasn't on the stairway to heaven after all.

I heard someone repeating my name, and when I turned my head I saw none other than Kit. He gently put his hand in mine. Squeezed.

I squeezed back. *Yep, he was real.*

I realized that his head of beautiful blond hair was shaved. *God, so was mine.*

'Waahhhhhhhhhh,' I said. 'Your hair.'

'I love you too, Baldie,' Kit whispered. 'Welcome back to the planet, Frannie.'

'Oh, it's good to be here.' Kind of, anyway. Except that my Simulated Reality heaven had been such a trip.

We were in the Dream Room, the same ward I had seen through the glass wall. A day before? Whenever. There were still about a half-dozen patients in headgear, wired up to flickering overhead monitors and a lot of other expensive equipment; cardiac monitors, respirators, arterial lines.

But no Dr Ethan Kane, goddamn him to hell! No ninety-four-year-old Harold Hauer!

I heard a loud ruckus, a stampede of hurrying footsteps out in the hallway.

Then I saw the kids! I quickly counted noses. Max and Wendy and Ic and Matthew and little Peter swarmed around my bed, their faces pushed up against mine. They were *cooing*, and it had to be the sweetest sound in the world.

'Hello, Mama,' said Wendy, and I almost lost it right there.

Then I did lose it. Big time. I sobbed and sobbed and tried to hold all five of them at once and nearly succeeded. Then I took things a little slower. One darling face at a time.

Max was smudged with soot, and dried blood caked one leg of her blue jeans, but she had a luminous smile. She hugged me and I hugged her back. It was just about the best hugging ever.

'We made it,' I finally said.

'Not everybody,' Max said and shook her head. I knew she was talking about Ozymandias. 'But I did get Ethan Kane. He's dead, Frannie. He won't hurt us again. I knocked his head off.'

I put my hand to Max's tangled hair, and as I did, I saw that I wore a plastic bracelet.

There was one very creepy word written on the plastic in fat black letters.

DONOR.

# CHAPTER ONE HUNDRED AND FOUR

Something very bad happened next.

Something unthinkable, and also scary as hell – or scarier – as if there was anything unusual in that, as if I ought to be surprised.

*Nothing* was written by the press about Resurrection, or the powerful men who had obviously been involved. Not one word in a major newspaper or magazine. It was as if it had never happened. As if we hadn't seen what we'd seen. As if we'd made it all up.

I'm not real big on conspiracy theories or paranoia – at least I wasn't until I saw what was happening.

*Not one word.*

Some of you might say 'That's unbelievable!' All I can say is – where have you been lately? And get your head out of the sand. Truth is not at a premium these days. Haven't you noticed?

*Not one word.*

Dr Ethan Kane/Harold Hauer believed he had changed the world for the rest of the century – but no one in the press seemed to notice or care, or maybe *believe* that monstrous things had happened.

Just as they had failed to notice the importance of biotechnology in the years leading up to the present. That biotechnology *is* our future. A done deal. Written in stone by *someone*, and not anyone I know, or you know.

Crazy things happened after I was set free, too. The men who we saw with our own eyes at the Hospital denied they were there, and seemed to have alibis, every one of them. What we had seen on the lower floor – gutted corpses, fetuses in bottles, incredible high-tech machinery – was all *gone* by the time law enforcement agencies went inside to look. The body of Ethan Kane/Harold Hauer was gone too.

*Or so they said.*

*So they said.*

Finally, and maybe most disturbing of all, the body of Ozymandias had disappeared as well.

The only stories, *the only stories*, were the hoked-up ones in the sensationalist tabloids. Now what the hell did that say about the current state of the world? And besides, stories in the tabloids *guaranteed* that nobody would believe what had happened, what we had seen.

*Another* month passed and nothing too terribly, earthshakingly insane, rambunctious, chaotic, or particularly dangerous happened. There was *still* no exposure about the Hospital or what had happened there. Kit and I went back to Denver. One more time – with feeling – we had decided to fight for custody of the children.

The five who had survived.

We had vowed to keep them safe.

And the children promised to do the same for us.

We solemnly promised – we made pinky swears – that we would get to the Lake House again, at least one more time.

# CHAPTER ONE HUNDRED
# AND FIVE

It was only a hearing, but Judge Dwyer had promised us he would review his previous decision and our lawyer was holding him to his word. So were the children.

On a scale of one to ten, the local media hullabaloo was nudging a hundred, and Bannock Street was crowded beyond belief, certainly beyond capacity. Everyone wanted a piece of *this* story. To hell with Resurrection, and whatever else Ethan Kane had done at Liberty General Hospital. The public couldn't get enough of the bird-kids.

Of course, neither could Kit and I.

We hurriedly made our way to Courtroom No. 19. Kit wore a navy-blue jacket, white dress shirt, gray wool pants. He looked good – a hint of Tom Cruise cockiness, a dash of Harrison Ford slyness, something kind of neat like that.

I had on a forest-green sweater dress and high black boots, and hoped that I looked like an adult – a hint of J.C. Penney, a dash of Dillard's.

Kit and I had both grown a half-inch of brand-new hair, giving us a 'prisoner of war' look that our lawyer said couldn't hurt.

We exchanged falsely cheerful hellos with Jeffrey, our faithful legal pit bull, then we found two seats on the left side of the oak-paneled courtroom.

Our old antagonist and foe, Catherine Fitzgibbons, dressed in serious black, was going over her notes across the aisle. The bitch of the Rockies looked ready for us.

Soon the children would arrive. With their other families, their biological ones. Also expected was the mother of Ozymandias, who would testify against Kit and me.

This was the hearing's second day, actually. The first day had been intense, to say the least. Catherine Fitzgibbons, *speaking for the parents*, had ranted, stabbed the air, and laced her arguments with hurtful accusations aimed at Kit and me. She had her shining moment when she spun on her well-turned heel, pointed at us and shouted, 'Judge, if those two hadn't kidnapped Oz, he would be alive today!'

Jeffrey Kussof shot out of his seat. 'I object, Your Honor, on the grounds that opposing counsel is out of her mind! And she's also dead wrong. *Was she there?*'

'Sustained,' said the judge. 'And both of you cut it out!'

Meanwhile, I had looked over at the kids and saw tears streaming down Max's cheeks. I knew she couldn't take this arguing about Ozymandias much longer. It was so cruel, so heartless and wrong. But that was our legal system, wasn't it? Anything goes. The end of civility, manners, maybe even civilization.

Then Jeffrey Kussof delivered our argument with great fire and resolve, and, I thought, intelligence and wisdom. He told the judge that the parents were laboring under the erroneous notion that their kids were 'normal' when they clearly were not. The kids were unique and had unique needs, and the parents hadn't been able to fulfill those needs. Wasn't it true that armed men had attacked Max and Matthew Marshall in their own home? And what had Terry and Art been able to do? Nothing. They slept through it.

On that second morning, I glanced up at the large oak-framed schoolhouse clock on the southern wall of the courtroom. In about five minutes, the judge would speak, or so we'd been told. What would Judge Dwyer say? Could the ruling possibly go our way? I doubted it. But we had to take our shot.

The atmosphere was heating up and getting ready to boil over.

Every time the doors opened, *more* people poured in.

Suddenly the kids, along with their lawyers and parents, filed into the room for the second day. As always, Max, Matthew, Ic, Peter and Wendy were magnificent to behold. They were also the best kids in the whole wide world and they deserved better than this public fiasco.

'Frannie! Kit! Hey, hey,' they called and waved to us. 'We *love* you guys. We miss you.'

'We love you too,' I called. 'Hugs and kisses!' Long live sentimentalism.

'Hello, Mama,' Wendy cooed. She *was* my baby; my sweetheart of sweethearts; my little girl.

I shot a grin and a thumbs-up as they climbed, jumped, and flew into their seats. Then a solemn hush fell over the court.

The bailiff took his place beside the bench and called the room to order: 'All rise.'

The judge entered from his chambers, and I swear he looked older than he had just *yesterday*. His wispy white hair was flying everywhere and his aged face seemed about ready to cave in.

'Hear ye, hear ye, the court is now in session, the Honorable Judge James Randolph Dwyer presiding.'

The judge dropped on to his chair. 'Please be seated,' he said. 'Please.'

The room became so still it was as if all the sound in the world had been turned off. It almost seemed a trick of nature. Judge Dwyer's voice was the only one that mattered. I could just about tell from the look on his face that he'd already made his decision. I prayed to whoever was listening that it was the right one for everyone involved.

'They can't take these kids away from us again,' I whispered against Kit's cheek. 'They can't, can they?'

Then Kit turned and looked me in the eye. His gaze was absolutely steely. 'We're going to be a family again. I promise you, Frances Jane.'

# CHAPTER ONE HUNDRED AND SIX

There had been several times in the past few weeks when I'd involuntarily called up the images of my Simulated Reality dream. Apparently, new neural pathways had been burned into my brain by that incredible vision of the earth, and sometimes remembering the awe-inspiring perspective from outer space was the only way I could find a center of calm.

I called upon it now as Judge Dwyer cast his heavy gray eyes around his courtroom. He caught my eyes, and oh-my-God, *the great man smiled*.

'Ladies and gentlemen, and children,' the judge said in his deep, resonant voice. 'This has been the hardest case I've ever adjudicated and all of you know why.

'Aleksandr Solzhenitsyn once said, "One can build the Empire State Building, discipline the Prussian army, make a state hierarchy mightier than God, yet fail to overcome the unaccountable superiority of certain human beings." Some people think they can destroy and manipulate human life with criminal impunity. A while back, a group of scientists right here in Colorado apparently believed this. Now, I've been charged with deciding the fate of these delightful children.

'All of the parties, Agent Brennan and Dr O'Neill, the natural parents, and especially the children, have exhibited extraordinary and unparalleled courage.

'I want to reward this courage equitably, to make everyone happy. And that, of course, is impossible.'

There was a rolling rumble from the gallery as people turned to one another to mutter their predictions.

Judge Dwyer banged his gavel loudly, calling out, 'Order. Please.'

In the chastened silence that followed, he continued. 'The laws of the State of Colorado are clear. *The best interests of the children are paramount.* The law also usually falls on the side of the parents. The parents of these children may not be prepared for what the future holds for Max, Matthew, Icarus, Peter and Wendy – but is anyone? I honestly don't know the answer to that. In any event, the parents of these children have demonstrated parental excellence. I asked myself over and over, how could I deprive them or their children of familial bonds?'

I edged myself into Kit's shoulder and felt like I was going to cry. My heart was breaking. It seemed clear to me what Judge Dwyer would say next. I tried to prepare myself, but I just couldn't. Not again.

The judge continued. 'While I deliberated, I remembered something that Max had said to me at the time of the first hearing. She said, "I know you're a good guy, but you've made a mistake. You're only human, right. And that's the problem, Judge – *we're not.*" '

I had pulled my face out of the crook of Kit's shoulder. I had also inched up toward the edge of my seat.

Judge Dwyer stopped for a breath, but then he went on. 'Well, I *am* only human. Maybe no one but the five of you kids can truly understand that *you are a flock,* and that you need to be together. And that Frannie and Kit *are* Mama and Papa for you. I don't know if I completely understand it, Max . . . but that's what I believe.

'And so, that is the judgment of this court – the children will go with Frannie and Kit. You're a flock again. You're also a family. Be a great flock, and a great family. I'm pretty sure you will be.'

The courtroom erupted in noise, which was mostly applause, and then the kids were all over Kit and me.

'We're a flock and a family!' Peter yelled for all to hear. 'Victory lap!'

And then the amazing kids flew once, twice, three times around the room.

# EPILOGUE

---

# THE LAKE HOUSE

# CHAPTER ONE HUNDRED AND SEVEN

And so, the seven of us finally went *home*. Isn't that something? The Lake House was where we had gone with the kids after we helped them escape from the dreaded School. It was secluded, high on a picture-postcard mountainside, overlooking our own private lake. I won't tell you where it is exactly. It's safer that way. Leave it at this: the kids love it, and so do Kit and I. My mother used to always say that there are two important things you can give to your children — one is roots, and the other is wings. I agree with that wholeheartedly. That was my plan. *Roots and wings.*

Then one afternoon I was toasting marshmallows in the fireplace with Wendy as feathery flakes of snow drifted across the sky. Kit and the boys watched a couple of college football teams trash each other on the fifty-one-inch Sony. They were cheering for 'the Buffaloes', whoever the Buffaloes were. Probably the University of Colorado.

Out of the blue, a nagging thought crossed my mind.

Max had been in her room almost all day, ever since just past breakfast. I worried that maybe something was wrong.

Then I thought I knew what it was: *she was missing Ozymandias again. We all were, of course. He was such a great boy, so much potential. Every time I thought about Oz I choked up myself.*

Max's room was upstairs in the southeast corner, and it had a special view of the quarry, the lake and the woods.

I went up there on tippy-toes.

At the door, I thought I heard her moan. *What was going on in there? What now?*

Every one of us had had night terrors and waking nightmares, post-traumatic stress syndrome that just wouldn't quit. The most graphic scenes from the Hospital and the School were still with us. They always will be.

'Max? You okay in there?' I called out. 'Max, sweetie?'

She didn't answer. So I opened the bedroom door a crack and peeked inside. I relaxed as I saw Max in bed under a lot of fluffy covers. She stretched out a hand and beckoned.

'Frannie, come in. Please, Mama. I need to talk to you.'

'Okay. I'm right here.' I shut the door behind me.

I could see that Max was flushed. She was perspiring. Then, to my shock, I saw blood on her outstretched fingers!

'I need your help, Frannie. I really need you right now. Seriously.'

I clamped down on my fear as I walked across the creaking bedroom floor. I dragged a chair up to Max's bedside and sat beside her. 'I'm here.'

I put my hand on her forehead. She was extraordinarily warm. Her long hair was matted and damp.

The doctor in me began to take over.

'Honey? What's the matter with you? What are you feeling? How long have you had a fever? Talk to me.'

'I'm not exactly *sick*, Frannie. I've just been working real hard,' Max said.

I must have had a puzzled look on my face.

'*Labor*,' she said. 'Labor is hard work. I had some babies!'

I gasped when I finally understood. I think I almost fainted. 'Oh Max, why didn't you tell me? Oh Max, sweetheart. Oh Max, oh God, Max.'

She shrugged and then said, 'I wanted this to be private. But I'm really glad you're here, Frannie. Just us two girls.'

'Just the two of us,' I promised.

Now I stared at a miracle never before seen in this world, at least I didn't expect so. *My God!* Snuggled right up to Max's body, lying in the crook of her arm, were two magnificent human eggs. *Oh Max.*

The eggs were quite large, the shells ivory white, with a pearly pink sheen. They looked to be three or four pounds and the sight of them made me weak with tenderness.

I imagined Max's precious babies inside the eggs, their arms and legs tucked in the fetal position. Two beautiful babies with wings.

'You're going to be a mother,' I whispered. 'This is so beautiful.' Then I started to choke up.

'They're mine with Ozymandias,' Max said, whispering too. 'I have to keep them warm. I don't know how I know that, but I do. Oh, I wish Oz was here to see this.'

I reached out and gently put my arms around Max, holding her, calling her name. I felt tears rolling down my cheeks.

Max's face was so joyful and radiant, so full of hope. 'Aren't they just the most beautiful things? Isn't life a miracle sometimes?' she said. 'OK, you can call the other kids now. And Kit. This is gonna blow all their minds, isn't it? I'm going to be a mother.'

# CHAPTER ONE HUNDRED
# AND EIGHT

O ver the next few weeks Max began to learn real honest-to-God PATIENCE for the first time in her life. She was going to be a mom, and she'd need it. It was so quiet in her part of the house that she sometimes thought she might be going a little mad. Going, going, *gone*.

Her mind was frayed from being alone too much, watching and nursing her eggs every minute, thinking about Oz constantly, missing him so much it hurt. Constantly and *for ever*.

But she had good reason to be extra watchful and careful. She was going to be a mother, and her children were going to be very special. Of course, Max knew, just about every mother felt that same way.

She was all cozied up in bed, re-reading *The Hobbit* by candlelight, when she heard a creak coming from the deck right outside her bedroom window.

Strange.

What was that?

Perhaps the low, steady whistle of the wind had frightened an animal. There were plenty of critters out there skittering here and there in the woods. If anything, her superior hearing was better than ever.

She touched the eggs with her fingertips, *one, two*.

*Buckle my shoe.*

*Going, going, gone.*

Max couldn't take her eyes off the two eggs. The babies were growing bigger day by day. They were also starting to move now. She could see their shapes pressed up against the shells. *That* got her every time. She was going to be a mom.

Max blew out the candle, lay very still, and *listened*. She heard the same funny creak again.

Probably nothing.

*Probably . . .*

It was like the sound of a branch or the wind pushing at the deck, but there were no overhanging branches out there, were there?

No, the creak was more like a damn footstep. Out on the deck.

A footstep she was imagining in her head? A bogeyman footstep? A fantasy footstep?

Max held her breath and listened closely again. *This was too dopey for words.*

Finally, she slipped out of bed. *Even dopier.*

She moved three paces to the window, waited, then parted the white eyelet curtains Frannie had made for her. She looked out on to the second-story deck.

Then Max jumped back.

She was staring into another pair of eyes!

Eyes she knew. And hated. A face she knew. And hated. *Yes, it's me.* The mouth formed words. *Hel-lo, Max. I've come for you.*

The window broke inward as a gloved fist smashed through it. Shattered glass rained around her. Then Dr Ethan Kane/Harold Hauer burst into the room, and she knew this just had to be a dream, like really *bad* simulated reality.

But it wasn't!

He was alive.

He was in her bedroom. He had come for her and the eggs.

# CHAPTER ONE HUNDRED
# AND NINE

'Get out of here!' Max shrieked.

But Hauer grabbed her around the waist and threw her backwards toward the bed. He had a scalpel in his hand. And he was strong – much more so than normal men. He *wasn't* normal.

Of course he wasn't! He had made himself over; he was the first to experience Resurrection; he was the new Frankenstein.

Max twisted her body as she fell, to avoid the pillow nest she'd made for her babies. She just missed crushing the eggs.

When she lifted her head, there was a sharp blade pressing into her throat. Hauer's free hand covered her nose and mouth. He was suffocating her. Did he even know how strong he was?

'Why, hello, Max. So nice to see you again, dear girl. Yes, I'm alive. You killed a clone, Max, not me. Of course, you probably don't know that.'

Then he warned, 'Don't you dare move, you fine-feathered freak. Don't even think of screaming for help because I'll kill *them,* too. In the blink of an eye. Fight me and I'll kill you. You'll die without seeing your babies. You're smart. You understand me. Don't you?'

Max nodded. Her lungs were aching. She needed air. Hauer finally took his hand from her mouth and she actually *growled*, a sound she'd never, ever made before.

'You're the freak. Godless creep. What do you want?'

'Well, I've come for a few of my papers, which Frances Jane

apparently swiped. And the *eggs* of course. I've come for your eggs, Max.'

'You can't have them,' Max hissed. 'I'll die first.'

Hauer shrugged. 'It doesn't matter to me. You die, you live. Either way, I have your precious eggs. I *am* Harold Hauer. Not a clone. Do you know why I'm here, Max? Do you know why I kept you alive all this time? Want to know the secret? You're even bigger than Resurrection. Really and truly you are. These eggs are more important than anything I've ever done before. I've seen the future, Max, and it flies!'

Max couldn't speak at first. Finally, she understood why she'd been allowed to survive. *I've seen the future, and it flies!*

'You're a sick ghoul,' she said.

Then Max found herself making the terrible *growling* sound again. What was that noise anyway? Her way of protecting the eggs?

'You're incorrigible, hopeless. I should have done this at the Hospital. Die, you little twit.'

'I don't feel like it!' Max shouted. She kicked out and sent the doctor reeling against her dresser. Taken off guard, he dropped the knife.

He recovered quickly though. Bearlike, he shook himself off, cursed and felt around for the scalpel in the darkened room. Found it in a fold of the scatter rug.

'Dead or alive?' he asked as he showed Max the sharp blade. 'It's your choice.'

'I choose my babies,' said Max.

She spread her wings, making a wall of feathers and bone between Hauer and her eggs. 'Get out of here! Get out of here now,' she screamed. 'I'll kill you, Hauer! Kane! Whatever your name is, you creepy bastard! Get away from my babies!'

He rushed her, and Max sidestepped the attack. Barely. He was quick, too.

She reached out and grasped for something. *What?* She felt a brass candle holder. She swung it very hard, very fast, very accurately, too.

There was a solid crunch as the heavy object connected with Dr Hauer's skull. She'd hurt him! He moaned and fell against her, pulling at Max with the full weight of his body, dragging her toward the far wall.

'Let go! Don't *touch* me.'

'You little son of a bitch,' he groaned through gritted teeth. 'I'll show you something. I'll show you pain. Then *death.*'

Max heard yells and footsteps in the house. Frannie and Kit were coming. Running. The kids, too!

Hauer was so strong, though, obviously something else he'd engineered in his lab. He was relentlessly pushing her backwards. Max lost her footing. She was going down.

She was falling right through the broken window behind her. No way to stop it. She reached out. *For something, anything!* Grabbed Dr Hauer with both hands. Held on to him as if her life depended on it.

'You're coming too!'

The bedroom was only on the second floor – that was the good news.

The bad part was that her window overlooked a steep cliff, a drop of another hundred and twenty feet into the woods, which was *so far* below.

Max and Dr Hauer crashed through the picture window, and fell several feet together – then she let him go. Just like that! Say goodbye to old rubbish! Max flapped her wings furiously, struggled, but then hovered as she watched the screeching doctor falling to the forest floor far below. He spiraled; he cartwheeled; he dived. It took a few seconds that seemed so much longer.

'Help me, Max!' he screamed. Maybe she would have if she could, but she couldn't dive and swoop up his falling body. Even if she'd wanted to.

She saw him hit a tree then carom to the ground with a sickening *thud*, then he lay very still. Crumpled, twisted, *still*. As she had hoped, as she'd solemnly promised Ozymandias – *she'd broken the bastard's neck*.

Dr Harold Hauer, ninety-four years old, was finally dead. Good riddance to the human monster, the creep of creeps, the sick prick.

The *real* deal, the *real* person, was dead as dogshit down there.

Max whispered, 'I've seen the future, too . . . and you're not in it.'

She finally had to look away. She caught a breath, and then flapped her wings and took off toward the bedroom window of the house.

Frannie and Kit were up there, with the other kids, and also her precious babies, her eggs.

Less than four weeks later they were born.

In the perfect, perfect spot.

At the Lake House.

A boy and a girl, just what she'd wanted.

The most special and beautiful babies in the whole world – tiny infants with gossamer wings like angels. Maybe they *were* angels.

Frances Jane and Ozymandias.

She couldn't wait to teach them to fly.